PRIVILEGE

RENZO + LUCIA, BOOK 1

BETHANY-KRIS

Published by Bethany-Kris

www.bethanykris.com

ISBN 13: 978-1-988197-78-4

Cover Art © London Miller

Editor: Elizabeth Peters

This is work of fiction. Characters, names, places, corporations, organizations, institutions, locales, and so forth are all the product of the author's imagination, or if real, used fictitiously. Any resemblance to a person, living or dead, is entirely coincidental.

For the youngbloods, and the young loves.

CONTENTS

PROLOGUE

Lucia Marcello

The baby hadn't been planned or expected, not when her oldest sibling had over a decade of years on her, and her parents had believed undoubtedly that they would not have any more children after their last daughter.

But here she was.

And God knew she was loved.

Maybe she hadn't been planned, but she had been *most* wanted.

Born in the early morning inside a private suite, the baby girl was wrapped in the softest muslin wrap after being warmed, and washed of any remnants of the birth. Tucked away in a Labor and Delivery Ward of a hospital where there was a doctor for every few patients, and three nurses to every laboring woman, her parents made calls to people who were probably still sleeping, and had their own children to care for.

Aunts, uncles, grandparents …

Despite sleeping, those people would still come.

They would come to welcome a new *principessa* to the Marcello family. They would come to congratulate her parents. They would bring her oldest brother, and two older sisters to say hello for the first time. They would bring gifts, and beautiful things to say *thank you* for being ours.

They would all hear her name.

Lucia.

And they would love her simply because she was alive. They would love her because she was born a Marcello.

Born rich, to a family that was both adored and feared, her parents would make sure she wanted for nothing.

That was the privilege of Lucia Marcello.

Simply because she had been born.

• • •

1

Renzo Zulla

The baby hadn't been planned or expected, not when his mother was barely past her sixteenth birthday and hadn't slept on a mattress with a sheet since before she found out she was pregnant.

But here he was.

And God knew he wasn't wanted.

Maybe he hadn't been planned or wanted, but his mother couldn't find it in herself to give him up, either.

Born on a warm evening in an Emergency Room triage bed because his mother had waited too long to go to the hospital, and the Labor and Delivery Ward was full, the baby boy laid wrapped in scratchy cotton. His mother explained tiredly for the third time that she didn't *have* an insurance card. With a smear of ruddy blood still staining the floor of a hospital where the hallways were currently full of the sick, and the nurses were overworked, one thought to ask his mother if there was someone she might like to call.

Grandparents, other family … the father, perhaps?

Those people would never come.

They wouldn't come to welcome a new baby they hadn't even known the teenager was pregnant with. They wouldn't come to congratulate his mother. They wouldn't come to help, or to show his mother how to love him or keep him alive. They wouldn't bring gifts, or any beautiful things.

They wouldn't hear his name at all.

Renzo.

Given the name his father hated when his mother told the man the ones she was considering for him in a dank alley months ago. Given a name that would already make his absent father hate him.

Born poor, to a mother who'd only stopped sucking on a pipe long enough to birth a healthy child she refused to give up, and without a home to keep him warm.

That was the misfortune of Renzo Zulla.

Simply because he had been born.

ONE

The one thing a person could never escape once they were born a Marcello?
Love.

Sometimes that love was soft, and supportive, and everything a person
needed to propel them into a world that was ready to tear them to bits. And
sometimes, that love was suffocating, and heavy, and everything a person
wished they could escape from because there was no growth when people
were holding you too tight.

Lucia Marcello liked to call that a double-edged sword. Maybe it was
because she was the baby, but she was on the receiving end of that *love* a
hell of a lot more than any of her other siblings when it came to her
parents. Like they were scared to let her fly, and so they were just going to
keep holding onto her until she broke free on her own.

She thought ... maybe it was time to do just that.

"*Principessa*," Lucian said, placing a kiss to the top of his daughter's head.

"Hey, Daddy," Lucia greeted.

She went back to the binder of information that she needed to study.
Apparently, volunteering for a women's and children's shelter for the
summer wasn't as easy as simply signing up for the job. Lucia had policies
to memorize, schedules, and a bunch more.

It was worth it. She wanted to help.

"Where is your mother?"

"Reading in her room."

Lucian pulled out a chair at the table and sat down beside Lucia. "I was
thinking ..."

Sighing, Lucia closed her binder and gave her father the attention he
wanted. Lucia, being the youngest child of four siblings, had always been
the baby. Her parents seemed to think she needed more attention and care
than her older siblings simply because there was such a difference in age.
Maybe they figured she felt left out. Lucia never had.

Being the family baby at only seventeen, almost eighteen, meant being
babied like one. She needed some breathing room, some time away from her
family and room to grow. She knew they didn't understand, and that they
would be hurt by her wanting to leave, so she chose her actions in quieter
ways. Like volunteering at a woman's shelter for the summer.

With her father's past, she knew Lucian wouldn't put the brakes on
Lucia spending eight hours a day, five days a week at a shelter to help. He
was more likely to donate a bunch of money, which she already did, and buy

3

her a car to get to and from the location every day. She wanted to volunteer, too, but it was a small step away from her family and their smothering.

"Thinking what?" she asked her father.

"About college in the fall," Lucian answered. "Couldn't you pick Columbia instead of a college out of state? It's a great school, Lucia, and it has all the programs you want for social development."

Lucia dropped her father's gaze. If he could see her eyes, he could see her lies. "But I fell in love with that campus when we visited."

Lucian made a sad noise under his breath. "I know, *bella ragazza*."

"I'll come back, Dad. Holidays, vacation, and some weekends."

"You're not making it better, Lucia."

She smiled. "I'm sorry."

"I worry about you being alone."

"Don't. I'm an adult. I can handle college."

"Graduating high school and being almost eighteen does not make you an adult, Lucia."

"But—"

"I'm sorry, sweetheart, I can't help but worry. I know you want to grow up, but I'm not sure we're ready for you to."

Lucia dropped her hands to the table with a smack and stood from her seat quickly. "That's the whole problem."

Lucian glanced up at her with surprise deepening the lines in his face. "I don't understand."

"*You're* not ready to let me go. *You're* not ready for me to grow up. You, Dad, not me."

"Oh."

Lucia picked up the binder off the table and said, "I'm choosing the college out of state, not Columbia. It's already been settled, tuition and first year is paid, plus I was accepted months ago. I have the grades for it, and I want to do this. Let me do it."

Lucian dropped his head. "Okay."

Lucia was surprised her father had dropped it that easily. It wasn't like Lucian at all. Lucia knew exactly where she had gotten her stubbornness and fight from—her father. The man had given her far more than just his namesake when she was brought into the world as her mother and father's unexpected surprise later in life.

Guilt chewed Lucia up inside.

"I'll be back, Daddy," she said softly.

"We have the summer, right?" her father asked.

Well, she did. Her father was a different story. As a Marcello *principessa*, Lucia knew what her father and the rest of the men in her family were

4

involved with. She wasn't blind or dumb. She had witnessed more than enough things over the years to know her family might as well be royalty in the world of organized crime. Her father and two uncles held three of the highest seats in the family. Even her brother was mixed up in it all. Thankfully, it kept her father busy. She had the summer off, but Lucian probably didn't. His job was non-stop.

"Sort of, yes. I have this volunteering thing, too."

"I'm proud that you took this on," Lucian said, reaching out to tap the binder. "I've always tried to donate to the shelters and organizations for women and children, but it makes me extremely proud that you've taken the extra step to do this."

The guilt flooded Lucia again. She'd done it because she needed the break from her family, and the fact it would look good on a résumé. She also did it for the experience. Lucia came from a ridiculously wealthy family. Her father might have lived some of his early years on the streets, forging for food and trying to survive, but she never had. She never worried about one single thing. Nothing was out of reach if she asked her mother and father for it.

Lucia wondered if she needed a wake-up call from real life.

Maybe this job would do that.

"I think you'll get something amazing from it," Lucian added when Lucia stayed quiet.

"I hope so," she responded.

Standing from the table, her father drew her in for a tight hug that said he still wasn't quite ready to let Lucia out of his sights. She let him hold on until he was ready to let go, because all too soon, her father wouldn't have a choice but to let her go.

Lucian was a good father—a great one, actually. But for once, Lucia simply wanted to step out of her family's shadow and be her own person. She didn't think her dad would understand.

Would he?

"I love you, Lucia," her father murmured. "You always were the easy one out of the four. I never had to worry about you getting in to some kind of trouble, or causing us any heartache. My good girl, huh?"

She had always been the good girl.

Lucia didn't know anything else.

Lucia sighed. "Yeah."

"Hmm, what was that?"

"I love you, too, *Papà*."

Releasing her from his hug, Lucian said, "I should go find your mother. I have news she'll want to hear."

"Oh?"

Lucian smiled widely. "Retirement is coming early for me. Your mother has been pestering me for years to do this, and I finally have. It feels good. She will be pissed off like nothing else if I don't tell her right away."

Retirement.

Lucia didn't know what to say.

"So, no more … *famiglia?*" Lucia asked, choosing her words carefully. Outright asking about the mafia or her father's involvement would likely get her nowhere. "None at all?"

Lucian shrugged, still happy. "Mostly, no."

• • •

Lucia poked her head into the state of the art kitchen and found the chef working behind a large stove. The man blinked a couple of times before he finally recognized her.

"Lucia?"

She nodded. "Hi. Is my cousin around?"

"Andino is in his office. I can let Skip know you're here, if you want."

"That would be great, thanks."

"Go find a table. Do you want something to eat?"

"No, I'm okay."

"Sure," the chef said. "Go, I'll let your cousin know you're here to see him."

Lucia wasn't surprised that the man was confused at her presence. It wasn't often that Lucia went to Andino's main restaurant in the city because her cousin was known to use the place for the more illegal side of his business. Like the mafia. More than once, Lucian had told his daughter to steer clear.

Quickly, she found a quiet table toward the back and slid into a chair. Resting her bag in the chair beside her, she waited for Andino to come out from the back. It didn't take him long. Her cousin strolled across the restaurant floor, waving at a couple of patrons as he passed, and then joined Lucia at the table.

"Hey, kid," Andino said, smiling.

Lucia forced herself not to roll her eyes. "Hey."

"Didn't your daddy tell you to stay away from this place?"

"So?"

Andino chuckled. "You should follow the rules, Lucia."

"I wanted to find out something, and I was in the neighborhood."

"Oh?"

"Yes," she confirmed.

Andino leaned back in the chair and fixed the buttons on his suit jacket as he asked, "Well, what do you need?"

"Where's Johnathan?"

Lucia had only seen her oldest sibling once since his release from prison. John was her only brother, but besides that, he was also the only person who truly understood Lucia and how suffocating their parents could be. For John, she knew it was an entirely different reason. But honestly, Lucia just needed a break, and John seemed like the right person to go to for it.

"Working today. Why?" Andino asked.

"I want to talk to him."

Her cousin lifted a single brow. "He's working, which means you probably shouldn't be around him, Lucia. I know how your father would feel to find out you were slumming it up with John while he was doing business."

Frustrated, Lucia grabbed her bag and stood. "Thanks for nothing."

"Hey, hey." Andino stood from the table, reaching out to grab Lucia's wrist.

"What?" she asked, snappier than she intended.

"What is up with you?" he asked.

"I want to see my brother. He doesn't answer my phone calls, and he never comes around to the house, so I can talk to him there. I figured coming to see you would probably point me in the right direction. I'm not surprised it didn't. All this family does is take care of business first, right?"

Andino's gaze flicked away. "Yeah, I suppose you're right."

"I'm sorry, Andi. I know I'm not allowed to be hanging around here. I shouldn't have come."

"It's fine, kid. Just keep quiet to your dad, huh?"

Lucia nodded. "I will."

"Where are you going after this?"

"I was going to go sit with Grandpapa while Grandmama ran some errands."

Cecelia, her grandmother, always felt uncomfortable leaving her husband home alone when she left the house, for whatever reason. Lucia didn't mind sitting with her grandfather. Then, he had someone watching him and someone to talk to. Antony, her grandfather, never minded.

Andino nodded. "All right. I'll give John a call. Let him know where you're going to be."

Lucia's anger ebbed away. "Thanks."

"No problem."

• • •

"Are you sure you'll be fine?" Cecelia asked.

7

"We'll be perfect," Lucia told her grandmother. "I'm sure he'll get in to his usual trouble."

Cecelia laughed, the lines around her eyes deepening in her joy. "Okay."

"Don't worry, Grandmama."

"He's been tired a lot lately," Cecelia explained quietly. "I can't help but worry."

Lucia frowned, saddened over her grandmother's concerns for her husband's health. Antony Marcello always seemed to be the strongest, most formidable person in their family, but truth be told, he wasn't getting any younger. A sharp tongue and a strong soul did not make for a healthy body.

"Just go do your stuff," Lucia said. "He'll be okay with me. I'll put on his music, and he'll be happy."

Cecelia smiled. "Okay. Thank you for coming today."

"I'll always come, Grandmama."

Her grandmother's hand patted her cheek gently. The leathery feel of Cecelia's palm reminded Lucia that her grandmother wasn't a young woman, either.

"Our good girl, huh?"

Lucia batted her grandmother's hand away lightly. "Go. You're wasting time."

"Going, going."

Lucia closed the front door to the large Marcello mansion the moment her grandmother stepped out into the marble entrance. Making her way back through the house, she found her grandfather sitting in the living room in his leather recliner with his feet up, a glass of water beside him, and a remote in his hand as he flicked through the television channels.

"Did she pester you about me again?" Antony asked, his voice raspy with age.

Lucia laughed. "Nothing gets past you, does it?"

"I only look old, Lucia. I may feel it at times, too, but my mind is the same as it was when I was twenty-five. Sharp, quick, and too smart for everyone else."

"That's all that matters, Grandpapa."

Antony waved a weathered hand high. "They all worry too much."

"I know what you mean." Lucia eyed the water her grandfather sipped from. "You didn't spike that with something when Grandmama wasn't looking, right?"

Antony smiled slyly. "Wouldn't you like to know?"

"No drinking, Grandpapa."

"Oh, it's just water. Stop it. She doesn't even give me wine anymore."

Lucia fake pouted. "Poor you."

"She worries too much," Antony repeated with a sigh. Flicking his wrist at the couch beside his chair, he added, "Sit, or your legs will get tired. Then I'll have to listen to your father go on about how I don't take care of you while you babysit me."

"I'm not babysitting you."

"Same thing."

Lucia shook her head, knowing better than to argue with her grandfather. Antony, no matter his age, was too stubborn for his own good. The man would choke on his words before he would ever spit out that he might be wrong about something.

Taking a seat on the couch, Lucia asked, "What do you want to do today?"

Antony smiled, reached over, and took his youngest grandchild's hand in his. "Sit here and enjoy the day with you, Lucia."

"Okay, Grandpapa. We can do that."

"Good." Antony nodded at the television. "They have a true crime marathon on today for the mob and the New York families."

Lucia couldn't have stopped her laughter even if she tried. "Really?"

"Yes. They made a show about my rise to power in the eighties and nineties, too."

"I know, I watched it when I was fifteen," she admitted.

It was how she learned most of her family's history and legacy in Cosa Nostra. The conversation that had followed with her father had been interesting, especially since Lucian didn't hide a thing when Lucia asked about it all. It was the only time they did talk about it.

"The whole show is lies," Antony said.

Lucia wondered about that. "Is it?"

Antony's old eyes twinkled with mischief. "No."

• • •

After saying goodbye to her grandmother, Lucia opened the front door to leave the Marcello mansion and begin her drive home. She froze on the stoop, finding a familiar figure waiting for her in the driveway. Her older brother leaned against the hood of what looked to be a brand-new Mercedes.

"I heard you were looking for me," John said, grinning.

Lucia took the front steps two at a time until she was close enough to run her hands over the shiny black paint job the Mercedes sported. It was a beautiful, two-door coupe with sharp lines and a hell of a lot of chrome.

She loved cars.

"When did you get this?" Lucia asked.

"Picked it up yesterday. You like?"

9

"A lot."

"I should have known what with you being the little car whore and everything."

Lucia flipped her brother the middle finger. "Don't call me a whore."

"I said a *car* whore, Lucia. It's a compliment." John chuckled. "Get in. We'll go for a drive, and then I'll bring you back to pick up your car."

"Okay."

Lucia didn't need to be told again. She jumped into the passenger seat, flinging her bag to the floor of the car. John climbed in his side and started the beauty, revving the engine until Lucia was grinning like crazy.

"I sincerely hope whatever man you find realizes that you have expensive taste," John told her.

"Yeah, I know. I blame it on Dad."

John smirked. "I blame it on Dad, too."

Lucia fiddled with the stereo system the car sported while her brother drove them straight back into the heart of the city. She barely noticed time flying them by at all. Despite the fact that there was a thirteen-year age gap between her and Johnathan, she always felt closer to her brother than she had her older sisters.

"So," John drawled, bringing Lucia out of her thoughts.

"Yeah?"

"Andino was pretty insistent you wanted to see me. What's up, kiddo?"

"Well, that, for one."

John's brow furrowed. "Pardon?"

"I'm turning eighteen next month. Can we cut out the kid nonsense?"

Chuckling, John said, "Sure. My bad."

Lucia settled back into the passenger seat, watching the buildings pass them by. "I haven't had any time with you since you got out. You're avoiding Mom and Dad, so apparently, that means staying away from me, too."

"Yeah," John said, cringing, "I hadn't thought that one out very well."

"Obviously."

"Sorry I missed your graduation."

Lucia shrugged. "It's okay."

"No, it isn't. I heard you graduated with high honors."

"I did," she said.

"And got an acceptance to every college you applied to."

"Yep."

John smiled. "Smartest one of us all, Lucy."

Lucia scowled. "I hate that nickname."

"I know, but you're not tough enough or old enough yet to stop me from using it. I dropped the kid one, but I am not dropping Lucy."

She whacked her brother hard on the arm. John grinned back.

"They do care about you, John," Lucia said.

"They do," he agreed. "Right now, I just want to focus on staying sane and good."

"Okay."

"But I'll be around for you, too."

"Good," she whispered, smiling.

"Also, I'll let Dad know you're loving hard on my car."

"Why?"

John made a dismissive noise. "Maybe he's looking to upgrade your car for your eighteenth."

"Maybe?"

"Maybe," her brother echoed with a wicked smile.

Lucia did a little dance in the passenger seat. "Yes!"

"Spoiled."

"Don't judge me."

"You make it hard," John teased.

Sighing, Lucia watched her brother from the side. "Does it feel weird to be out and everything?"

"No, but everyone keeps trying to make it that way."

"I don't get it."

"I feel like a bug being watched as it climbs up a wall. Someone is probably waiting with a shoe to swat me when I get too close. It makes me feel like I'm living in a bubble or something, like I'm going to blink and suddenly go insane."

Lucia hated that for John. "You're not crazy."

John blew out a harsh breath. "Thanks."

Before Lucia knew it, they were driving through a dirtier part of the city. The shady part of Brooklyn that her father had always made it clear to Lucia that she was not allowed to go. Like the smart girl she was, Lucia always followed those rules because she didn't want to find out what would happen if she didn't.

"What are we doing here?" Lucia asked.

"Just keep quiet," John replied. "I've got some business to handle. I knew that you were wanting to chat and see me, or whatever, but I still have work to do all the same. Turn cheek like Dad always told you to do, and we'll be fine."

Lucia chose not to respond to her brother on that front. "*Working*, working?"

"I don't have any other job, Lucy. I'm a Capo, and nothing more."

Great.

John parked the Mercedes in front of a shoddy apartment building. He repeated to her to stay put and leave the car locked until he came back. Then, he climbed out of the car, and Lucia watched him disappear into the building. Less than ten minutes later, her brother emerged from the building with a black duffle bag in hand. John unlocked the car and tossed the bag to the back.

Once he was settled back into the driver's seat, he said, "Just ask."

Lucia peered into the back seat. "What is in that bag?"

"A couple of things."

"Like what?"

"Money and substance."

"Um ..."

"Coke," her brother clarified. "I need to pick up some stuff and hand it off to the people who run with it. Do you understand?"

"Not really."

John shook his head. "Then stop asking."

Lucia could do that.

"I have a couple of more pickups to do before I can take you back. Is that okay?"

"Perfect, John."

Her brother pulled out of the parking space. "Good."

For the next hour, Lucia sat quietly in the car while her brother did whatever it was he did. He often disappeared in and out of buildings with his black bag in hand, and no one ever passed him a second look. Apparently three years in prison really wasn't affecting her brother's ability to do his job.

Sticking a spoonful of a hot fudge sundae in her mouth as John drove through what looked to be a park of some sort, Lucia noticed a group of older kids hanging around a convenience store. Well, she didn't think they were kids, but they were probably around her age or a little older.

John parked his car and beeped the horn once. He flashed his lights twice. Confused, Lucia watched as an older boy broke away from the group and approached John's car. Since the sky was starting to darken, she really couldn't see the guy's face all that well. But the closer he came to John's window, Lucia had a far better view of him.

Sharp, strong lines shaped the man's face. Wild black hair, like he'd been tugging on the ends, hung down to his eyes. Dark russet eyes peered into John's opened window, finding Lucia instantly, while the guy's lips pulled into a cocky smirk.

Lucia glanced away.

"Hey, Ren," John greeted.

Ren.

Lucia took the guy's name in, and chanced another look at him. He

12

wasn't looking at her anymore, but instead, focusing on John.

"Skip," Ren said.

"You got anything for me today?"

"Always, boss."

Ren's hand disappeared inside his coat before he pulled out a white envelope. It passed into John's hand like nothing was amiss. John opened it up, counted the cash that was inside quickly, and then handed over a stack to the man. Then, Lucia's brother tossed the envelope onto the backseat.

"Go see, Tucker," John said. "He'll get you set up for next week for whatever you need."

"Will do, Skip."

Ren's hand hit the top of the car, but before he turned away, he shot Lucia another look. Lucia fidgeted in her seat as her brother took notice of the stare that was passing between the two.

"Ren," John snapped.

Clearly, her brother was not playing around today. He'd never been one for boys being around Lucia, anyway.

"Sorry, Skip," Ren said. "I'm going. Next week?"

"Yeah. Get gone, kid."

John was backing up before Ren had even moved away.

Once they were back on the road, Lucia's curiosity ate away at her.

"John?"

"What?" her brother asked.

"Who was that?"

"Renzo?"

Lucia would recognize an Italian name anywhere.

"Yeah, him," she said.

"A street kid," John informed like it was nothing. "A solider who probably isn't going anywhere but right where he is. It sucks, but that's how it goes."

Lucia picked at her manicured nails, still curious. "Why?"

"Because that's what his father did for our father, and his grandfather for our grandfather. It's a circle, Lucia. It's vicious. It's the kind of life they can't get out of even though they try damned hard. What does it matter?"

She didn't really know.

"Just wondering," Lucia settled on saying.

John's gaze cut in her direction before he said, "Keep wondering. Nothing more."

"Huh?"

"Stay away from guys like Renzo, Lucia."

"I didn't even say—"

"Take it as future advice," John interrupted. "Remember it."

She would try.

But …

Marcellos didn't follow the rules all that well. They were far too filthy for that.

John reached over and turned the radio on. Lucia took in the sight of her brother seemingly happy and carefree. She couldn't remember a time when John looked like he did right at that moment.

"What is going on with you?" Lucia asked.

John flashed a smile. "Huh?"

"You're happy."

"Why wouldn't I be?"

Lucia shook her head. "It's nothing."

John laughed. "My happiness is that confusing for you, huh?"

"No, but usually you're not as … open about it," she settled on saying.

"I'll give you that."

"So what is up?"

John drummed his fingers on the steering wheel with the beat of the music. "Nothing, Lucy. I just think it's going to be an interesting few months in this family. Something feels different. Things are beginning to happen. I'm looking forward to the changes."

She had no idea what her brother was talking about, but he was happy. Lucia took that for what it was, and chose to leave the rest alone.

"Whatever you say, John."

TWO

Everyone likes to say you can choose your own path. But that would be a lie. No one chooses to be born poor, disenfranchised and struggling before they even know their own name. No one wakes up one day and decides to be born to an addict mother who can't seem to control her ability to produce children she can't care for, or love. No one chooses to be a child on the streets, or a child neglected.

No one chooses those things.

So, what did Renzo Zulla choose?

Renzo chose to step up where his mother didn't. For every bad choice she made, Renzo worked twice as hard to correct it. Not for him necessarily. He had two younger siblings that needed a hell of a lot more than he did.

Everything he did was for them.

It always would be.

"Ren!"

Renzo sucked the last drag from a cigarette, and tossed it to the ground. Glancing up, he found his usual guys waiting at the corner store. Calling them friends might be a little too much. And calling them coworkers would be illegal. Or that's what Vito always liked to say.

"Are you heading over to do the drop off today?" Noah asked.

Perry and Diesel, the youngest two of the group, continue their conversation like Renzo hadn't even arrived. Not that he minded. As long as they did what they were told, he didn't give a shit what they did on their spare time. And since work hadn't started today, he still considered this their spare time.

Besides, they did behave.

They fucking listened.

Vito let Renzo run the guys whenever he wasn't on the streets doing business, and these fools knew how this worked. Noah, Perry, and Diesel … well, they came from the same trash Renzo did, in a way. Their home lives weren't any better than his had been growing up. There was a reason each of them met up at this corner store every single day to take their cut of product, and get it on the streets. They needed cash in their hands.

They all had a reason to be here. They all had reasons for why they did this.

Nobody just decided one day that they wanted to be a drug dealer peddling dope to people who were already too far gone to save. It wasn't like the money was good enough to justify the whys of it all, either. Sure, Renzo made a ten percent cut on everything he sold, and another five percent cut for handling this small crew of guys who worked under Vito Abati. And for every pickup or drop off he made, he got another handful slapped into his palm for his *troubles*.

Again, that's how Vito liked to put it.

As if calling the risks Renzo took to move dope from one end of the city to another *troubles* was adequate or accurate. He didn't think it was, but this was his life. And these were the choices he made considering no one was looking at the almost twenty-year-old white boy from the Bronx for fucking anything.

He came from trash.

All he was going to be was trash.

He'd heard it enough times in his life to know it was true, or rather, that it was exactly how everyone else looked at him. All he had to do was slap his address on a job application, and that was enough to make someone look at him like he was the lesser between them. Once they figured out he hadn't made it far enough in the twelfth grade to get his diploma, as he had to drop out to make sure his brother and sister got fed three times a fucking day, he was already screwed.

This society wasn't built for people like him. Already poor, and struggling all the damn time. Already marked with stains from circumstances that pushed him to make choices that would affect the rest of his life so that his siblings could have *something* good in theirs.

But nobody cared about that. Those were details. Nobody liked those.

"Well," Noah asked again, "are you?"

"Yeah," Renzo said, his voice coming out gruffer than he intended. "Later."

He probably should have grabbed something to drink, at the very least, but he was already late taking his little brother, Diego, to the shelter that morning, so he'd be safe for the day. It wasn't like Renzo could count on his mother to take care of her four-year-old, and the chick on their block who watched him had shit to do today. At least at the shelter, they had a free daycare as long as the spots weren't filled by the time he got there. He'd much rather have Diego there than walking the streets with him all day, anyway.

"Well, when will we—"

Renzo turned his sharp gaze on Perry. The youngest of all of them at seventeen, Perry was a handful sometimes. Sure, he got the job done, and he was sneaky as fuck when it came to staying out of trouble, but still … a *handful*.

"You'll get your packages tomorrow. Don't you have a bit to carry you through?"

Perry shrugged. "I guess I got enough."

"Yeah, all right."

Giving the rest of them a look as if to silently ask, *Anyone else?* None of them spoke up.

Renzo stuffed his hands in his pockets, and eyed the quiet streets. Across the way, a man slept in the mouth of an alleyway tucked inside a dirty sleeping bag. Every day, that man and his pigeon stayed in the same exact spot. And every fucking day, it was a reminder to Ren.

He'd been there.

More than once.

Shortly after his birth, his mother sucked on a meth pipe, blew a positive, and got kicked out of the shelter where she'd been staying with him. She called it an act of kindness that the shelter hadn't called CPS for four-week-old Renzo.

He just called it bullshit.

At thirteen, he slept inside the tunnel of a slide at one of the city parks, and used a public bathroom to wash his face every morning.

His sister, Rose, had been around then. She cried all the damn time. She was cold, and hungry. Sometimes, their mother showed up with enough money to keep them warm in a pay-by-the-hour motel but that was just as much a blessing as it was curse.

Especially when they had to step out of the hotel room every so often, and listen to the sounds that slipped out from under the door when each new man would randomly show up.

Renzo made a choice, then. That was the first time he went out on the streets, and looked for some kind of work to give him money to keep his sister warm, and feed her. At first, it'd just been chasing dregs and homeless away from businesses that didn't want that kind of problem in front of their windows. One day, a guy in a leather jacket handed Renzo a package, and asked if he'd run it up to the man sitting in a bakery in Queens.

No questions, he'd been told.

Don't open the package, he'd been warned.

He ran that package, and without ever knowing what it was, had a thousand dollars in his hand by the time he got home.

That man was Vito,

Vito came back, too. Renzo kept saying yes to jobs. He put money away, worked from the time the sun came up, until the streets were pitch black. He kept walking and moving and running for people who wore better clothes than he did and drove vehicles he could only dream about because they paid well, he didn't ask questions, and he needed to do better.

He needed to do better for his sister, and then later, his brother, too.

The rest was fucking history.

His life was not a pretty one.

It was the only he was given.

And fuck anyone who said he didn't try because he did. All he ever did was *try*.

"I'll get your shit to sell," Renzo told the guys, "right after I make a trip into Brooklyn."

Noah and Perry nodded like that was enough for them. Diesel, on the other hand, decided he wanted to test Renzo's already thin patience by running his mouth. As he usually did.

Nothing new.

"Say hi to Rose for me, yeah?" Diesel punctuated that smartass comment with a smirk. "Haven't seen her in a while."

Renzo turned a bit, ready to leave, but not before tossing a remark over his shoulder he knew would cut the other man. "Rose ain't coming back to these streets for nothing, man. And everybody knows those who walk these streets aren't going anywhere but right on these goddamn streets. Where she is, you're never going."

He'd made sure of that.

Dropped every cent he had into lodging and food and books and whatever else his sister needed when she won that scholarship to a private school in Brooklyn for the arts. No matter what, he was going to keep making sure Rose could stay right where she was for as long as she wanted to be there.

"Like you, too, right?" he heard Diesel shout out behind him. "You're walking these streets, too, Ren. Where the fuck are you going, huh? Right here, man."

Was that supposed to hurt?

It didn't.

It wasn't news to Renzo where he was going to live and die. These streets had been mean to him for his entire life. Maybe they'd be kind when they finally killed him.

He wasn't holding his breath.

• • •

Renzo stepped off the city bus, and kept his head down as he walked through the people waiting at the bus stop. He wasn't sure what it was, but he always felt out of place when he wasn't walking his own streets. Maybe that shit was all in his mind, but it still felt very real to him and not something he could escape.

It didn't take long before he was passing a row of brownstones with carefully manicured flower pots on the steps, and shined railings leading up to the front doors. Rose was already waiting at the very end of the block on the front steps of a brownstone that had been converted to an apartment of sorts for students of her school. Like a dormitory off school grounds. Rose could stay at the private school, and it would be cheaper, but the rooms were full. They had to make due elsewhere.

Renzo dropped down on the steps to sit beside his seventeen-year-old sister, and handed over a doggy bag full of sweets from her favorite bakery in the Bronx. He made the trip up to visit her once a week just to make sure she was okay, and had everything she needed. Usually, he dropped off cash and took care of whatever it was she needed until he would be back around again. He never forgot to bring those sweets, either.

Rose smiled as she peeled open the bag to peek inside despite already knowing what would be there waiting for her. "Smells like *heaven*."

Renzo laughed, and leaned back on the steps. "Diabetes is in your future, Rose."

His sister shrugged. "Whatever. I'll die happy, then."

"Pretty sure that's not how diabetes works, actually."

"Stop judging me."

She said that through a mouthful of half-eaten puff pastry. Renzo could only shake his head, and enjoy the moment he had with his sister. All too soon, he was going to need to catch another bus, head across the city, pick up a package of drugs, and get back home so he could put Diego to bed. Tomorrow, he'd get up before the sun had even risen in the sky, and get out on the streets to make sure his guys had their product to deal, so no one was chasing his ass for that. He'd get to his own territory, and wait to make some extra cash, too.

It was a never-ending cycle.

"How's Diego?" Rose asked.

Renzo sighed. "You know how everybody says the twos and threes are terrible for a reason?"

"Not really."

"Well, they do. The fours aren't much better."

Rose grinned a little. "But he loves you."

Good thing.

Next to Rose, the only person Diego cared for was Renzo. He blamed that on their neglectful, addict mother, honestly. She barely looked at Diego when she did show up at their apartment, and that was usually just long enough to sleep before she was gone again. Although, lately, she'd been around more.

It was just enough to make Diego hope his mother would stick around, and then she'd take off once more. Renzo was left picking up all the broken pieces of a four-year-old boy who was learning far too young that there was nothing in this world for people like them.

Not even love.

"How's school?" Renzo asked.

"Good. I painted a naked man yesterday. That was interesting."

Renzo's head snapped to the side, and his gaze narrowed. "*What?*"

Rose let out a laugh. "Relax. Art class. They're professionals."

Professional *what?*

Nude people?

"He was like forty," Rose added. "Chill out."

That only made it slightly better. Renzo decided to just keep his mouth shut, though. What else could he do? His sister was in a far better place than he and Diego were at the moment. His goal was, hopefully, by the time Diego started school … Renzo might have enough money to put him in a decent school that would keep him busy for the day.

He just needed to keep Diego out of trouble, right? Make sure his little brother never had a reason to go out on the streets like he did to make up the difference, and take care of his family. Diego wouldn't have to do that at all if Renzo was doing it for him.

That's all that mattered.

Rose offered him a donut, but Renzo shook his head. He brought those for her, not for him. He should have grabbed food at some point over the day, but he ended up getting busy and shit like feeding himself fell to the wayside. He'd make sure to have something for Diego later, and maybe then he could eat for the first time all day.

But even that was a toss-up.

"So, hey," Rose said, closing up the bag of sweets and giving her brother all her attention again. "I was talking to someone …"

She looked like their mother, he thought. Soft-features, dark hair like his, and brilliant green eyes with gold flecks. He'd taken their father's russet eyes—darker than night itself. Renzo also took his sharp, strong jaw from their shared father, but everything else—high cheekbones, and straight noses to even the way their eyebrows quirked with a mind of their own—came from their mother. But you know, before drugs had taken away the beauty their mother had once been, dulled her skin, and took all the life out of her eyes.

"You were talking to someone, huh?" Renzo rolled his eyes, and shifted his shoulders a bit to get more comfortable. "Didn't I tell you that talking to people gets you in trouble?"

Rose smacked him lightly with the back of her hand. "Just *listen*. It was my counselor at school. She said there's a program at the Y coming up. High school equivalency, you know."

"I don't have time for that."

And he didn't.

Rose grumbled. "Don't say I didn't try."

The knot between his sister's brow tugged at his heart in a painful way. She worried about him far more than she should. He wished she wouldn't concern herself over him and his affairs at all. It would be easier on both of them.

Pushing up to sit straight, Renzo bumped Rose's shoulder with his own, and grinned in a way that had her smiling back. "Remember, kiddo, I look out for *you*. That's how this has always worked. Not the other way around."

"But someone's gotta look out for you, Ren."

"Maybe, but it isn't you."

With that said, he stood from the steps and dug inside his leather jacket to pull out a yellow envelope. He held it out for his sister to take. Rose did, but not before eyeing it first. This was their thing—a few minutes of chit chat every week, he handed over some money, and then he left her to her life until he came back around again.

It was better that way.

"Where did the money come from this week?" Rose asked.

"Does it matter as long as it keeps you here, and not in the Bronx?"

His sister didn't reply.

Renzo didn't need her to.

• • •

Renzo ignored the way the grease on the underside of the fast food bag seeped through to his palm as he balanced it with the rest of the shit he was carrying, and tried to unlock the door of his apartment. It took him entirely too long to realize he didn't need to unlock the door at all because it was already unlocked.

Fuck.

Bad sign number one.

The second bad sign was the mess he walked into as soon as he opened up the front door. Papers and takeout containers scattered across the entryway floor. Discarded clothes beside the laundry basket he'd left out to wash later after Diego went to bed.

And the smell ...

Sickly sweet.

Too sweet.

Renzo knew that smell, and it instantly turned his fucking stomach. As much as the smell of meth made him sick and *angry*, it also made him concerned. He dropped the bags he was carrying onto the chipped

21

countertop in the kitchen as he passed through, and headed right for the living room on the other side.

Sure enough, he found his mother strung out on the couch. One leg had been tossed over the arm of the couch, while the other was bent at an ungodly angle under her backside like at one point, she'd been sitting up straight and fell over. One of her arms hung limply over the side of the couch, while the other was wrapped around her middle. Sunken in cheeks moved with each shallow breath Carmen took, and her hair looked like she hadn't washed it in a couple weeks.

She probably hadn't.

Her scant clothes didn't look much better.

Meth made people stay *way* up.

So, when he saw her sleeping, he instantly looked for signs of something else. His mother was predictable that way. Without trying very hard, Renzo found the reason why his mother wasn't up and climbing the fucking walls with paranoia.

A track mark in her arm dried with a dot of blood, and a forgotten needle that had somehow rolled under the couch. The burnt spoon on the coffee table and rubber band that had loosened and fell down to her wrist was just more proof.

Carmen went way up.

But then she had to balance it out, and go way down, too.

It was a dangerous game. How many times had Renzo called for an ambulance because he found his mother overdosed? Too many to count or care, anymore. It got to the point that he now kept a couple doses of Narcan on hand, but his mother always raged whenever she woke up after he used it.

Narcan put her right into withdrawals, and she was fucking mean, then. Mean, and violent, and *sick*.

He couldn't help it, though. Maybe he should let her die—God knew she wasn't doing anything to help them like she was. She only caused her kids heartache and pain time and time again.

Except he couldn't just let her die. There was a part of Renzo that still clung onto hope that someday—maybe—his mother would wake up from whatever hell she was in, and want better. That she would want to do better. That she would somehow remember she made three people, brought them into the world, and in a way, they still depended on her.

Life hadn't always been like this, either. Renzo could remember brief bouts of time where his mother somehow got herself sober, gave a shit, and *tried*. Usually, when she was pregnant or even shortly after the birth of her kids. Well, for Rose, anyway.

Maybe that was the stupid part of him. That was the part that kept clinging to hope Carmen would get better.

He checked her pulse quickly—a slow, but steady, beat thundered against his fingertips. He took a moment to look her over, and wonder if he should get the Narcan out, but everything pointed to the fact she was probably going to be fine, but strung out all damn night.

Too bad she wouldn't find another place to do this at. She knew the rules—he paid for this place, and his damn name was on the agreement. She wasn't supposed to come here high, and fucked up using it as a place to sleep. He didn't want Diego seeing that shit anyway.

Diego.

Shit.

"Diego!" Renzo darted through the one-bedroom apartment to the room he kept for his little brother. It was tiny as hell, and all he kept in there was a small double bed, a banged up dresser, and a few scattered toys that Diego wouldn't give up for the world. He found the bedroom empty. "*Shit.*"

"Get the fuck up, Carmen," Renzo snarled, heading back into the living room. His mother barely reacted to his shouting at all. Not that he was surprised. He leaned over her, and shook his mother for all he was worth. He slapped her cheek a couple of times with his palm until her eyes started to flutter open. Already, he could see the drugs staring back at him. Confusion, and disorientation. "Where the fuck is Diego?"

"W-what?"

Renzo tried his hardest not to kill the woman right then and there. He'd put up with a lot of shit from Carmen, and had for most of his life, but Diego was *not* one of those things. Ever. That was his hard line.

"*Diego*, Ma," Renzo snapped. "You promised to pick him up from the shelter tonight when the daycare closed because you knew I was going to see Rose. I wasn't going to get back until late. You said you would pick him up. Where the fuck is he?"

Carmen blinked.

Too many stupid, high blinks.

He knew she was going to drift out again before she would even answer him or explain herself. Tomorrow, when she woke up again, she probably wouldn't even remember what she had done, and it would be pointless to argue with her about it then, too.

He should have known better than to trust her to pick up Diego, but he really didn't have a choice today. No one else was available, and she had been trying to stay clean. Or so he thought.

"Is he still at the shelter?"

"What sh-elter?" Carmen slurred.

Fuck.

Renzo stood, and turned fast to head for the front door again. Fuck his mother. She could die there tonight for all he gave a damn.

Someone more important needed him.

Diego would always be more important.

THREE

Laurie chatted on as her arms swung out one way to show Lucia something, and then just as quickly gestured the other way at something new. The woman was a fast talker, and she walked at just about the same speed she spoke. Lucia found she either had to pay close attention to everything Laurie said, or she missed far too much.

"Fridays and Saturdays, the shelter has a group of tutors who come in for the women that need an extra boost to pass their high school equivalency."

"Could I help with that, too?" Lucia asked. "On Fridays, since I won't be working weekends, I mean."

Laurie shrugged. "You could, if you have time between everything else you're doing. I don't see why not."

"And you said the kitchen is open seven days a week?"

"Yes, and you'll get a schedule for two weeks ahead that show which shifts you're helping out in there. It might seem a little overwhelming at first, but ..."

Lucia just laughed as the woman trailed off. Overwhelming was not really the best way to describe this place. It was kind of amazing, honestly. The shelter housed twenty women who were very much in need of help to get back on their feet. Nearly all of them had at least one child, but Lucia had noticed a couple with more than one. A great portion of the women were young—some close to her age, and others, only a couple years older.

As Laurie had explained when they first began their walk-through tour of the facility, it was not *her* responsibility to tell Lucia the different women's stories and what caused them to end up in the shelter. If they felt comfortable enough, they would explain it to her themselves.

But that didn't stop Lucia from *wondering*. She was only human, after all. And her first thought was not to ask what had caused the women to end up here at the shelter, but rather, how she could help.

She was never more aware of her privilege than in that moment. She'd been born rich and to fairly good parents. Society had already given her a hand up by way of both a mother and father in a stable home. She wasn't one of the ones who would get kicked when they were already down.

That's not how it worked for people like her.

Right now, that was obvious.

"And since the kids are gone for the day," Laurie continued, opening the steel double doors that lead into another section of the shelter, "now is a better time to let you see the daycare."

"You know, that's what had me most interested about this place."

Laurie smiled over her shoulder. "I noticed you mentioned it in your application to volunteer. Do you like children?"

"I've actually never been around a lot of young kids," Lucia admitted. "I'm the baby of my family, so someone always felt like they needed to take care of me. I just thought it was interesting that the shelter has managed to run a daycare here alongside everything else they do, so it was an interest of mine."

"Well, you'll get lots of practice with the littles while you're here."

Lucia had to smile at the way the woman called the children who attended the daycare *littles*. "I look forward to it. You said earlier that the shelter daycare takes kids from low-income families around the area, too?"

"We're allowed to have four children per adult. Typically on any given day, we usually have five paid adults and five volunteers. The daycare has two sections—one for four and under. One for five and up. We don't take kids older than twelve, either. But yes, that allows us to take forty children which we try to divide between the two age groups. At the moment, we only have twenty-nine children in the shelter with their mothers, and not all of them need the daycare on a daily basis. Some have made other arrangements, and some are still in the process of finding a job or getting prepared to go out and look for a job."

"That leaves a lot of space open."

Laurie stopped at a second set of double doors with colorful flowers and small handprints painted on the window. "It does. I found we usually have about ten open spots, and knowing this area like I do, because I grew up around here, there are always more people in need than what we see. I put out word that the shelter daycare was going to be taking children from morning until evening, Monday through Friday."

The woman leaned against the doors, and her gaze drifted over the hallway where cubbies had been set up with a row of small closets. Each one had a rack for shoes, and a small hook to hang a tiny coat.

"I knew by not putting it in the paper, we wouldn't have an influx of those who really didn't need it. Instead, I told a select few who would pass the word around to those who might not otherwise be able to afford daycare for their kids, and were barely scraping by with the arrangements they had. Some of those probably weren't safe. I made it a first come, first served sort of thing to allow those who truly needed a safe space for their children while they went out to work, or whatever was the case. Come that first Monday, the eleven spots we had open were filled within fifteen minutes of the daycare opening."

"And that was it?"

Because that sounded like a way for people to *abuse* the system, really. Lucia wasn't exactly rude enough to say it out loud, of course, but she could think it. If all someone needed to do was get up early enough and arrive at the shelter before anyone else to get their kid into the daycare, then *anyone* could do it. Not just those who really needed it.

Laurie laughed like she knew exactly what was going through Lucia's mind without being told. "We have a file on each child—those from within the shelter, and those who come into the daycare from the outside. A questionnaire has to be filled out, and everything a parent or guardian puts on it has to be validated or confirmed in one way or another."

"Things like what?"

"Residency. Job situation. School. Whatever the case may be that causes the person to need the daycare. We also want to make sure this isn't just a drop off for people who don't want to see their kids for the day, you know? I get needing a break from your kids—I have three teenage boys of my own—but that's not what this place is. But having the open spots in the daycare *does* help the community, so despite the logistics that we have to keep up on, I do allow it to continue."

Lucia nodded. "I get it."

"Good. You're going to be a great addition here, Lucia. And I'm sure it's going to look great in your portfolio, as well."

She couldn't hide the cringe that flitted over her lips at that statement. Laurie wasn't wrong. The shelter would look good on her portfolio to the kind of people who would never matter to the people who needed to use this shelter. But to people like Lucia who needed as many good marks on her portfolio as she could get to show a board of people who someday might decide whether or not she was good enough to join their ranks—be it for furthering her education, or a job—then this volunteering gig for the shelter would certainly be great for that.

That was only part of the reason she was here. Another part of it was her need to have a little bit of freedom before she finally went off to college later in the year.

But right now?

Lucia was thinking she needed a dose of reality. She was so sheltered in her life that she'd never even had to think about what happened to people who weren't as fortunate as her. She'd never once had to consider anything other than getting good grades. Her parents would take care of the rest.

"It's not about the portfolio," Lucia said as the woman opened the doors to the main section of the daycare, "I want to be here. I'd like to help."

Laurie let out a quiet sigh. The sound reminded Lucia of the one her mother would make whenever her older brother apologized for doing something wrong, and promised not to do it again when he still lived in the house. As though their mother wanted to believe John, but history proved different things.

The woman gave Lucia a look as they stepped inside the daycare. "I sincerely hope you keep that attitude once you really get started here. It seems like one thing when we're operating during quiet hours. It's quite another when the place is full, we're at capacity, and people are knocking on the doors asking for help."

Lucia blinked.

What could she say to that?

Nothing seemed appropriate.

"Hi, Laurie!"

The soft, boyish tone drew Lucia's attention away from the shelter's manager, and instead to a little boy she hadn't even noticed was inside the daycare. He sat at a small, circular table in a tiny chair meant for children with a crayon in his hand as he colored what looked to be a purple and blue cat. Beside him, a woman typed something out on her phone before she slipped it into the bag at her side.

"Diego," Laurie replied, a wide smile splitting her lips. "How are you, buddy?"

"Good. I made my cat purple and blue."

He was the sweetest thing, Lucia thought. Big, dark russet eyes and pink-tinged cheeks. His dark hair curled at the ends like they could use a trim, but he looked terribly sweet with the longer hair, too. He was still small enough that the backs of his knuckles had dimples. They matched the ones on his cheeks when he smiled, too.

For some reason, Lucia thought the child looked familiar, but she didn't know why. There was no possible way she'd met him before, but it felt like it.

Diego chattered on, and scribbled his crayon against the paper as Laurie looked to the woman sitting beside him.

"Late again?" she asked.

The woman shrugged. "I didn't mind sitting with him."

"Still, he knows the rules."

"Is my brother coming soon?" Diego asked suddenly, his sweet face popping up expectantly.

Laurie shot the quiet woman a look. "I thought the mother—"

"You know he *rarely* asks about her."

Lucia didn't know what the two women were talking about, and she didn't feel like it was her place to ask, either. Not that it mattered. Laurie had other things for Lucia to handle, it seemed.

"Listen, you can get a good look at the daycare tomorrow, Lucia," she told her. "Could you finish up those papers for me, get them all filled out, and drop them off at the front before you head out for the evening?"

"Sure," Lucia murmured.

"Great. Tomorrow—six sharp."

"You got it."

Lucia shot one more look over her shoulder as she exited the daycare, and found Diego was staring after her and smiling. He waved one chubby hand as if to silently say goodbye. She waved back.

• • •

The Cartier watch on Lucia's wrist had just ticked past nine o'clock when she finished filling out the papers with her signature on the final line. Beyond the usual info that she had already provided to the shelter, these papers had just been a recap of policies and things that she needed to agree to adhere to while she volunteered at the shelter.

Things like appropriate behavior, no substance abuse, and other details that didn't even cross Lucia's mind on a daily basis. She had found the relationship policy rather interesting, though. Volunteers and workers were, under no circumstances, allowed to become romantically involved with the women in the shelter.

She wondered how many times that had needed to happen before someone decided to make a policy about it? And just how effective was said policy?

Shuffling the papers into a neat pile, Lucia scooped them up from the counter she'd been using as a makeshift desk, and headed into the hallway. She was reading over the papers to make sure she hadn't missed anything when she first heard his voice.

God knew she hadn't expected to ever hear it again.

Maybe that was why heat shot through her body as her spine stiffened like someone had shoved a rod through it. It was confusing, and disconcerting that someone's *voice* could make her have that kind of reaction.

Lucia brushed it off, and picked up her steps to head for the front of the shelter where she needed to drop off her papers. And where that familiar voice was coming from.

Angry and bitter, the noise picked up as she rounded the final corner.

"I apologized, didn't I?" he demanded.

"You know that's not the point, though."

"I get it—I was late."

"It wasn't even supposed to be you picking him up today, Renzo. It was supposed to be your mother."

29

Lucia came into the main reception area of the shelter in just enough time to see Renzo's gaze flash with fire as he shoved his fisted hands into the pockets of his jeans. His jaw was stiff—like something strong and sharp carved from marble. If not for the scowl etched on his lips that kept twitching like he was trying to hold back words, she thought he might have been a statue.

Cold, and beautiful.

Despite knowing whatever was happening near the entrance doors between Renzo and Laurie was none of Lucia's business, she couldn't help but peek over her shoulder as she approached the desk. The woman there seemed to be doing an even better job at minding her own business as she took the papers from Lucia without ever acting like there was a whole *very loud* argument happening just a few feet away.

Lucia was not that good.

She dared another peek over her shoulder. Standing directly behind Renzo with a blue backpack on was Diego. He stared up at the scene in front of him with his tiny brow knotted in confusion. It was plain to see the tiredness in the child's eyes. How old was he? Maybe four, but he couldn't be any older than that.

Lucia briefly wondered if the little boy was Renzo's son, but then she remembered what Laurie had just said. Their *mother* was supposed to come and pick up Diego. So, a brother, then.

"She can't be counted on, clearly," Renzo said dryly. "I will make sure—"

"This is the fifth time this month that someone has been late picking him up. I even held the spot last week in the daycare for him because I knew you were dropping him off as you'd called ahead to let me know."

"Listen—"

"No, *you* listen, Ren," Laurie countered just as fast. "I know he needs a safe place to go in the day time, so you can … do whatever it is you do. It is only because you were able to provide a statement from your mother showing you take care of the majority of the child's needs that I even allowed him a spot here without confirming other things that everyone else who gets a spot has to prove, Renzo. But I can't keep stretching rules for you when you can't even follow the basic policies of the daycare."

Everything about Renzo's posture *screamed* defensiveness. Lucia wouldn't even have needed to hear him speak to know that just by looking at him.

"He'll be picked up on time," Renzo muttered through a still stiff jaw.

Laurie sighed. "You have one more chance. And no more calling in for me to save the spot, either. He either gets here on time, or you don't get it."

Renzo sucked air through his teeth, and his gaze swung down to his little brother who had come to stand by his side. It seemed that just by seeing the look of worry on little Diego's face, Renzo quickly fixed his scowl and offered a smile to the boy. He tousled his hand through Diego's hair, and winked.

"Is that understood?" Laurie asked, breaking the two brothers' moment.

Renzo let out a grunt, but didn't take his attention away from his brother. "Yeah, I fucking got it."

Laurie only sighed again. Renzo gave the woman one last burning look before he bent down to scoop Diego up to carry him out of the entrance. He'd never even seen Lucia, or so she thought, but she had seen him. That was more than enough for her. She couldn't begin to explain the strange desire in her chest that made her want to follow him just so she could speak with him, but it was there.

It grew with every passing second.

Every *breath*.

Lucia wasn't even sure why. She didn't know anything about Renzo except the fact he worked for her brother, and that didn't mean good things. She'd literally watched her brother give the man money, and Lucia wasn't so young or stupid that she didn't know what her brother did for a living. Like every other man in her family.

And John basically said it, too.

Renzo was bad news.

The streets made him.

Yet, all Lucia could think was that the only difference between what Renzo did to get by and what her family did to make their money was the fact they dressed better than he did. So, she really didn't see the difference.

And besides, right then, all Renzo had looked like was a young man struggling and at the end of his rope. That made her chest ache for reasons she couldn't explain.

"I think that's all, Lucia, thank you," the woman behind the receptionist's desk said. "We'll have your identification card and everything ready for you here at the front tomorrow. Okay?"

Lucia blinked back into reality fast. "Okay, thanks."

By the time she turned back around, Laurie was already gone from the entrance. Probably back to her office, but who knew for sure. It was only the phone buzzing in her pocket that took Lucia's attention away from the doors for a second. She answered the phone as soon as she saw her father's name flashing on the screen.

A lie was already on the tip of her tongue, too.

"Hey, Daddy," she said, "something came up at the shelter, so I might be a little late. That's okay, right?"

Lucian chuckled on the other end. "All right. I was just calling to see if

31

you were going to drive yourself home, or if you wanted someone to come get you because I figured you might be tired."

"I'll drive."

Right after she spoke with the man who just left.

Yeah, right after that.

FOUR

"Can I come back?"

Renzo glanced down at his little brother. Diego's big, worried eyes stared back at him waiting for the inevitable answer he figured was going to come. It sucked that at only four, his brother was already figuring out the world was not made for people like them. He had to learn far too young that disappointment was really the only thing he could count on.

Fucking hell …

God knew Renzo was trying to change that for his brother. He'd managed it for his sister, in some ways, and Diego was next on his list.

The thing was, the daycare was something Diego enjoyed. He had made friends with some of the other kids who attended, and the adults always kept him busy with some new activity each time he attended. He looked forward to going to the daycare a lot more than he did staying with the chick down the block.

Getting kicked out would break his heart.

Renzo wasn't going to let that happen.

Bending down to one knee on the sidewalk, he was eye-level with his little brother once he leaned forward a bit. Renzo grabbed hold of Diego's shoulders, and squeezed just tight enough to give his brother the feeling of a hug.

"I promise, you can come back," Renzo said.

Still, it felt like a lie on his tongue. He was going to try his hardest to make sure Diego didn't lose his spot. He'd guarantee that if not him, then someone else would be here every single day to pick the kid up even if he had to pay someone to do it.

Diego shifted the little backpack on his shoulders, and held tight to the straps. "You're sure?"

"Do I ever lie to you?"

His little brother shook his head.

Renzo grinned, and patted the boy on his grinning cheek. "Exactly, no. Besides, they like you too much in there to kick you out, right?"

That really had Diego lighting up.

Renzo could only chuckle.

"I guess," Diego said, showing off all kinds of teeth as he smiled.

Yeah, he guesses.

Already, the boy was humble.

Life taught them that shit, too. Way too early.

"All right. You hungry?"

Diego nodded. "Yeah, a little."

The food he'd grabbed earlier was probably cold and soaked in grease by now. Although, Diego wasn't fussy when it came to food. He'd eat anything as long as it wasn't green, and it hadn't spoiled. He could pop those burgers and fries in the microwave, and they'd be good to go. Diego would be happy.

Except …

Their mother was still passed out on the couch. If the crazy bitch hadn't already woke up from her stupor, and headed out for her next fix. Or overdosed right where she slept. Either was a very real possibility, but it was more likely that she had probably woken up by now and headed out.

Still, the idea that Diego might see their mother strung out—or worse— was not something Renzo wanted after a day like today. Already, the kid's mind was probably too heavy with all the other worries he'd picked up. There was no need to add their mother to that when she wasn't even worthy of her four-year-old's concerns, frankly.

Diego glanced up at Renzo again.

Big-eyed, and tired.

That much was obvious.

Renzo sighed. The kid just needed to get home, be fed, and put to bed. If he was quick about it, Diego might not even see their mother on the couch if she was still there by the time they got back. The hallway to the bedroom was in the front of the apartment, anyway.

"I'm tired, Ren," Diego said, shifting his little backpack again so that this time, it slipped off his arms and hit the cement sidewalk. "Will you carry me home?"

It was about four blocks.

Diego was a good forty pounds.

God knew Renzo had done enough running around today, and shit. He'd been on his feet all day working. He was tired too. He needed to eat— since all he'd shoved into his mouth today had been a coffee in passing— and a bed.

Soon.

It didn't matter.

Diego was most important.

Renzo reached out, and swept his tired brother into his embrace. Diego's feet lifted from the ground, and he wrapped his limbs tightly around Renzo's waist and neck.

"Thanks, Ren," Diego mumbled against his neck.

"You got it, buddy."

Renzo grabbed that tiny backpack, and let it dangle from his fist as he turned to give one last look at the shelter before they turned off the lights.

He had not been expecting to see *her* coming his way.

Renzo stiffened all over. Oh, sure, he'd seen her out of the corner of his eye while he'd been in the shelter arguing with Laurie, but he didn't know why the hell she was there except to maybe write a fucking check, and go on her way feeling better about herself. Wasn't that what her kind did?

More fucking money than brains.

Lucia—yeah, he knew her name; everybody who worked the streets under people like the Marcellos knew *all* their names—lifted a hand as if to wave, and offered a small smile. Renzo stayed like a cold statue as she came even closer, seemingly unbothered by his cool reception and unwelcoming stance.

"Is Diego okay?" Lucia asked, her gaze skipping to his little brother.

The boy popped his head up, and smiled brilliantly. Always willing to make someone else happy even when he was anything but.

"He's fine," Renzo replied gruffly.

What was this chick even doing out here? Or in this part of town, for that matter? It was a bit of a step down for her considering the last time he saw her, she'd been sitting in a black two-door Mercedes with her brother.

The young woman *screamed* money. From the Cartier watch on her wrist to the diamond studs in her ears. Even the way her wavy light brown hair had been streaked with red and blonde highlights looked like something that had been done in a proper salon. And that was before Renzo thought to figure out what brand of jeans she had decided to paint on that morning, or if that was actual silk she was wearing for her blouse.

Yet, even with the money she might as well have been draped in, Renzo wasn't so distracted that he couldn't see Lucia was pretty.

That was a bit rude, really.

Beautiful was a better description.

She was tiny featured. Small lips with a perfect cupid's bow. A button nose. High cheekbones. Soft lines on her face, and an even softer smile. She was petite in height, maybe only reaching his chin, but that didn't detract from the shape of her hips or the tight cinch in her waist.

Shit.

He needed to get laid if he was noticing how nice looking some spoiled little rich girl from the other side of the city was. And he really didn't need to be thinking about getting laid while he was holding Diego.

"Hi, Lucia," Diego said. "Miss Teresa said you're gonna work here now."

Oh, for fuck's sake.

Lucia nodded, and smiled back at Diego. "That's right."

Her gaze drifted to Renzo again.

"What?" he asked.

"I was thinking about offering you two a ride home. It's late, and your little brother looks like he's had a rough day. I don't know how far you live from here, but do you really want to carry him the whole way?"

Renzo's jaw stiffened. "Like I don't do it every other day?"

Lucia didn't miss the bite in his tone if the way her smile faded was any indication. Maybe he took a little bit of satisfaction in that, but he wasn't about to admit it. Renzo wasn't the type to be an asshole just to be an asshole. But here he was.

Something about this chick made his nerves stand up on fucking end. Like little hairs that felt something annoying or bad, and were reacting to it being too close.

He knew exactly where Lucia Marcello came from, and she was nothing like him. A privileged little girl who probably never knew what it was like to struggle, or walk the streets day after day because she wouldn't eat otherwise.

He doubted she knew any of that kind of shit at all.

And for some reason, it just irked him like nothing else that she was so willing to stand there like she was and act as though there was no difference between the two of them. As if the two of them were somehow on level ground when it came to the rest of the world. Like she wasn't wearing designer and silk while he was running around in frayed jeans and a leather jacket that he'd won from a bare fist boxing match three years ago.

Like her heels didn't have red soles.

And his combat boots weren't scuffed all to hell.

He was the poor kid from the Bronx.

She was the trust fund baby with mafia connections.

Oil and water.

Lucia seemed to pick up on his hesitance to take a ride from her, and she shrugged. "It's just a ride, you know. You seemed angry inside, and I thought maybe I could make it a little better."

Renzo arched a brow high. "Better?"

"That's what I said."

"A ride isn't going to make my life better, Lucia."

He didn't miss the way her throat jumped when he said her name, or how her pretty mouth drifted open a little more. He was noticing too much about this chick, and at the moment, his brother was getting heavier by the second on his arm.

He figured, why not let Diego decide? His kid brother always had a better feeling about people than Renzo did. It was a talent, really.

"What do you think, Diego," Renzo started to say, "should we ride with *her?*"

Lucia huffed a bit.

Diego just smiled. "Yeah, Ren."

That was that.

"Guess we'll take a ride," Renzo muttered.

Lucia's hazel gaze glittered when she smiled brilliantly all over again. She even did a little bounce on her feet that only added to her sprite-like joy.

Yeah.

He was noticing *way* too much.

• • •

Renzo did well with silence. He liked it when things were quiet because that meant no one was yelling at him or demanding something. It meant the day was over, and he could try to relax a bit. Silence was his best friend, really.

Lucia was not the same.

He wasn't sure if it was the fact that he was quiet, or because Diego had somehow fallen asleep in the back seat in the span of two blocks, but the woman wouldn't *shut up*. She just chatted on like she was having a full-on conversation with him even though he hadn't opened his mouth to say anything at all.

Renzo didn't even know what she was talking about because he had started to tune her out about a block back even if she did look so animated about whatever the hell she was talking about.

Finally, he got tired of being quiet and asked, "Are you even old enough to drive?"

That shut her up.

Lucia's gaze cut to him, and narrowed. "Would we be in this car otherwise?"

Well ...

"I don't know the kinds of strings your people can pull," he said, shrugging one leather-covered shoulder. "Fake license, maybe. A guy I used to work for got me one when I was sixteen, so I could get into places that required me to be at least eighteen."

Lucia rolled her eyes. "I'm almost eighteen. I do have my license, but I had to have some strings pulled to let me drive at night since I'm not eighteen yet. But that won't matter soon, anyway."

Renzo blinked.

All he heard in that was *almost eighteen*.

Which meant she was seventeen.

Jesus. H. Christ.

Before he could mull that over, though, Lucia was speaking again. "And

37

how old are you, Renzo?"

"Old enough to know I have no business sitting in this fucking car."

Lucia frowned. "Why?"

"Many reasons." He waved that question off. "Turn right at the next stop light."

She followed his direction as she hummed under her breath. "I'd say you're about eighteen, right?"

Renzo made a noise in the back of his throat. "Close. Nineteen, almost twenty."

"Huh."

Yeah.

Like he said ... old enough to know better.

Another block passed them by in silence before Lucia was the first one to break it. Color him surprised. The girl didn't seem to know how to sit in peace and quiet.

"I'm sorry if I made you uncomfortable by offering you a ride," she said.

Well, he hadn't been expecting that.

Renzo glanced over at her, but he found all he could see was her profile since she was so focused on what was ahead of them on the road. It didn't matter, really. The lights from the dash were enough to halo her soft features, so he could linger a little too long on the shape of her lips and the length of her eyelashes.

She really was something to look at.

A part of him wondered what else made up this young woman, but the rest of him figured ... *not very fucking much*. Money could give a person a lot of things, but it couldn't magically turn them into a human being or tune them into the reality of the world around them. That was the thing about those who lived in the rose-tinted bubble of wealth and privilege ... they never had to face *life*. Comfort, stability, and protection was simply paid for, and expected.

The very second he thought those things, his mind was quick to point out that he didn't know if those things were true about Lucia. he was only assuming because of the image she presented to the world. A lot like people just assumed whatever the fuck they wanted to about him because of where he came from.

Where was the difference?

It didn't matter. That bitterness was bred as deep as it could be into Renzo's very fabric of being. He couldn't even cut that shit out.

"You didn't make me uncomfortable," he lied. "I just figured you probably had better things to do than haul my ass around."

Lucia shrugged, and finally glanced over at him. There was honesty staring back from her when she murmured, "Not really."

Renzo swallowed hard, and took in their surroundings. "Next parking lot on the right—that's our apartment building."

"Okay."

Thankfully, Lucia was soon pulling up in front of Renzo's apartment building. He wasn't sure what might be said next between them if he didn't get the hell out of that car, and *soon*. He was also getting a little tired of having his own foolishness shoved in his face.

Lucia quieted as she put the car into park. He turned to thank her— because frankly, he might not have had a mother who raised a half-decent guy, but he still was one at the end of the day—and noticed her gaze skipping over the front of the building.

God knew the place was an eyesore. Two steps from being condemned, too. Broken bricks, and cracked cement stairs. Two apartments on the bottom had their large windows broken out, and covered with plastic garbage bags because the landlord was a lazy fuck. There were always a few dregs hanging around the outside. Selling dope—Renzo never dealt where he lived just because that could cause problems.

He could see it written all over Lucia's face.

The harsh reality that the two of them were not anything alike. They came from two entirely different worlds.

This was his.

It was nothing like hers.

Renzo scoffed, drawing Lucia's gaze to him as he muttered a quick, "Thanks."

Stepping out of the car, he didn't say another word to her even as he opened the backdoor, and unbuckled his sleeping brother. He didn't have anything to say.

Lucia seemed to think the same.

Good fucking riddance.

• • •

"Come on, Ren, it was a *mistake*."

"Fuck off, Carmen."

That was all Renzo offered his mother before he slammed the front door of the apartment. He'd already run Diego down to the shelter daycare in just enough time before they closed the open spots. Laurie wasn't screwing around the day before when she warned him that they wouldn't be holding a spot for Diego anymore.

As much as that sucked, Renzo did understand. It just pissed him off, too. It wasn't Diego's fault that his mother was a fuck up, and Renzo made a mistake in thinking he could trust his mother to do anything. Honestly, he should have known better.

"You little asshole!"

Renzo kept his back turned to his shouting mother as she opened the apartment door just to lean out in the hallway, make a damn scene, and scream at him. This wasn't anything new. And the whole floor knew what Carmen Zulla was like on a good day.

"Remember what I said," Renzo warned. "I come home one more time and find you strung out, and I'll personally drop your ass outside. I don't give a fuck who you are to me, Carmen."

Because mothers ... they didn't act like that. They didn't abuse or neglect. Not a *real* mother, anyhow.

Renzo was done feeling guilty for treating his mother like the abusive addict she was simply *because* she was his mother. The woman deserved what she got—she either wanted to be good for her kids, or she could fuck off.

That's just how it was going to be.

Carmen made a screech—a little too high, he thought. She wasn't strung out as badly as she had been the night before. But she had definitely smoked something to keep the shakes away and make sure she was *up*. She hadn't been home when he took Diego to the daycare, but she was there by the time he got back.

Someone was feeding the bitch's need for a fix. And it was somebody close.

That was probably going to be a problem. One Renzo would eventually have to deal with, but today was not that day. Already, he was late for the daily meeting with his guys down by the corner store. He was already edgy enough considering he had a whole brick of cocaine in his messenger bag, a half a pound of weed, and a bag of opiate pills that were all too popular on the streets lately.

He hadn't had time to drop that shit off individually to each guy who needed to deal it. He preferred to do that late at night when he could just skip from building to building without being seen until he had nothing left but his own shit to sell. He certainly didn't like walking around with this much product in broad daylight.

If someone thought to jump him, and they took it?

He'd be the one who had to fix it. Come up with the money to pay it back—impossible, there was at least a hundred-thousand dollars' worth off drugs in his bag—or something. If he thought to run from the higher ups who kept him supplied with drugs, well ... that wouldn't end well for him.

They'd hunt him down.

Like a dog.

That's all he was to them, anyway.

Just a fucking dog.

Renzo kept his pace at a normal speed as he left his apartment building. He didn't do any more or less glancing around than he normally would. There was no fucking need to draw unneeded attention to himself because he was acting strange.

Somehow, he made it to the corner store without any trouble. As he expected, his guys were waiting, and they looked like they weren't pleased about it.

Renzo jerked his head to the side, and without needing to be told, Perry, Noah, and Diesel slipped into a connected alleyway. He wasted no time pulling out the packages from his bag, unwrapping the plastic wrap around the bricks of drugs, and handing each person their take for the week. They'd go home, weigh and package everything, and get to work. In a week, they'd all meet up again to hand over money and get their take of the cash, too.

There was a bit of trust involved in all of this. He had to keep up with the street price of *everything*. That way, when the guys came back with empty bags but hands full of money, he knew whether or not they were stealing from him.

So far, none of them dared to.

A while back, he had four guys. The other three got to learn really up close and personal what happened when someone stole from Renzo. It hadn't been pretty, but really, it couldn't be.

He needed that lesson to *stick*.

"Thanks, Ren," Noah muttered, shoving his take into his own bag.

The other two echoed the same thing.

Then, Perry said, "Hey, guess what we heard?"

"I imagine a lot of things," Renzo replied. "And probably nothing that I'm very interested in hearing."

Diesel laughed. "Right, I bet. Anyway, we heard you got dropped off last night with Diego. Quite a fucking car, we were told. A Mercedes, right? Who are you messing with that they're driving you home in a Mercedes?"

Fuck.

Not the kind of attention he needed. It would not do him any favors for these guys to think he was reaching higher than they could. He didn't need to be seen as out of their league in any regard. It would make discontent, and he couldn't fucking trust or control any of them when they thought he was hiding shit like *money*.

Renzo glanced up, and gave the three a look they would recognize as him reaching the end of his very thin and frayed rope. "Get to fucking work, and stop listening to the nonsense you hear on the streets."

FIVE

"Just make a choice, Lucian," Jordyn said. "It shouldn't be this hard."

"Well, it is, *bella*."

Lucia was drawn from her mind at her parents' voices filtering through her thoughts. In the back seat of the Rolls-Royce, she watched familiar streets pass them by from the safety of the vehicle. It was the smell of new leather that she liked the most in a car. Considering the Rolls had been a gift to her mother for their last anniversary from her father, the car still had that smell. Usually, it would comfort Lucia, but right then, it wasn't doing that at all.

"You liked the one in the Maldives," Jordyn pointed out.

Her father grunted under his breath. "Chicago has business down there, though."

"Holy fu—"

"On our way to church, Jordyn. Try not to swear."

Lucia glanced at her mother who was currently sitting in the passenger seat—despite it being her car, she liked being driven around more than she drove—who gave Lucian a look that would burn a lesser man.

"Get over the Chicago thing," Jordyn muttered. "That's all I am saying."

"I am over the Chicago thing. I let Liliana get married to that Rossi kid, didn't I?"

"You're calling him a kid, *really?*"

"Well—"

"And *let her*, Lucian. Let her, though."

Her father sighed loudly. "It's not about Chicago, but the fact they have business there. I don't want it to seem like us buying that vacation home would be … us trying to step on their toes in some way."

"Well, I liked the home in the Maldives. Far more than the other ones we looked at. And it's over the *water*, Lucian. I want the Maldives home. Call Tommas—"

Her father let out another one of those grunts. He only did that when he wasn't pleased about something. Lucia might typically find an exchange like this between her parents amusing. But right then, she was just thinking about someone and something else.

"Make that sound to me one more time, Lucian," Jordyn warned. "Call Tommas in Chicago, let him know we're looking at a home to buy in the Maldives, and it has nothing to do with business. *Simple*."

"Yes, everything about the mafia is exactly *that* simple, Jordyn."

Lucia had absolutely no reason to open her mouth and join their conversation. It wasn't like her parents had invited her to do that, or anything. They also hadn't said she couldn't join in, either. She was seventeen, not five. If they didn't want her to hear their conversations, they wouldn't be having them with her within earshot.

"How many homes do we have?" Lucia asked.

She watched her father's gaze shoot to the rearview mirror, so he could get her in his sights. Her mother, on the other hand, never even looked away from the passenger's window as she said, "A few."

"But how many is a few?"

Lucian hummed under his breath. "That depends on what you want to know, *Tesoro*. Just vacation homes, or … properties as a whole."

Lucia blinked.

"Is there a big difference?"

"*Big difference*," her mother said.

Huh.

"We have three vacation homes in Europe—one in England, another in Italy with an attached vineyard, and a smaller penthouse in Paris. We also have a large cabin in Canada. They call it a cabin, mind you, but that is only because it is made out of logs and not because it sits on a hundred acres of private property, and has three floors."

"There's also the one in Maine," Lucia said.

She remembered that one because she'd visited it more than once as a young girl.

Jordyn nodded, and shot her daughter a look over her shoulder. "We bought that to have somewhere to stay when I visited my biological father, but after he passed, we rented it out and have not been back."

"One in Vegas, too," Lucian put in after a moment.

Like it was nothing at all.

Like they hadn't just admitted to having *six* fucking vacation homes, and were considering buying a seventh.

What kind of a waste of money was *that*? Sure, she knew her family was well-off. They were beyond the simple title of *rich*. The Marcellos were vastly wealthy. But sometimes, it didn't always look that way from the outside when they simply lived in beautiful homes tucked away in normal suburbs with luxury cars in the driveway.

It was what people didn't know and couldn't see where the Marcellos hid their wealth.

"Do you even visit them all every year?" she asked.

Lucia was pretty sure she knew the answer to that question. Her parents went on the occasional vacation, and she typically went with them.

So no, no they did *not* visit all their many homes.

43

"We try to visit a different one each year, if they're not rented out to someone else," her father said. "They are good investments, which in turn, means a good profit in the future. That's why they were purchased and added to our portfolio. Maybe with all you kids out of the house, we *will* be able to visit more than one a year."

He'd offered that with a joking tone, but Lucia was still feeling heavier than normal in her chest. Even her shoulders seemed to slump a bit. Her parents went back to discussing the Maldives vacation home like she hadn't even been talking to begin with. But right then, she didn't mind.

She had other things to think about.

It was no wonder why Renzo—she'd learned a day after seeing him at the daycare from the shelter's manager that his surname was Zulla—had looked at Lucia like she was something from another world. And not necessarily a world he wanted to know or visit, either.

She'd dropped him off at his place that night, and found herself concerned by the people loitering near the front of the worn down building. Mostly because they hadn't exactly looked friendly, and she was concerned they might cause Renzo problems since he had a four-year-old in his arms.

Yes, she'd noticed the fact there was nowhere for Diego to play but a parking lot. Yes, she noticed the shape of the building. And yes, it made her take a second look.

She hadn't meant to offend him, but that's what his scoff and hard slam of the car door said she did. But maybe she understood now … he looked at her and saw things he did not have, and things he would never be.

Or that's what he thought.

Lucia was lost in those thoughts of hers until her father finally pulled the Rolls into the parking lot of a familiar church. Every Sunday, never failed, this was where Lucia was supposed to be. Her father stepped out of the car first after parking to head for the passenger side and open the door for her mother.

Her mother, though, took that time to turn in her seat a bit to look at Lucia with a curious expression. "Are you okay? You seemed upset earlier … but then quiet."

No, not really.

Lucia decided to lie, anyway. "I'm fine, Ma."

• • •

"Lucia, you saw the schedule change, didn't you?"

Lucia's head popped up over the counter where she was currently working to pull out dishes that would be needed for the morning rush at the shelter. She had learned, since she started work there a few days earlier, that thanks to donations of food and money, they were able to serve an average of a hundred people per mealtime. It was more than the shelter housed, so it was the only time that the doors were opened for anyone who needed fed off the streets.

She'd figured that the kitchen would probably be her least favorite place to work in the shelter. She didn't do well in chaotic situations—that wasn't where she did her best work, frankly. Yet, she found the kitchen and serving food to be one of her favorite parts. Maybe it was because each face had a new story to tell, and they were always kind and grateful just to be there. Plus, they liked having someone to talk to.

Lucia liked listening.

She was good at that.

It always seemed like everyone working the kitchen made it a point to have fun, too. Music was always filtering over the chatter of people and the clattering of dishes. It didn't matter if you were in the back scrubbing out pots, or at the front on the serving line … someone would make you smile and laugh.

"Did you see it?" Laurie asked again.

"Um, no," Lucia admitted. "I just came right back here to get started and didn't double check. Sorry."

Laurie smiled as Lucia set another pile of plates on the metal counter. "Yeah, I don't blame you. I never get to work in the kitchen as much as I want to anymore. It's still my favorite place to be, but now I get to push all the papers and make sure everyone is doing what they're supposed to be doing. Like *you*."

Laughing, Lucia wiped her hands across the apron. "Where am I supposed to be, then, and could I *maybe* convince you to let me stay here instead?"

The woman had the decency to pretend she was considering Lucia's request before she fake frowned, and shrugged. "Sorry, can't do it. They really need an extra adult in the daycare today since it's at capacity, and you know how it can get in there. Besides, you're great with the kids and most of them who are regulars already know your name. I am sure they would be super excited to see you walk through the doors."

Well …

Lucia nodded. "All right."

Laurie laughed. "Yeah, I didn't figure you'd have a problem with switching."

Not really.

The daycare was Lucia's second favorite place to work in the shelter. She did enjoy the kids a lot, and it was another place that was all about fun, and it kept her moving from one thing to another. She enjoyed being busy.

Time passed faster, and she got to feel like for a few hours, she was making an impact for someone else.

With those kids, she wasn't Lucia, the mafia *principessa*. She wasn't some rich girl who people looked at and figured she was just there to get a good mark on her portfolio for volunteering before she headed out to college in California to start the second semester.

She was just *Lucia*.

Lucia found that she wanted to just be herself here a lot more than she wanted to be the thing people saw her as when she walked in the doors.

"Okay, hurry over to the other side of the shelter, and get in there to help," Laurie said, turning to head back to whatever she was doing for the morning.

"Aww, Lucia's leaving!"

The echo came out from the kitchen behind Lucia, traveling over the noise of the latest song on the radio and the laughter from the joke someone had just told.

Lucia laughed as a half of a dozen voices echoed the same sentiment as she shrugged off her apron, and pulled the gloves from her hands.

"Bye, Lucia!"

Yeah, she enjoyed the daycare.

The kitchen was still her favorite, though.

· · ·

"Will you be here tomorrow?" little Rowen asked, her big brown eyes and corkscrew curls bobbing in her excitement as she stared up at Lucia. The girl's mother apparently had a shift change this week, and so, she needed someone to look after her while she did her morning hours. The daycare it was. "I hope so."

Lucia smiled as she bent down to help the girl slip her pink, sparkly backpack on. "I'm pretty sure I'm in here working tomorrow, too."

"Awesome!"

Rowen's exclamation was punctuated with a tiny fist pumping into the air. The girl's mother smiled at the doorway, and as soon as she called out her daughter's name, Rowen gave a little wave before heading off.

Lucia checked her watch to find it was time for her lunch break. The thirty minutes wasn't much, but it allowed her to grab something from the kitchen, and relax for a few seconds. After letting one of the other supervisors know she was taking her break, she headed out of the loud and busy daycare.

"Loud down there today, isn't it?"

Lucia popped her head into Laurie's office because she figured it would be rude to just agree and pass on by. "It is, but they're having a great time. Finger painting today, so *messy*."

The woman never took her gaze away from the paperwork on her desk. From what she understood, Laurie had started this shelter out of her home a decade or more ago. It had since grown into the amazing organization it now was. The woman was always the last one to leave, and the first one to arrive.

This place would never fail with Laurie running it. Not to mention, Laurie was a motivator for everyone around her, including Lucia. Focused, driven, and always wanting to help. The woman never asked for something from someone else. She simply went out, and got whatever it was that she needed for her shelter, or whatever the case may be.

"I was meaning to ask you something," Lucia hedged.

It had been on her mind for a few days, but she'd swallowed down her questions thinking that Laurie likely wouldn't tell her anything—if she even did know something—or the woman wouldn't have anything to say.

"What's that?"

"I noticed Diego Zulla hasn't been around in a few days. He was here the day after I first started, but not since. Is that … usual for him?"

Really, she was trying to find out where the boy and his brother were at the moment. With every day that passed where Lucia didn't see Diego show up at the shelter's daycare, the more concerned she became.

For him, *and* Renzo.

Plus, Lucia was worried that maybe their awkward interaction that night in her car caused Renzo to avoid the daycare altogether. She hadn't meant to make him feel badly about his situation. He, like everyone else in this damn world, was doing the best they could given what he had.

No one could expect anything more.

Laurie finally glanced up from the paperwork in front of her with a soft gaze. "It is a little unusual for him to go this long without attending the daycare, but that's not my business, and it isn't *your* business, either. That's important to remember here, Lucia. There is only so much you can do, and becoming too involved with one person in particular can cause a problem. I hope you understand."

Sure, she did.

That didn't mean she was going to listen to the advice, or heed it, for that matter. If Renzo was avoiding the daycare because of her, then she was going to let him know that was pointless, and it only really hurt Diego in the end.

She knew where he lived. She could go right over there and let him know that as soon as she was done with her shift.

She certainly wasn't going there just because she wanted to see Renzo again.

No …

It wasn't that at all.

• • •

Lucia wasn't sure which thing bothered her more. The fact that the guys loitering on the steps of Renzo's apartment building were leering at her car like they wanted to get their hands on it, or that their attention *instantly* switched to her the second she stepped out of the car.

Jesus.

"Well, look at *that*. Damn."

One of them even whistled.

Lucia was quite aware that she was pretty. She took after her mother with her soft features that were made even more dainty by the fact she was sprite-like in size. She also learned how to wield a makeup brush and hair tools from the time she was little because her two older sisters, Liliana and Cella, thought that was an important skill for her to learn.

That didn't mean she enjoyed being leered at like a piece of meat walking down the sidewalk. She was pretty sure no woman enjoyed that feeling.

"Bit of a step down for a chick like you around here, ain't it?" someone else called.

Lucia clenched her jaw, and tightened the coat around her waist as she headed for the steps of the apartment building. The guys' comments only picked up more the closer she came, but she just tuned them out until she was standing right in front of them.

"I'm looking for someone," she said.

The guy in the middle with the longer hair and beady blue eyes sneered. "You're in the wrong place then, girly."

Girly.

Lucia couldn't even try to not be offended at that statement. "First, don't call me that. Second, I know Renzo Zulla lives here. That's who I'm looking for. I need an apartment number, if that's not too much to ask."

Looks passed between the three guys, but the one in the middle was the only one who seemed to want to do any talking for the time being. Lucia didn't really give a shit who talked, as long as someone did, and they gave her the right apartment number. The less time she had to spend outside with them, the better.

"Since when does Ren hang out with someone like *you?*"

Lucia lifted a single brow. "What does *someone like me* even mean?"

"How much does your car cost?"

"I don't know. I'll ask my father, and let you know the next time I come around. If you're done making comments about my money, an apartment number would be great."

The guy scoffed under his breath, and glanced away from Lucia like she wasn't worth looking at anymore. He could try to save his pride all he wanted. She didn't care as long as she got the apartment number.

"Floor three, apartment five," the guy muttered. "Don't chip a fucking nail on your way up there, princess."

Lucia moved past the guys sitting on the steps, and replied, "It's *principessa*, actually. If you want to insult me, at least do it right."

She was all too aware that she really shouldn't be antagonizing people she didn't even know from a hole in the ground, but they weren't the only ones who had too much pride. She didn't want to be insulted just because she looked like an easy target. No Marcello would stand for that, woman or not.

Lucia entered the building and made sure not to look back at the guys she'd left behind. She didn't want to give them the indication they bothered her or got under her skin. She figured that probably wouldn't be to her benefit. Bullies, no matter what kind, were all the same at the end of the day. They only kept being pests because they believed they were getting somewhere.

Soon, Lucia had climbed the three flights of stairs and opened the heavy metal door to the hallway belonging to a row of apartments. The first thing she saw when she opened the door was a woman passed out down the hallway.

And by passed out, the woman was *out*.

She didn't know from what, but given the hallway smelled like cheap beer and the woman had an empty bottle of Colt 45 beside her, Lucia figured it was probably alcohol.

It took Lucia entirely too long to realize the woman was passed out right in front of Renzo's apartment. On the hallway floor.

Great.

She was careful not to touch the woman as she leaned over her to knock on the door, but that didn't stop her from glancing down. Pale, and with a bit of vomit on the side of her mouth, the woman looked like a sore fucking sight.

And it just made Lucia sad.

Who was she?

SIX

Renzo was done with being on his feet for the day. Entirely fucking done. As much as he loved his combat boots, he was starting to think he needed to wear something else on his feet if he was going to be running all over the place. With his head down, and his hands shoved in his pockets, he wasn't paying attention to what was down the block. He was intent on checking in with his guys, then getting home to drop off the bag of shit hanging over his shoulder, and then he could go pick up Diego from the chick a few apartment buildings down who had agreed to watch him for a couple of weeks.

Renzo sighed, and dragged a hand out of his pocket to scrub down his face. God knew Diego would much rather go to the shelter daycare, but the idea of running into Lucia again put Renzo on edge. There was something about that woman that made his hackles rattle, and he felt like she was taunting him just by being alive.

He knew it was irrational. It wasn't her fault that their lives were entirely different. She hadn't chosen to be born to the family and wealth she had been given, just like he hadn't chosen to be born like he was.

It didn't matter.

Renzo figured the easiest way to move on from all of that shit was to put as much distance between himself and Lucia as he possibly could. That, unfortunately for Diego, included the daycare. Although, how long this would last was anyone's guess. The woman babysitting Diego this week could only do so because she had time. Next week might be a different story, and Renzo would either have to figure something else out, or take Diego back to the shelter daycare. Which would make the kid happy as hell.

"You always lookin' at the ground whenever you're walkin' somewhere, or what, shithead?"

That fucking voice.

Renzo reacted to that voice in such a visceral way, it was impossible for him to hide it. Like nails raking down a chalkboard, or a damn spike being driven right into his spine with as much force as possible. He got cold all over, and yet hot with anger at the same damn time. Stiffening like a board, and fisting his hands at his sides, he came to a stop as he lifted his head to find a familiar man leaning against the brick of a corner store. The same store Renzo used to meet up with his guys every morning before they headed out to work, and then again in the evenings when they had to check in.

In fact, Perry, Noah, and Diesel were there waiting for Renzo *now*. Which only put him on a steeper edge as his gaze drifted between his guys down by the payphone, and his father who couldn't have worse fucking timing.

What was he even doing here?

Renzo swore this asshole only showed up in his life when he wanted one of two things—to either remind Renzo of the shit he came from, or to get money. A habitual gambler, a drinker, and an all-around abuser, the man was absolute scum. He'd never taken care of the two children he'd helped create with Renzo's mother, and he only caused chaos and problems whenever he did show up into their lives.

It was like looking in a mirror as he regarded this man. Well, an older and *shittier* mirror, maybe. A disappointing, useless, cocksucker of a mirror.

Dark hair that hadn't been washed in a few days.

Russet, bloodshot eyes.

Defensive posture.

Toothpick hanging out of the side of his mouth.

"Son," Charlie muttered around his toothpick. "Heard you'd be walkin' past this way around this time. Thought we should chat."

Renzo's jaw clenched, and ached from the force. "We don't have anything to talk about. Pretty sure the last time we talked, you told me to *fuck off, and stay there.*"

And all he asked for was a place for Rose to stay after she had a blowout fight with their mother. Charlie had laughed, told his son to fuck off, and then slammed the apartment door in Renzo's face. That was after it took Ren a few days to track this asshole down because God knew where he was on a regular basis.

Charlie shrugged, and tipped his head to the side to peer at the waiting guys. "That your crew, or …?"

"That's none of your business. What do you want?"

Better to get his father on track, figure out what he could do to make the man go away, and be done with it. Renzo didn't need Charlie's brand of trouble, but especially not out on these streets where he worked.

"Want to know what you're up to," Charlie returned, those dark, bloodshot eyes darting back to Renzo's. "I can't come around to check up on my son? Maybe I was thinkin' about you, and wanted to see you."

That toothpick in his father's mouth bounced with every word, and for some reason, the sight of it made Renzo's blood boil. The man was so cool, calm and unbothered. Like he wasn't standing there talking to one of the two kids he just fucking abandoned. Renzo had the strangest urge to take that toothpick, and stab it through his father's eye just because he could and he bet it would feel damn good to do it, too.

He wasn't the kind for violence. He *could* be violent, when the time called for it. A lot of his business on the streets was violent, in some ways. That was how he stayed on top, but it was also how he made sure no one else fucked around with him.

But he didn't want to have to do any of that. He didn't want to resort to breaking someone's face just because he needed to survive. That was the thing, though—this was life for him. And yet, he found it was extremely easy for him to want to absolutely *slaughter* this man in front of him. Consequences be damned, they would be worth it.

The only thing that held Renzo back was thoughts of his siblings. Rose would be screwed out of her private schooling, and Diego would likely go into the system the first time someone found him alone without their mother because she fucked off to get high again.

"Listen, if you want to meet up or something," Renzo started to say, "then let's figure out a way to do that, but I am busy today. I have to go pick up Diego, and—"

"How's the little bastard, anyway?" his father asked.

Renzo felt the pain in his chest at that question. It bloomed fast, and harsh. Entirely unforgiving as it wrapped around his heart to crush it like a dead weight that meant absolutely nothing.

How flippant and cold Charlie could be whenever he decided to ask after little Diego. The only one of the three Zulla kids that didn't belong to him, Charlie liked to make sure none of them forgot it whenever he did come around to show his unwanted face. Usually, he just outright ignored Diego, which made the boy confused because even though Charlie wasn't his dad, Carmen tried to say he was.

They didn't know who Diego's father was.

"Diego," Renzo said lowly, "his name is *Diego.*"

"Yeah, that one."

Renzo clenched his fists so tightly at his sides, that his fingernails cut into his palms. It was only that little shock of pain that kept him from flying across the sidewalk to break his knuckles on his father's face.

"Hey, Ren?"

The call of his name drew his attention to the payphone again, and his guys loitering there. He tipped his chin as a silent greeting and acknowledgment which Perry returned.

"Head out, yeah?" Ren called back. "We'll meet up tomorrow instead. Shit came up."

Clearly.

The guys nodded, grabbed their backpacks from the ground, and headed down the street. Although, not without looking back a couple of times. Renzo really didn't need people thinking he had problems—personal or otherwise. That was not the image he wanted to project when he came out onto these streets to work.

People saw weakness, and they exploited it.

That's just how it worked.

"So, what do—"

Renzo swung back to his father before the man could even finish his sentence. "*What in the fuck do you want?*"

Charlie's gaze widened momentarily before he smirked a bit. Maybe even appreciatively.

Renzo didn't care. He was done with this man, and playing whatever games Charlie wanted to play. He had better shit to be doing, and more important people to take care of—simple as that.

"Your mother, actually," Charlie mumbled around the toothpick.

"*What?*"

What the fuck would he want with *Carmen?* The two never spoke, and didn't even hang around the same junkie circles. In a way, Renzo considered that a good thing because it was one less thing for him to worry about.

Sort of.

Charlie pulled the toothpick from between his lips, and flicked it to the ground as he looked at his son again. "Your mother—she owes people money, Ren."

Not that he didn't already know for what, but he still asked, "What does she owe for, then?"

"Probably for whatever shit she's smoking or shooting into her body lately, but that's not the point. They're coming to me for it because they know at some point, I took care of her. They know she pushed out a couple of my kids, so they think I'm still ..." His father gestured with one hand as if to wave at him, saying, "Coming around, looking after you all, if you get my drift."

"Too bad for them, then, I guess," Renzo said, deciding he was done with the conversation. He turned on his heels, and started down the sidewalk again, leaving his father behind. "Good luck with that, Charlie."

Renzo probably shouldn't have turned his back to the man—he likely wouldn't have done that on any other day but today was just *one of those.* He was tired, not thinking right, and he had better shit to do than stand there and chat with an asshole like Charlie.

It wasn't like his father would try to lay a lickin' on him or anything. Charlie stopped doing that when Renzo turned fifteen. He hit a fucking growth spurt, and broke his father's face on a kitchen table after he showed up one day, slept on their couch, and then called Rose a slut for wearing a skirt he didn't like.

But the man might just be stupid enough to try.

"*Ren.*"

His father's call was punctuated by footsteps a second before a hand landed hard to his shoulder. *Fuck.*

Just having this man touch him—even if it wasn't in a violent way—was enough to make Renzo's rage spike as high as it could go. There was no one who made him want to go out and catch himself a felony like Charlie did every time his stupid face showed back up for one thing or another.

Swinging around fast on the street, Renzo's hands came up to shove against his father's chest. Charlie hadn't been expecting the move if the way he stumbled back a few steps in order to catch himself was any indication. Renzo took a bit of satisfaction in that fact.

"You keep your fucking hands off me," Renzo warned.

Charlie sighed, and shook his head as he righted himself. "You got the viciousness of your mother, but all that anger is *me*, Ren."

"I'm nothing like you."

His father tipped his head to the side like he was considering those words. "That may be true enough, son."

"What do you need, huh?" Renzo asked. "How much cash is going to get you away from me for a while?"

"It ain't for me. You want to keep those lookin' for your mother away from your little brother, and your sister, too, don't you? Stop acting like a prick, Ren, and use your head. You know what *you* do when somebody owes you, yeah? Well, *she* owes somebody. I'm the first place they came to. Who do you think they're coming to next?"

Was this his father's fucked up way of trying to take care of them in a roundabout way, or was this just another stunt of Charlie's? That was the thing—it was damn near impossible to tell the difference.

"*How much?*" Renzo demanded, his teeth clenched.

"Right now, she's two-Gs in the hole," Charlie returned.

Fuck.

Renzo had it, sure. Stuffed away in a container he kept hidden in the apartment freezer. The only place his mother wouldn't look because she couldn't cook worth shit, and instead of consuming food, she just pumped drugs into her body. But that small bit of money was the only savings Renzo really had. It was his backup if something came up, or whatever. If he took two grand out of it, that wasn't going to leave him very much left.

"They're not nice people," his father added quieter, "a lot like the people who you work for, I'd say."

Renzo stiffened.

That sealed the deal, really.

"Fine. I've got it at the apartment. Keep the fuck up, Charlie."

That was all Renzo said before he turned around, and walked off. He made sure to keep a good ten strides between him and his father, though.

He didn't even want to share that man's *air*.

Renzo wished the couple of blocks it took to get to the apartment went by faster than it did. Instead, it felt like they crawled the entire way. All the while, his father chatted on behind him like Renzo was listening, or gave a damn.

Neither of which he was doing.

Charlie closed the distance between them as Renzo climbed the entrance steps to the run-down apartment building. Maybe it was because of the people sitting on the steps that eyed Charlie, but not Renzo. Charlie hadn't visited this particular apartment since Renzo started renting it, so no one who usually loitered around the front would recognize his face.

New faces typically meant trouble around here.

"Yo, Ren!"

Renzo, having just grabbed for the handle on the door, leaned back to see who was shouting at him from a window higher up. The man leaning out the window with a blunt between his fingertips and white smoke trailing higher gave him a nod.

"Had a girl asking about you a while ago—that's her car, yeah? Pretty thing, but she shouldn't be around here, you know?"

Oh, for fuck's sake, please don't tell me—

Renzo didn't even get to finish his thought because he turned to see which car the man was talking about, and yeah, there it sat. Lucia's black Mercedes, locked up tight. He didn't even have to wonder how he missed that car when he passed it by. His mind was on other things—like getting his father the hell out of his hair.

Shit.

Charlie whistled low. "That's a nice car. And you know the chick driving it, do you?"

This day could not get worse.

"Mind your business," Renzo snapped at his father.

Charlie only shrugged. "Just sayin'—"

"And stay out here. I'll bring your money out."

Renzo just expected his father to listen to him and follow directions because Charlie didn't have any reason to follow him inside. He hoped for too much because his father came inside, anyway, and gave him a look that dared him to tell him to go again.

"Stay in the hallway, then," Renzo said.

"I'll think about it."

Asshole.

Renzo wished he could say that when he got upstairs, the sight of Lucia inside his apartment taking care of his strung-out mother was easy to take ... but it wasn't. She didn't even see him standing there in the apartment doorway. She didn't notice him as he watched her wipe down his mother's face with a wet rag.

She didn't know he was there at all.

And maybe that was for the best. Those first few seconds let him have all those emotions he didn't want her to know he was feeling. All the shame and embarrassment was that nearly always constant whenever his mother was involved. The anger that ... Jesus Christ, why was she here again? She'd be far better off staying on her own side of the city, and not trying to fit in on *his*. And oddly, he also found himself feeling *grateful*.

Because what Lucia was doing for Carmen in those moments, Renzo couldn't even be bothered to attempt to do anymore. He'd lost all empathy for his mother long ago. His ability to worry and love her had gone out the window right along with his respect for her, too. Every overdose ... every time he had to pick up the pieces of Diego ... all this fucking shit she had done to them meant he just couldn't afford to care anymore.

Lucia didn't know those things, though.

Apparently, she was just the type to *care*.

How sweet.

"How did you get in my apartment?" Renzo demanded.

Lucia's head popped up, and her striking hazel eyes found his in an instant. He could see the concern and softness reflecting back in her gaze, but he couldn't be bothered to deal with that right now.

She shouldn't be here.

He needed her to go for more reasons than she would ever be able to understand. Because he didn't want her to see what his life was like. Because his father and mother didn't even deserve to know who this young woman was, never mind her *name*. Because in those few seconds, Renzo realized Lucia Marcello might just be exactly what he thought she was— better than him.

Not because of money.

Or status.

Or *anything like that*.

No, because she could care.

He stopped doing that long ago.

"The landlord was doing a walk through the apartment," Lucia explained. "He said it was your mom, that she's like this ... pretty often. He let us in, and I got her cleaned up. Sorry, I didn't mean to—"

"Why are you even *here*?"

Lucia blinked, and hurt marred her features. He wished it didn't affect him like it did to see the water that lined her lashes, but it bothered him all the same. He didn't want to be mean to this girl, but Christ, they were two entirely different people from worlds that would never mix. She could keep being sweet and kind all she wanted because at the end of the day, Renzo was still going to be the same asshole wearing a leather jacket and combat boots.

He *had to be.*

He didn't know how else to survive.

"Oh, don't worry about Carmen, pretty thing," Charlie said, moving past Renzo in the doorway. He didn't miss the way his father *leered* at Lucia, either. That hot shot of anger that burned in his gut wasn't *new*, but it was a hell of a lot stronger than what he'd been feeling earlier. Now, he really just wanted to get Lucia out of his father's sights. "She's always strung-out, or drunk … or a mixture of the two. Leave her be."

Charlie came closer to Lucia, who kept looking between his father, and Renzo. "Now, who are *you?*"

"It's time to go," Renzo said to Lucia.

Firm.

Dark.

Cold.

He wasn't accepting no for an answer. He needed her *out.* And it would be to all their benefits if she just stayed fucking gone.

Renzo didn't know what did it. It could have been him speaking, or his father still leering at her, but Lucia got up. She grabbed her bag, and headed past Renzo in the hallway without a look back at his mother. She did slow down as she passed him by, though.

Just enough to whisper, "I only wanted to check on you and Diego. You hadn't been around—I was worried. I wanted to make sure you both were okay."

Yeah, sweet.

Kind.

Pretty.

All things Renzo really didn't deserve or need.

"Does my life look okay to you?" he asked.

Lucia didn't break his gaze as she replied, "I didn't say your life. I said *you.*"

"They're the same thing."

"But are they, Renzo?"

She didn't give him a chance to think that over, or reply. She was already gone.

Renzo kind of hoped she stayed that way.

And he also wondered if she might come back.

Fuck my whole life.

• • •

"Ren, where's Ma?"

Renzo kneeled down to tug the blue blanket back over Diego's tiny body. The only bedroom in the entire apartment, and he always made sure Diego was the only one who got to sleep in it. It was his space—safe from anything happening outside.

Diego didn't have much in there. Just his bed, a beat-up dresser full of clothes that had been either bought at a thrift shop, or passed down from someone else, and a few toys. What he cherished the most were his books, and the model car that Renzo had bought him last Christmas and spent seventeen hours putting the damn thing together piece by piece.

"Uh, Ma's ... out," Renzo lied.

Carmen had started choking on her vomit shortly after Lucia left, and an ambulance had to be called. Which made Renzo late to pick up Diego at the babysitter's, and caused the chick to rant at him for a minute too long about making sure to pick Diego up on time *or else*.

Fuck it all.

Maybe later, he'd call the emergency room where he knew Carmen had been taken, and ask if she was awake and lucid. That was about the only thing he was going to do, though. It would be in her best benefit if the doctors recognized her for what she was—an addict in need of help—and forced her into inpatient rehab.

But that was unlikely.

It wasn't how the system worked.

"Okay," Diego said, holding tight to the book that Renzo had just finished reading him. "Night, Ren."

Renzo leaned over the bed, and pressed a quick kiss to his brother's forehead before he stood up, and left the bedroom. He didn't bother to close the door. Often, Diego would wake up and walk the apartment to find his brother.

He rarely ever looked in the bathroom first which was the place someone could always find Renzo when nighttime fell, and he could finally go to sleep.

Yanking open the small closet in the hallway, Ren pulled out the pillow he kept hidden in there. Given there was only one bedroom, and it belonged to Diego, Renzo was not going to fit on the boy's small bed. He also wasn't sleeping on the floor. God knew he'd slept on the ground too many times as it was.

He also wouldn't take the couch because for one, his mother used it when she was around, but right then, it still smelled like a mixture of bleach and vomit. It needed cleaned *again*. Or just tossed out altogether.

That was a more likely option.

But he'd have to go get another one.

So yeah, no bedroom, no floor, and definitely no couch. That really only left Renzo with one option, and that was the bathtub.

He'd slept in more bathtubs over his lifetime than he cared to admit, but out of all the things in his life, it was the one thing he didn't find very much shame in. He found it *comforting*.

Climbing into chipped porcelain, resting the pillow behind his head, and unloading the shit in his pockets that he'd gathered over the day. A roll of small bills, a grinder for herbs, the small baggie of weed and papers he kept on hand for days like today, a lighter, a pack of smokes, and the gun he kept tucked into the back of his pants. He rested all the items on the edge of the tub, tucked his arms behind his head, and stared up at the yellow-tinted ceiling.

He should light up a joint, and smoke the bathroom out.

He should go to sleep.

He should worry about tomorrow.

He should have done a lot of things.

Instead, when he closed his eyes, he thought about red-soled shoes, hazel eyes, and a girl that asked him a question he really wasn't ready to answer.

Was his life who he was, too?

Did it make *him*?

He'd always thought yes.

She said it like the answer was *no*.

SEVEN

Streams of light basked in flecks of gold and streaked with slashes of white crawled across Lucia's face. She wasn't the type to enjoy sun on her face first thing in the morning, not when that meant it was time to get up. She wasn't sure how long she had been sitting here staring at the light peeking between the opened slat in the curtains. Long enough that her alarm clock had run its course, and then went off again five minutes later in an effort to remind her that she needed to get up.

She never even turned it off. It played itself out.

"Lucia!"

Her gaze drifted from the window, to the closed door of her bedroom. Her father's shout echoed from down the hallway, but she didn't answer him back. She knew what he wanted.

Not that she hadn't gotten up yet.

Not that she might be late for work.

No, it was her birthday.

He had a surprise for her.

Lucia could always bet on that when it came to her parents and her birthday. They never shied away from buying her beautiful things to remind her just how much she was loved by them. Maybe that's what had made her pause that morning when she first opened her eyes and realized today was her eighteenth birthday.

Instead of being flooded with thoughts about herself, her life, the shit she had to do today … or anything at all that she would usually think about first thing in the morning, she saw the sunlight coming in and thought about something else entirely.

Renzo.

Where was he waking up this morning? Was he already up? She didn't have to wonder if he was sleeping in a California king-size bed like her. She didn't have to wonder if he would have to walk down two flights of stairs just to reach his kitchen. And she knew—without a doubt—he didn't have someone calling for him to wake up because they likely had something expensive to give him.

This seemed to be Lucia's life now. Thinking about a guy who made every effort to point out that he either didn't like her, or *wouldn't* like her.

Funny how that worked.

"Lucia!"

"I'm up," she called back to her father.

His shout had been closer that time. Before he came and knocked on her door, she figured she might as well just get the hell up. The last thing she needed was her parents thinking something was going on with her. They were predictable in the way they would likely pry into her issues until they found what the source was.

She loved them for that, really.

But not for this.

Lucia listened for the sounds of her father's receding footsteps before finally kicking the blankets off her body, and sitting up in the bed. Instead of getting ready for the day right away, she continued staring at the light streaming in through the window until she was forced to blink because her eyes were getting too dry.

She'd tried, hadn't she?

Tried to make Renzo see she didn't think lesser of him because of where he came from, or the stuff he was dealing with in his life. She fully believed people weren't defined by the number in their bank accounts, never mind the situation around them. A person could only make due with what they had. They couldn't do anything with something they didn't have in the first place.

And yet, she couldn't act like she didn't see the contempt in his gaze every time he looked at her. He couldn't even be bothered to try to hide the heat in his tone whenever he had to talk to her.

Maybe that was his pride, or whatever, but at least she could say she tried. For now, though, Lucia was done trying. She didn't need to keep making an effort where it seemed entirely pointless.

Even if everything about Renzo Zulla made Lucia want to get close, and learn more. Bad news was still bad news at the end of the day.

Though she didn't want to admit it, Lucia was trying to protect herself a bit, too. The closer she tried to get to Renzo—because God knew curiosity was determined to kill the cat—the more he pushed to get her away.

That hurt.

Except, it shouldn't hurt at all.

He didn't owe her a thing. Not about himself, or his life.

So, yeah, she was done trying. If what he wanted was for her to stay far the hell away from him, then that's exactly what she was going to do.

Or *try*.

Christ.

It took Lucia longer than it normally would to get ready for the day. She took extra care to make sure she painted the tiredness from under her eyes with careful strokes of a makeup brush; that her eyes looked wider and more open than they were with mascara and smudged eyeliner. She tossed her hair up in a high pony, and instead of her usual skinny jeans and blouse, she grabbed a dress instead.

A flowy, white dress because it was her birthday, and why the hell not. She might have been set to work in the kitchen that day, but it was her birthday, and she wanted to wear a damn dress.

Simple as that.

"Took you long enough," Lucian grumbled as Lucia came down the stairs. "I didn't think you were ever getting up, *dolcezza*."

It was hard to ignore the fact her father was grinning, and looked like a kid in a candy store. It wasn't often her father got excited about *anything*, really. Always cool, calm, and collected. That was Lucian Marcello in a nutshell.

"Why are you looking at me like that?" she asked.

As soon as she was close enough for her father to reach out and grab her, he did just that. Pulling her into a tight hug, Lucia relaxed in her father's embrace.

He felt like love, and home.

"Happy birthday, Lucia," her father murmured, kissing her on the top of her head. "I just wanted to tell you happy birthday, that was all."

"Eighteen, eighteen!"

It was only the sweet, sing-song voice of her mother that made her father step back from their embrace to let Jordyn in on it. Just like Lucian had done, Jordyn swept her daughter into a tight hug. Only this time, Lucia's face was peppered with kisses from her ma.

"Makeup, Ma," Lucia groaned, trying to pry herself away. It was pointless. She just ended up sighing, and letting her mother do her thing. All the while, her father stood a couple of feet back, chuckling. Soon, her mother stepped back, too. "Thanks."

"Ready for your present?" her father asked.

Lucia gave him a look. "It's a car, isn't it?"

Lucian scowled. "John told you, didn't he."

It wasn't even a question.

Lucia shrugged. "I have many informants, Daddy. *Many*."

Lucian grumbled under his breath, and pulled a pair of keys with a familiar *L* symbol dangling from the attached fob. "Many, right. John. It's John. Here—I know it's not the Mercedes you might have wanted, but the Lexus is better. Coupe. Black with chrome. Better for you in California than the Mercedes will be since it's a little smaller, and has better get up and go, so to speak."

Lucia looked at the keys in her hand, silent for a moment. Was it sad that her father offered all that info to her about a car because he thought she might be disappointed he hadn't gotten her a Mercedes instead? Like a Lexus wasn't just as amazing … and expensive, too.

It was never more apparent to Lucia how much she was given in life while others had so little than it was right now.

"I love it, Daddy," Lucia assured him.

Lucian smiled a bit, and passed a glance to her mother. "You haven't even seen the car yet, Lucia."

She shrugged. "It came from you—that means I'll love it, anyway."

"Mmhmm. Well, we were thinking dinner tonight to celebrate your birthday. How does that sound?"

"I'm at the shelter until nine."

"Late dinner, then," her mother put in.

Lucia nodded, still staring at the keys in her hand. "Yeah, okay. A late dinner."

• • •

"How are we doing for potatoes and carrots down there?"

Lucia finished filling the plate of the waiting woman, and then replied to the kitchen's manager. "A little low, actually. Maybe three more servings of each."

"Okay, go grab more and then take your break, Lucia."

They were nearing the middle of the lunch rush, and that was when it seemed like *everyone* decided to show up to be fed.

"I don't mind staying on the line, if you need extra hands."

The manager shook her head. "It's fine. You've earned your break."

The woman had an almost conspiratorial smile on her face when she said that, but Lucia just brushed it off. There was always one scheme or another going on in the kitchen. They always made it their first mission to have fun, and make sure the people who came in to eat were having a good time, too.

"Oh, and happy birthday, princess!" the manager shouted at her back as she headed into the kitchen.

Lucia just shook her head as the rest of the kitchen and dining area echoed that same statement. *Happy birthday, Lucia.* They'd already told her five times or more, but they just had to remind every single person that came through the line that it was her birthday, so she could be told again.

She really did enjoy working here.

As for the princess thing … well, she didn't mind that so much when it was her coworkers. They never said it with malice, just amusement.

Lucia made quick work of grabbing the waiting containers of heated potatoes and carrots, and bringing them back out to the line to get them ready for whoever would handle her station while she took her break. She was just pulling off the apron, gloves, and hairnet when she first felt it.

Like whispers crawling over the back of her neck, and making all her fine hairs stand on end. Like a clenching in her chest, and butterflies beating in her belly.

His voice only confirmed it when he finally spoke.

"You got a minute, *princess*, or ...?"

Lucia spun around to find Renzo leaning against the food line. He wore his usual leather jacket, and worn jeans with holes in the knees. His typical T-shirt had been replaced with a white button-down. It pulled the whole look off and gave him that *I-don't-give-a-damn* vibe that he didn't even have to try very hard to put off. With his hair pushed back like he'd been running his fingers through it, and his dark gaze on her, Lucia thought Renzo probably had no idea what he looked like standing there.

A woman's walking wet dream, really.

Bad boy appeal.

Lazy smile.

He looked like trouble all around.

Lucia had settled herself with *not* trying anymore where this guy was concerned. He was determined to tell her to fuck off at every turn, and frankly, she was tired of being told to fuck off.

So, why was he here?

"Ren," Lucia greeted, "what can I do for you?"

"I just told you. I want a minute. Do you have one, or not? Seems busy."

Lucia could have lied, said she'd be working the line, and sent him on his way. Something inside of her felt like a hand clamping around her throat to keep her from spilling that lie, though.

"I'm on a break, actually."

Renzo nodded. "Outside, then?"

"Sure."

It was only as she was following Renzo outside that she realized what he called her when he first greeted her. *Princess.*

"How long were you in the dining room?" she asked.

He shot a smirk over his shoulder. "Long enough, princess."

Like her coworkers, there was no malice to his tone when he said it. His gaze still glinted with a bit of enjoyment when her eyes narrowed in on him.

"Where's Diego?"

Renzo pushed the doors open that led to the outside, and warm air brushed along Lucia's bare legs. She didn't miss the way he turned to speak, but hesitated in his words because he was too busy taking in the dress she wore. Maybe she liked it a little too much when his gaze lingered on her legs, and then higher until he finally stopped on her face.

"I took him to Brooklyn to spend a couple of days with our sister."

"You have a sister?"

"Rose," he said. "She's seventeen. Smartest one of us all, I think. Got a scholarship to a private school for the arts, so she stays there all the time. I just run her up cash or whatever she needs."

Huh.

As fascinating as Lucia found that information, she couldn't help but be a little defensive, too. She didn't know why Renzo was here, but none of their previous encounters had gone particularly well.

"You didn't come here to be an asshole again, did you?" Lucia asked. "Because I was only trying to help with your mom, and the night I offered you a drive. I mean, I didn't intend to overstep your boundaries or anything. I was *just* worried—that's all."

Renzo cleared his throat, stuffed his hands in his pockets, and glanced down the quiet alleyway that led to the main street in front of the shelter. Maybe it was the fact that she'd grown up around a lot of men who took great effort in hiding their emotions when shit was rough, but she recognized Renzo's movements for what they were.

Nerves.

"I didn't come to be an asshole," he murmured, glancing back at her. It was his eyes, she thought. His face was beautiful. He looked like something out of a magazine, and he didn't even have to try. But it was in his eyes where she found her heart skipped beats. It was disconcerting and strange that she couldn't even look at him without those damn butterflies coming back. "And I'm sorry I was a dick before."

Lucia folded her arms over her chest as Renzo leaned against the brick of the building. "Go on."

He laughed, and the sound was *spectacular.* All deep, rumbling bass. He tossed his head back, and she didn't think he'd ever looked so careless, and happy. She really wanted to see if she could make him laugh again, but he broke her daze by meeting her gaze again.

Her thoughts went silent just like that.

All with a stare.

Lucia felt like she was frozen in place as Renzo's gaze traveled over her face, lingering on her mouth before he looked away altogether.

"Not really sure why I came here," he admitted.

Lucia swallowed hard. "Apparently, to apologize."

Renzo made a noise under his breath. "I just decided to do that when I saw you inside, if I'm being honest. I wasn't even going to come talk to you, or anything. I just wanted to … well, I don't know."

"Yes, you do. What did you want to do?"

He sighed hard, and let out a dry chuckle. "Check on you, I guess. Make sure you were okay. I owed you that, didn't I?"

Lucia's heart skipped beats again, and she smiled a little. "I'm okay, Ren."

He passed her another look, the heat in his stare obvious. "Yeah, I guess so, huh?"

"Was there any other reason you came looking for me?"

Renzo took a second, then two. He opened his mouth to speak, but he was stopped from saying anything at all when the door to the kitchen was opened, and Laurie popped her head out with a wide smile. The woman at least had the decency to hide her brief surprise at seeing Lucia and Renzo talking together.

"Renzo," Laurie greeted, "how have you been, and how is Diego?"

Renzo cleared his throat, and straightened his posture. "He's good. Took him to the school last week to meet the teacher he will have next year. Made him less nervous to start kindergarten."

Laurie's face softened. "That's great, really."

"Yeah."

The woman glanced Lucia's way. "Lucia, you're needed inside for something. But Renzo, you're welcome to join us for this."

"I probably should head—"

"Come in," Lucia told him before he could refuse. "For a second, anyway."

She was pretty sure he was going to tell her something else just now, but Laurie had interrupted him from doing just that. She really wanted to know what he was going to tell her.

Renzo's tongue peeked out to wet his lips, and he nodded. "Yeah, sure. For a minute, anyway. Then, I gotta head back out. Work to do, you know."

He didn't offer a further explanation, and Lucia chose not to ask even after Laurie went back inside the shelter. Only because she was pretty sure Renzo didn't want people knowing what he did on the streets to make money. Lucia only knew because she'd been a witness to him taking a cash payment from her brother.

Otherwise, *she* wouldn't know.

"Thanks," Lucia murmured, stopping next to Ren's side as they came to the doors. The lift of his eyebrow made her shrug, and explain, "Just … for coming here."

She pulled open the doors. Somehow, over the sounds of people shouting happy birthday, and Laurie coming forward with a cake, she was pretty sure she heard Renzo reply, "Still not sure why I'm here, honestly."

But she couldn't be sure, and she was already being pulled further into the dining room to check out her cake while everyone sang her happy birthday. She didn't know where they'd hid the cake—it hadn't been in the fridge earlier. Still, she was grateful.

"Thank you, you didn't have to do this," Lucia told Laurie.

The woman smiled. "Of course, we did. You're part of the family, Lucia."

They certainly made her feel like it, too.

Glancing up, Lucia searched for wherever Renzo had disappeared to for the moment. She didn't find him in the crowd, or even leaning against the wall.

Instead, she just caught sight of the back of his leather jacket as he headed out the doors. He didn't look back, either.

• • •

Lucia waved over her shoulder as a goodbye echoed out from behind her. Walking out of the shelter's main doors into the darkness of the parking lot took her a second to adjust to the lack of light.

But when she did, she froze right where she stood. Leaning against her brand new, two-door black Lexus, Renzo shot her a grin, and lifted one hand in a silent hello. He was still wearing his leather and jeans ensemble from earlier, and still making her insides do the craziest things.

She should really get this under control.

She hadn't known what to think when he slipped out earlier without a goodbye, but she really didn't know what to think about him standing where he was right now.

"What are you doing?" she asked.

Renzo pushed off the side of her car, and flicked the cigarette he'd been smoking to the ground. "Waiting on you."

Lucia wasn't sure she needed the whiplash that came with this man like a second bag he carried around twenty-four-seven. One minute, he was making her heart do the strangest things, and then in the next, he left her feeling cold.

"I didn't realize today was your birthday," he said, coming closer.

Lucia stayed rooted right to the spot. "Eighteen, yep."

"I felt like I … intruded earlier."

"Why?"

Renzo shrugged as he came to a stop entirely too close to Lucia. There was still a few inches of space between them, but he was close enough that she could smell his cologne on the breeze, and she had to stare upwards to look at his face.

He was a complex waiting to happen. All wrapped in a pretty package to distract her from the heartache he was probably going to cause her. She didn't know *why* she felt that way, but she just did.

Silently, Renzo reached over to tuck a stray strand of wavy hair that had fallen from Lucia's high pony back behind her ear. There was something amazing about the feeling of his rough fingertips gliding along her skin.

Electric, even.

She shivered.

"Figured maybe later would be better to talk," Renzo said, "you know, when I wasn't taking time away from you doing your job, or whatever."

"They're actually pretty easy-going here. It's fun."

"Yeah, Diego loves it."

"You should bring him back. I don't know if you stopped bringing him because of me, or—"

Renzo made a harsh noise, and glanced away. "We'll see. Anyway, new car, I see."

She didn't miss his attempt at distracting her, but Lucia was fine with letting him think that for now, she would drop the Diego conversation. She peered over at her black Lexus, and smiled.

"Yeah, a birthday present. How did you know it was mine?"

Renzo laughed, but it didn't sound bitter when he said, "Who else around here is going to drive a car like *that*, Lucia?"

Well, then …

"That's fair," she admitted.

Then, with no warning at all, Renzo turned back to her and said, "Do you wanna go out—have some fun for your birthday, I mean—with me tonight?"

Lucia blinked.

Renzo only stared, waiting.

Finally, her brain caught up with the rest of her.

"Like a date?"

Renzo grinned. "Yeah, let's call it a date."

She didn't even have to think about it, but she was more than willing to make him work for it. "That depends, Renzo."

"On what, exactly?"

"On what you had in mind."

EIGHT

"On what you had in mind."

Renzo found Lucia grinning in a way that said she was probably joking with him, but he couldn't quite tell for sure. It was very possible that his idea of a good time was not going to be up to her standards, not that those thoughts had been enough to stop him from asking.

There was something about this chick that Renzo really needed to just get out of his system, or *try to,* anyway. Maybe then, he could stop being so up in arms every time she was around, and he could quit thinking about her when he had no business doing that at all.

And maybe—although, he wasn't quite ready to admit it out loud just yet—Renzo wanted to know what it was about Lucia Marcello that made her who she was. Or see if he could find those pieces that made up who she was, anyhow.

What was it about her that made her coworkers want to bake her a cake and sing her happy birthday, along with all the people who'd stopped into the soup kitchen to eat, when she'd only been working at the place for a short time. He'd been bringing Diego here for a while, and that didn't happen often. Also, why did his little brother constantly ask after her when he'd only met her *twice*? Why was she so willing to help an obviously troubled woman—his *mother*—when it would have been far easier to leave her right where she lay on the ground?

Yeah, he had a lot of questions.

Lucia was the only one with the answers.

"Well?" she asked, drawing him out of his thoughts.

Renzo shifted in his combat boots, and stuffed his hands in his pockets. It was far from cold for August, but he still wore his leather jacket. It felt like an armor, of sorts. It gave him a certain appearance, and allowed his *don't-fuck-with-me* attitude a bit more credence. On these streets, sometimes a guy needed all the help he could get to make sure no one screwed with him on the regular.

"I know where there's going to be a party tonight," Renzo said. "Thought you might want to have some fun."

Lucia smiled in that sweet way of hers, and yet, it still managed to look coy. He wasn't sure how she did that, but it kind of drove him crazy. He liked that look on her face. He liked it even more that *he* was the one who made her do it.

Was that going to be a problem?

Renzo had yet to decide, really.

"*Your* kind of fun?" she asked.

Renzo let out a laugh, and took a step closer to her. "I don't really have time to go out and find fun, if we're being honest. It's usually me working, or doing work for someone else to get paid. But yeah, if I were going to go out and do something, I'd probably find myself a party where no one is going to bitch about your music, or how much your weed stinks. Seems like the better choice than an over-filled club with over-priced drinks."

Lucia lifted a single eyebrow. "You're not even old enough to get into a club."

"Neither are you. How many have you been inside?"

That sweet, coy grin of hers was back in an instant. "I plead the fifth."

Yeah, he bet her family was familiar with that line for more reasons than he wanted to get in to at that moment. Not that right then was the right time to get in to all of that. It most certainly was not, and he had other things to get started on.

Like figuring out what in the hell it was about this woman that had his head in such a mess. He needed to get a handle on that first, and then he would go from there.

"Where is this party, then?" Lucia asked.

"Here in my stomping grounds. A few blocks away."

"The Bronx."

She said it simply—just as though it were fact, and not that she had an opinion either way. Not like she was judging the area, or concerned about the trouble that might find her if she went down that way with him.

"It'll be like nothing you've ever experienced," Renzo said, "I can promise you that."

Lucia nodded, and dug in the pocket of her white dress to produce a pair of keys with a familiar *L* emblem on the fob. Not saying a word, she tossed the keys to him, and Renzo caught them easily enough. He shot her an inquisitive look to which she only shrugged.

"You wanna drive?" she asked sweetly.

Renzo stared down at the keys in his hand. The most expensive car he had ever driven was a friend's secondhand Jeep to help the guy move some shit from one apartment building to another. He never really needed to drive a lot in his work. The city was always congested as fuck with traffic, and another accident was usually right around the corner to make it worse than it already was. There wasn't anywhere he couldn't get to by using the city bus, or subway and it was typically a faster way to travel.

He did have his license, though.

He could drive.

Lucia laughed the longer Renzo hesitated to answer. "It's insured. You wreck it, and it'll be fixed. Try not to wreck it, though ... because it won't be the car that someone will be pissed about, you know. More like the woman in the passenger seat. They'll be really pissed about that."

Renzo met her gaze, and expected to find that same joking amusement he found earlier. Instead, she was stone-cold serious, and not even a hint of mirth reflected back in her eyes.

Well, then.

"All right," he said.

Lucia nodded, and the smile of hers that he was enjoying so much came back like it had never left in the first place. "A date, then?"

Yeah, shit.

Renzo hit the unlock button on the fob, and the Lexus lit up on all corners. "A date, Lucia."

• • •

"Oh, my God."

Renzo nodded to the guy who'd just taken two twenty-dollar bills from his hand without as much as a word about who he was, his age, or where he came from. Then again, the guy was a regular at these things. He usually watched the door, and on more than one occasion, probably saw Renzo walk through wherever they popped up once or twice to make a sale or two.

"Not what you expected from the outside?" he asked Lucia.

She turned slightly to look at him, but her gaze was quickly drawn back to the light show happening just down the main hallway of the warehouse. "No, I can't say it is."

Renzo figured that.

Placing his hand at the small of her back, he pressed and pushed her forward. Walking in step with her, he chuckled as the music ramped up a bit louder, and he swore he felt the floor of the old building start vibrating as people shouted in response to the fast beat of the next song.

Knowing she wouldn't hear him otherwise, Renzo moved closer to Lucia to murmur in her ear, "Fair warning, there's going to be a *lot* of people."

And when he said a lot, he meant a fucking *lot*. That was always a guarantee with these things. Given the fact these pop-up parties—some people still liked to call them raves—were illegal, that was one of the major factors that drew people in. It also helped that no one was there to police anybody's behavior or business. It was a free for all, in a way. As long as everybody was safe, stayed hydrated, and minded their own business, nobody had a problem.

"Some of them will be high as fuck," Renzo continued on, and hand curving tightly around Lucia's waist as they came closer to the large main section of the warehouse. "Some of them are going to be *getting* high. Some of them won't be high at all. Some might be hooking up in a corner, or on the floor, or … wherever they can find a spot."

She made a noise under her breath, but Renzo still heard it over the loud music nonetheless. It sounded like a mixture of curiosity and disbelief all rolled into one. Maybe a bit of embarrassment sprinkled on, too.

Funny, he thought.

He liked that sound, too.

What other kinds of noises might she make if he—

No, Renzo was not going there. Not yet, anyway.

"Really?" she asked.

Those hazel eyes of hers glittered under the neon green and electric purple lights that flashed, blinked, and moved in every which direction. The softness of her features and the gentle curve of her lips froze under the movement of the strobes. For a moment, she looked like an unmoving angel—perfect, and beautiful.

"What?"

Lucia shrugged, and a hint of pink tinged her cheeks. "People … fucking. *Really?*"

Innocence?

God.

That—probably more than anything else—made him want her. Because how amazing would she be, if he turned her into a sinner like him; if he made her dirty like him.

"Really," he told her. "Happens more often than it doesn't at these. Thing is, they like being watched, so don't feel like you're intruding if you do find yourself staring. That's the whole reason why they do it—they want to be seen. Or, just avert your stare, and pretend like you didn't see anything in the first place."

Lucia blinked. "Huh."

"Not a single one of them will care who you are, or why you're here tonight as long as you don't mess up their evening," he finished.

Lucia grinned. "So … have fun, then?"

"That's the point of it, babe."

The word—*that endearment*—slipped from his lips easily. Like he'd said it a dozen times before to her, but he could guarantee he hadn't said it to anyone *ever*. And yet, it felt easy to say it to her, and maybe he liked the way her tongue peeked out to wet her lips right after he dared to let the word come out of his mouth. Or maybe it was the way her throat jumped as she swallowed the longer he kept staring at her.

Maybe he liked a lot of things about her.

Even if that wasn't really the plan.

"Can we go in?" she asked.

Yeah, that was a better plan than what was going on in his crazy head.

"Lead the way. Don't take a drink from anyone but me."

They stepped into the main section of the warehouse, and Lucia's voice agreeing to Renzo's demand about the drinks was nothing more than a buzz in his ears. There really was something to be said about the loudness in these parties. Add in the strobe lights, the DJ with a mask over his face, and the people crowded together like sardines in a can as they danced ... it was a sight to see.

Intoxicating, maybe.

People chased these parties. Invite-only by way of a text message, a person never really knew when one was going to come up, or where the next location would be. Everything was portable, so it could be easily packed and unpacked when shit needed to be moved. No one really knew the names—only the aliases—or the faces of the people running the damn things.

Lucia was headed right for the swell of people dancing, and Renzo moved to catch up. He caught her wrist in his hand, and winked when she tossed a look over her shoulder to make sure it was him who had grabbed her. He wanted to make sure he kept at least one hand on this girl just in case she felt like trying to get lost.

God knew he wouldn't find her in the people.

"Do you dance?" she asked.

He didn't hear her voice over the music, but her moving lips were enough for him to discern what she said. Renzo shrugged one shoulder, and nodded.

He could dance.

He just didn't do it often.

Lucia wasn't going to give him a choice, apparently. She pulled him onto the makeshift dance floor, and before he knew it, the rest of the warehouse disappeared as all he cared to focus on was Lucia in her white flowy dress as all her soft curves pressed against him and moved in the *best* way possible. Her gaze locked on his as the song changed again, and he dragged her closer still.

She was prettier like this.

Carefree, and relaxed. Grinning in that way with a laugh on the tip of her tongue. Equal parts sweet and coy.

And none of that mattered when her body grinded against his, and his cock perked at the sensation. None of that mattered when he could get his hands on her skin, and all he could see was her under the strobes.

He didn't even think about it, really. The next time she came in close with the swell of the beat, Renzo's hands came up to cup her throat and jaw. He moved in fast because all he could think about was *what does she taste like?* The second his lips touched hers—soft and slow at first—electricity zipped through his body like a jolt waking him up from a dead sleep. That first taste wasn't nearly enough. He only wanted more. Add in the fact Lucia fisted his leather jacket to drag him closer, and her sweet lips parted so that her tongue could strike out against the seam of his mouth, and he was fucking *done.*

There was no hesitance in her kiss—just a burning heat that seared him from the inside out as her tongue warred with his, unafraid of the way his equally lashed back to find more of her taste. Soft curves pushed against his hard lines, and for a second, he was pretty sure he forgot where he was.

He was right, though.

She did taste like sweetness and sin.

It was only a *whoop* from the crowd that finally broke their kiss, but the second it was done, he was ready to drag her back again for a second round.

Lucia's head tipped up, and a slow smile spread across her features. "There's an upstairs?"

He looked up, too.

"Guess so."

"Let's go see what it looks like from up there."

Who was he to argue?

"Let's go, babe," he murmured.

Lucia tugged him along, and Renzo was all too happy to follow given the view he had of her ass swaying under that dress. He didn't even realize he'd climbed a set of metal, spiral stairs until Lucia was leaning over a railing with hooded eyes looking his way. In a blink, she'd gone from looking entirely too innocent to something else entirely.

And that was from a kiss.

What might she look like if he stripped her bare?

Christ.

"How long do these go?" she asked.

"Til the sun starts to peak."

That smile was back.

He wanted her to keep smiling.

"Ren! Hey, man, you working tonight?"

Renzo turned fast to see a familiar face coming his way. The guy was a regular for Renzo—liked just a pinch of something extra in with his hydro when he smoked. He was more of a social user than an addict, and Renzo preferred that kind of customer, really. They were easier to deal with, and they always *paid.*

"Not tonight, Kirk," Renzo said.

74

Kirk's gaze drifted to a quiet Lucia. "Something else tonight, then?"

"Something like that."

With a nod, the guy passed him by and headed down the spiral staircase. Lucia stayed quiet until the man was gone altogether, and it was just them side by side leaning over the railing. Up there, he could really feel the heat of the crowd rising in the warehouse. It almost made him want to take off his jacket.

Almost.

"You deal for John, then?" Lucia asked softly.

Too softly, he thought. He barely heard her at all.

"Does it matter what I do to make a living?" he asked back.

Lucia looked his way, but he didn't find anything that said she was about to bolt on him staring back from her. Maybe that was what surprised him the most. She *knew* he wasn't exactly a good guy, but she was still tucked into his side like that was exactly where she wanted to be.

"I'm curious," Lucia said. "About why, and other things."

"Because we all need to eat," he said, "and I never learned anything different."

"Neither did John or my dad … none of us, really."

Renzo's brow dipped. "What?"

Lucia met his gaze again, unashamed and bold. "My brother and father, or my uncles. The rest of my family. This life is what we've always known. We were never taught anything different, either. There's not much difference between them, and you. Not when you really think about it."

"I can think of one glaring difference," Renzo murmured.

"The fact they have money?"

"Exactly that."

Lucia nodded, and leaned in close enough that her lips were just a breath away from his. "And yet, take it all away, Ren, and what does that still make them?"

Criminals.

Bad people.

All that and more flew through his mind.

Lucia answered with something else entirely. "People surviving in the only way they know how—that's what it makes them."

He kissed her again.

Just because he wanted to.

• • •

"You can't do that!"

Renzo chuckled as he shifted the pick in the lock just enough to hear the

75

familiar *click* of the tumblers falling into place. Just like that, he was able to pop the lock on the gate, and push it open. "But I just did."

Lucia's eyes went wide in the moonlight as she glanced around like someone was going to come up on them at any moment to catch them. "But, that's—"

"Illegal?" Renzo nodded. "A little, yeah. Are you coming?"

"Can you promise me that we won't get arrested?"

"Highly unlikely."

"That you'll make the promise, or that we'll get arrested?"

Renzo shrugged.

Honesty was the best policy, after all.

"Both," he said.

Then, he cracked a smile and laughed. Without warning, Lucia struck out and hit him on the back of his shoulder with an opened palm. "That's not funny!"

"It kind of is, and so is your face. Calm down. I know the guy who owns the place. Are you coming, or what?"

She glanced around once more, and then finally, nodded. "Yeah, I'm coming."

He took her hand in his, and wove their fingers together tightly as they stepped beyond the gate of the restaurant's outside veranda. He moved in between tables and chairs that wouldn't be filled with patrons for another few hours, all the while keeping a tight hold on Lucia's hand, and a firm grip on the takeaway bag they'd grabbed from a roadside truck down the block.

"So the guy you know," Lucia said, "he doesn't mind you *breaking in?*"

Renzo tossed her a look over his shoulder. "Well, no. I lost the key he gave me, and he's never gotten around to replacing it, but since I can pick the lock, he isn't in a hurry."

"Did you work here, or something?"

"Or something," he muttered.

"*Ren.*"

It was the gentle squeeze of her fingers and the tug of her hand against his that softened his stance, and lowered his walls. That was the thing he was coming to learn about this woman. She didn't care about the shit he did, or where he came from. She just wanted to understand, but that required he open his mouth and talk about it all. Which was not something Renzo did very often, if at all.

It was easier to keep that shit locked up tight.

"He used to help me out when I was younger," Renzo said. "Let me wash dishes on the weekends to keep me out of trouble, and he'd keep a plate warm for me to eat at night. I used to stay down the block, so he saw me around enough, and thought to give me a hand out, I guess."

He didn't miss the way Lucia's brow furrowed as he directed her to a staircase at the far end of the veranda that led to a seating area on top of the restaurant.

"What?" he asked.

"I just ... there's no apartments down this block. There's a park, or whatever. Where was it you were—" Maybe it was the expression on his face, or the way he stayed quiet, but Lucia's question cut off abruptly, followed by a soft, "Oh."

"It was a couple months in the summer. Shit was rough. The park was mostly safe, and there were public bathrooms to wash up, or get water. Carmen couldn't stay clean long enough to blow a negative on a drug test, and the shelters wouldn't let her stay with kids when she was using. They kept calling CPS, and she kept moving on. It's not a big deal."

Sadness echoed in Lucia's features.

"Yes, it is," she whispered. "That's terrible, Ren."

Renzo shook his head. "Don't do that, huh?"

A simple tug of her hand brought Lucia closer to him on the staircase. Until she was tucked against his chest, and staring up at him with those glittering eyes of hers. Her palms laid flat to his chest, and he tipped his head down to catch her lips in a kiss.

Although he would much rather stay just like that, kissing her, the food was probably getting cold, and he really just wanted to get her mind off all of that other shit. So, he pulled away and dragged the pad of his thumb over her pink lips.

"That was then, yeah? This is now."

Lucia smiled. "Yeah, *now*. You know, when you break into the outside seating section of a restaurant to give a girl a place to eat."

"Better than the side of the street."

"Anywhere with you would be great, Ren."

Yeah.

Damn.

It was the way she looked at him, he knew. That, and how her voice alone could soften all the barbed wire he'd put up around his being just to keep himself safe.

The urge to kiss her again was unmistakable and undeniable. Problem was—he knew what was going to happen if he kept kissing this woman. He knew exactly where it was going to lead.

"Renzo," Lucia whispered.

"Hmm?"

"You keep staring at my mouth. But it looks a lot better when you're kissing it."

"You don't know that."

"Logical assumption," she countered.

"I want to do a hell of a lot more than just kiss you, Lucia."

"Yeah, I know. So, do that."

His gaze jumped up to hers.

Lucia smiled, and shrugged one shoulder. "Greasy food is always better when it's lukewarm, anyway."

Well, then …

He kissed her again, but this time, it wasn't soft or sweet at all. More like a war between the two of them—frantic and brutal. She only pushed closer to him to get more as his tongue lashed in and out of her mouth. And she didn't seem to mind a bit.

But that was the thing about kissing Lucia, Renzo realized all too soon. Once he started, he couldn't fucking get enough. He wanted more—more of her taste, and the way she didn't shy away from kissing him just as hard and deep as he did to her. He kept a tight hold on the bag of food but his other one wanted more of her to touch. Wrapping a hand in her hair, he had her pinned against the small stairwell wall as he learned just how sweet and sinful her mouth tasted when she was hot as fuck for him.

"Shit, yeah," Lucia breathed, tipping her head back as his kisses trailed down her neck. "Are we going up, or …?"

"Yeah, definitely up higher."

He pushed against her side, making her walk up the stairs with him following. It was only his hands keeping her steady that kept her from tripping on the stairs as she walked backward. His hands skimmed under the skirt of her white dress to find the outside of her thighs where he could grab on tight. The feeling of soft cotton meeting his fingertips was enough to make his dick perk up and try to punch a hole through his jeans.

By the time the two of them had reached the top of the stairs, she'd already yanked his shirt open, and had his leather jacket pulled halfway down his fucking arms.

"Not shy at all," he murmured against her lips.

Lucia grinned. "Do you want me to be?"

He didn't even have to think about that one.

"Not at all."

"Good."

She punctuated those words by grabbing his face, and yanking him in for another burning kiss. There was something about the way her gaze locked on his, all sure and filled with want. All it did was add to the craziness that was his brain when it came to this girl. He didn't know what to fucking make of her, but he knew that he liked her.

A lot.

But especially *like this.*

He liked her hot under his hands, and gasping for breath when his fingertips found the silkiness between her thighs. He only pulled away from her just long enough to shrug off his jacket, and let it fall to the ground where he shoved it against a wall with their bag of food before he was on her again. He liked how she pulled him back to the wall on the roof that looked like rocks, and didn't even blink at the ache it must have caused when her spine connected with the hard surface. Above them, the sloped roof of the roof's dining area protected them from the sudden downpour of rain when thunder cracked in the sky, and a streak of lightning lit up *everything.*

Water poured, sloshing off the roof and making a canopy all around them. Hiding them from view, not that it fucking mattered. The whole city could have been watching Renzo slip his fingers under Lucia's panties right then, and he wouldn't have given a single shit at all. He was too caught up in the way her hazel eyes darkened, and a whine clawed its way out of her throat as he found her wet, and so damn warm. Her pussy hugged his fingers tight when she widened her legs a bit to let him in.

God.

He just wanted to look at her while he did this.

See that flash of heat in her gaze.

The desire in her face.

All bliss.

Sin.

Want.

"Right there, huh?" he asked, speeding up the thrusts of his fingers. Her nod, and harsh exhale had him grinning. He used the pad of his thumb to flick at her clit with each push and pull of his hands. Her hips ground against his hand while the pretty noises fell from her lips one after the other. *Damn.* She sounded so good like this. Perfect, really. "Fuck, you're so wet, Lucia. Come so I can get a taste of that, baby."

"Oh, my God, *Ren.*"

He bet everybody thought this girl was *good.* Not at all wild, and sweet to her very core. He had news for them, she was just as dirty as everybody else, and he kind of liked that, too.

He really liked that he was the one who got to see it.

"Almost, *almost,*" Lucia breathed.

His hand skimmed her side, and came up to land on her throat. There, he held her, pinned against the wall as his fingers fucked her harder, and his name fell from her lips in a mantra. The way she said it, it could have been a fucking song. It sounded *that* good. When she did finally come, he thought she looked even better.

A little wilder.

A bit freer.

As she tried to catch her breath, he was busy pulling his hand out from between her thighs, so he could finally get a taste of her on his lips the way he'd promised. Lucia dragged in a shaky inhale as his fingers—wet with her—disappeared between his lips, and he sucked them clean.

She tasted like he thought.

Sweet.

Tart.

Uniquely her.

That was the best way he could describe it, really.

"Holy fuck," Lucia mumbled.

"You like that?"

"You just sucked me off your *fingers.*"

"I'd like to lick it right off your pussy, but another time."

Because right then, all he really wanted to do was bury his cock as deep as he could get it inside her pussy. He ached, and not in a good way. The water was still coming down, but that sloped roof kept them from getting the bulk of it, really. That didn't mean they weren't both getting soaked from the after spray, though.

Her hair was damp.

His shoulders were chilled, and wet.

He still didn't care.

Lucia reached for him, and he lost himself in the taste of her mouth again. He supposed she got a nice taste of her own come on his mouth, and her soft moan was enough to make him pull her to a bench next to the wall. It was the only place safe from the rain, really. He shuffled down his jeans, but not before grabbing a foil packet he always kept in his back pocket just in case.

Renzo fell on the bench first, but Lucia quickly followed. Her hands were already slipping beneath his boxer briefs as she straddled him. A hiss fell from his lips when her soft palms found his length, and tightened in just the right way as she stroked him from base to tip. Her tight body shifted on his before she snatched that condom out of his hand, opened it up, and rolled it down his cock.

He wasn't about to stop her.

He sure as fuck wasn't going to slow her down.

She could take what he wanted, and he was more than happy to go along for the ride. That's exactly what she did, too. Not even bothering to slip her soaked panties off, she simply shoved them aside before readjusting on his lap, and sinking down on his length.

"*Fuck,*" Renzo grunted.

How long had it been since he'd had sex?

A while.

He didn't remember it being *this* good, though. Not like silk under his hands when he held onto her hips, or like insanity in his mind when she started riding him wild. Her fingertips drifted over his lax features, and all he could do was grab tight to her hips, and let her fuck him the way she wanted.

She'd go from riding him hard, to soft circles when she had him buried as deep as she could get him inside her tight, warm sex. All her noises swallowed him up, and made him drunk.

So fucking *high*.

Still, he heard himself say, "You like that cock, huh?"

"God, yeah."

She kept up that pace until she was shaking and shivering again. Until his name was falling from her lips again. Until he could feel her coming undone around him again.

Then, he pulled her down, so her back was on the bench, and he could really pound into her. That's what he needed to come.

That, and her sweet pleas in his ear.

"Please, please."

She never sounded better.

He had never come harder.

NINE

Lucia's eyes peeled open as something shifted under her. Something warm, firm, and *hard*. And when that something *groaned?* Memories of the night before flooded back into Lucia's sleep-filled mind like a rushing wave coming up on the shore of a beach. Uncontrollable, fast, and ready to drag her back out into the ocean to drown her.

That felt apt, really.

Renzo was sort of like the ocean. Expansive, and deep. Crystal clear, and yet still murky enough to make her cautious. Beautiful to look at, sure, but beautiful things were sometimes made that way just so you didn't see the dangerous parts.

It only took the feeling of him moving under her to make Lucia hot and breathless all over again. She wasn't exactly *experienced* when it came to sex, and men. But she wasn't a virgin, either. Not entirely innocent. And yet, Renzo could make her feel like none of that mattered at all. She had no need to be shy, or anything like that. She just had to want something, and use her mouth to tell him exactly what it was she wanted.

And he would give it to her.

Hadn't that been what he said last night?

As quickly as those thoughts came, they were gone. Like the wind had ripped through the car somehow—though the windows were rolled up—to blow it all away, and leave Lucia feeling chilled.

"Shit," she heard Renzo mutter. "I gotta get up, move."

Lucia blinked at his sharp tone, but did what he told her anyway. Shifting off him in the back seat of her Lexus so that he could move without her on top of him, she realized just how cramped the two of them had been sleeping in the back seat together. Not that she had minded when they climbed in the back of the car after getting down from the restaurant's roof, really. She hadn't really cared what they did as long as they were doing it together. He hadn't been complaining, either.

Sitting at the other end of the backseat, Lucia rubbed the sleep out of her eyes, and tried to figure out what had just happened. Renzo paid her no mind as he grabbed the shirt he'd discarded the night before, and yanked it on. Leaning over the front seat, he found the leather jacket he'd used to keep her warm as they came down from the roof, and shrugged it on, too. He said nothing as he fished a cheap burner phone from his pocket, and checked the screen.

"*Fuck*," he muttered. Then, he shot her a look, asking simply, "You good, or ...?"

"Uh ..."

Renzo stared blankly at her. "I don't have time for this right now. I have to go. Are you good to drive home, or what?"

Wow.

Something cold washed over Lucia as she peered out the back windows. Right then, it was easier to stare at literally *anything else* but him. Last night, he was all too willing to do whatever the fuck he wanted with her, but right then, he seemed like he didn't want anything to do with her at all.

Lucia shrugged, and finally nodded. "Yeah, I'm good to drive home."

Why wouldn't she be?

Renzo gave her another look, but it wasn't lost on Lucia how he didn't stare at her the same way he did the night before. There was no *want* ... no curiosity. Nothing that made her feel those raging butterflies, or a heat that made her feel like she was about to burn up right where she sat. Wasn't that just a damn shame, too? She thought so—she much preferred the Renzo from the night before to the one sitting across from her now.

This Renzo was the same one who seemed to make a game out of seeing just how much of an asshole he could be to her before she said enough was enough. Lucia had no interest in going back to *that.*

None at all.

"All right," Renzo grunted, shoving his phone back into his pocket. Seemingly oblivious to her confusion and hurt, he made quick work of lacing up his boots. He was already pushing the front seat forward and reaching for the handle on the door when he spoke to her again, saying only, "See you around, Lucia."

She blinked, not sure how to respond or if she even wanted to, and then he was gone before she could decide what to say. Out of the car, and slamming the door behind him without a look back at her. She caught sight of his back as he headed down the street, but just as quickly, he darted into an alleyway, and that was that.

Lucia wasn't entirely sure how long she sat like that—cold, and staring blankly at the quiet street where the morning light was just beginning to color it with the day. Too long, probably. Her mind ran a million miles a minute as it tried to desperately catch up to what had just happened.

Not just the morning.

The night before.

That man.

Lucia was not the type to make stupid choices. She didn't do reckless things just because she could, and she would probably get away with it. She had a plan when it came to her life, and she really couldn't afford for things to get in the way of that, so she tried to always make smart decisions. She was not something to be used, and then discarded whenever someone felt the need to do just that.

And yet, that was exactly how she felt as she sat there alone, tender between her thighs, in an empty backseat while she stared out the window at the street.

Used.

Discarded.

Entirely *cold*.

It was only the buzzing of her phone somewhere on the floor of the Lexus that reminded Lucia she too had other shit to deal with. She'd been gone all night, and hadn't even thought once to call her family or let them know she was fine.

That's not like you at all, her mind taunted.

She found the phone under the passenger seat, and it only took one look at the locked home screen to tell her that she was right. She'd muted the phone the night before, but after her usual alarm went off—silently—the phone automatically unmuted itself.

Fifteen phone calls.

A whole list of texts.

All from her mother and father.

Great.

Lucia took one more minute to gather her thoughts—or try—and then she climbed into the front seat. Better to just move the hell on than to waste more time trying to figure Renzo out. She was convinced that man didn't want to be figured out, anyway.

At least, not by her.

• • •

Lucia certainly expected a conversation with her parents when she finally arrived home, but she hadn't thought her father would already be waiting on the front porch when she pulled into the driveway. What was more surprising was the fact Lucian *rarely* dressed down, and when he did, it was typically dark wash jeans and a silk dress shirt rolled up to his elbows. She didn't think she had ever seen her father in anything less than his best, except for right then.

Lucian folded his arms over his chest as Lucia parked the Lexus, and exited the vehicle. In a plain white tee, and dark sweatpants, her father looked ready to hit the gym rather than chew her out for the night before.

"Dinner, remember?" he asked.

Lucia's brow dipped. "What?"

"Yesterday was your *birthday*."

"I know, Daddy."

Lucian nodded. "Yes, and we were all going to have a *late dinner* with you for your birthday. That's what we had planned, Lucia. Or did you forget?"

Mentally, she cursed herself because yes, she had done exactly that and forgotten about her plans with her parents. Clearly, she had gotten distracted by something else entirely.

Renzo, that was.

She still wasn't sure if it had been worth it. Especially not with the way her heart was feeling entirely too heavy, a little painful. It was strange to her that she even felt this way in the first place. She'd never had to be *good enough* for someone before. She'd never had to prove her worth to anyone or anything.

That man made her feel like she had to do exactly that for him every single time she was put in his presence. Lucia wasn't sure if she wanted to keep playing that game. She didn't like being made to feel worthless.

"What happened?" Lucian demanded.

Lucia shrugged her bag over her shoulder, and headed for the porch steps. She figured this conversation would be better held in the house— even if she didn't plan on telling her father where she had been, what she had done, or *who* she had been doing it with—instead of out here where the neighbors could see them.

Instead, her father didn't budge from his spot at the top of the stairs. He blocked her path entirely, keeping her two steps lower than him, and staring up at his hard expression. As much as he tried to appear *only* angry, she would see he was worried, too. That was as clear as day.

"I'm sorry I forgot to call," Lucia said, "it won't happen again."

"That's not what I asked," her father returned.

If she was a smarter girl, Lucia would have just made up some lie and been done with it. It wasn't like her father ever stepped in on his children's choices or made them go one way or another when it came to relationships. If anything, he made every effort to stay out of all that. Lucia appreciated it, and she knew her older siblings did, too.

It wasn't at all common in their culture, or within the suffocating life of *mafioso* for parents to do that in the first place. It was almost expected that men like her father would decide who their child could or could not date, and who was or was not appropriate for their lifestyle.

Lucian had never done that—*ever*.

But Lucia was apparently not a smart girl lately. Wasn't her recent actions proof enough of that? She didn't want to tell her father anything at all; partly because she didn't know what in the hell she was thinking, and partly because she didn't think it was any of Lucian's goddamn business.

Here she was.

Safe and sound.

That should be good enough.

"I'm eighteen," Lucia said, moving up the stairs and pushing past her father to enter the house. "I don't have to answer you when you ask where I go, or what I do. I'm an adult, Daddy."

Her father made a noise under his breath, but Lucia didn't care. She reached for the door knob to twist it open, but her father was there first. Once again, he blocked her path. She was forced to stare up at him, and tried her best *not* to glare, but probably failed.

Lucian looked entirely unbothered by her attitude. She'd never gone a round with her parents before. She was not the rule breaker of their family. She knew what was expected of her, and followed the rules to a T.

She had the distinct feeling this was not going to be the same at all. Her father looked like he knew it too, if his stiff posture was any indication.

"I want to go inside, shower, and have a nap," Lucia said dryly, "so excuse me."

Lucian shook his head, and folded his arms over his chest again. His telltale sign that he wasn't going to be moved *at all*. She'd seen him use that same stance over and over again throughout the years with her stubborn brother, John. Lucian was a brick wall, and no-fucking-body was getting through him.

Simple as that.

Lucia just wasn't in the mood today.

"*Daddy*, move," she said.

He didn't.

"Do you know," he murmured, "that despite how much freedom I have given to all of my children over the years—including you, Lucia—that it is only an illusion for you bunch. Sure, I let you make your own choices, mistakes, and paths. I step back, and watch from afar as you fall, get back up again, and succeed the next time you try. I don't hold your hand as you figure out life, or whatever else you need to learn. I've let you all do whatever you need to do to be happy, and to *thrive*."

Lucia swallowed hard. "I know."

"But the freedom you all think you have is an illusion," Lucian continued, colder than ever. She didn't think she had ever heard her father so cold, really. "Because no matter how *you* see me at the end of the day, whether it be just a man, or your father, or your mother's husband ... I will always be who I am, Lucia. And do you know who that is?"

"No."

"A *made* man. A man who will forever have a target on his back because of the life I chose, and because of that, so will you and anyone else I have brought into this life. So, yes, I give you the illusion of freedom, but at the

86

same time, when you think I am only watching from the sidelines, I am also keeping you safe in the best way I can."

"I don't under—"

"I wouldn't expect you to," her father interjected sharply. "Because what good would the illusion *be* if you're able to see right through it?"

Lucian let out a dark laugh, and softened his posture a bit. He scrubbed a hand down his unshaven jaw, and glanced back at the front door like he expected it to open up any second. Lucia wondered where her mother was in those moments.

"You have people who keep an eye on you," her father said quietly, not looking at her as he spoke. "People who you don't see, but that keep me informed when needed. You lost them last night—no, sorry, not *you*. You weren't driving, were you?"

Lucia blinked, silenced.

Her father met her gaze, then. Seeing right through her shit, even if he wasn't about to call her out on it.

"It's not the first time they noticed the young man around, or that you had sought him out," her father continued, unbothered. "Renzo Zulla, his name is. He's got some ties to your brother, it seems. I figured I would let you work it out, you'd learn quickly enough that he wasn't where your attention was best spent. You're a smart girl—you know to stay away from people who might cause you unneeded trouble. And that, Lucia, is all Renzo is. *Trouble*."

She stiffened as a hot shot of disbelief and anger rocketed through her spine.

"Why?" she asked.

Lucian's gaze narrowed. "*Why?*"

"That's what I asked, Daddy. Why is he *trouble?*"

"You've spent more than a few minutes with the young man to know who he's hanging around, and some of the things he's doing. You know exactly why he's trouble, Lucia."

Was that so?

"Like you, then?" she pressed.

Lucian straightened like someone had shoved a rod into his spine. "I beg your par—"

"Like John, too?"

"Lucia—"

"Uncle Dante, or Uncle Gio? Granddaddy, too? Andino, maybe? Like all of *you*, too? He's like you, too, right? If you're going to throw stones, make sure your house is not made of glass, Daddy. I hear that doesn't work out very well."

It took her father a second, and then two before he finally found his words to respond.

"That is not the same thing."

"I think it is."

"Lucia—"

"I think it's exactly the same," Lucia interrupted, unwilling to budge on her point. "And you can phrase it however you want. You can paint our family with whatever golden brush you would like to—God knows we can afford to paint ourselves however we want society to see us, right? But he can't. He's who he is, so you see him as he is. He's not covering up the things he doesn't want the rest of the world to see like you do—like the rest of our family does. It's exactly the same; I don't care what you say."

She had no reason to defend Renzo. After the way he left her that morning, she could have just thrown him to the wolves and said fuck it while she did so. That might have been the better way to handle it, really.

Still, she *couldn't*.

If she put this morning out of her mind, and thought about all the other things she knew about Renzo, then the truth was far clearer to her. He struggled. He was barely keeping his head above water. He had the responsibility of taking care of his siblings, and keeping himself alive. He was doing the best he could with what he had been given, even if it wasn't very damn much.

Nobody had the right to judge him for that.

Certainly not her father.

"Lucia," her father said as she opened the door to the house when he stepped aside, "you're to stay away from that young man. I'm not asking. I am *telling* you this. Stay away from him."

Nope.

Definitely not.

And if she did, it would because she chose to keep her distance. Not because someone had told her to do it.

Simple as that.

• • •

Lucia shifted the messenger bag hanging over her shoulder to ease some of the weight. She was focused on making sure she didn't trip over the edge of the shelter's entrance as she came out of the front doors instead of staring straight ahead.

Maybe she should have done that.

It would have prepared her for *him*.

But probably not.

"Got somewhere to be, princess?"

Lucia's head snapped up, and she found Renzo leaning against her Lexus. As usual, he looked like bad news standing there in his ripped jeans, combat boots, and a leather jacket thrown over a simple, white T-shirt. Like he didn't have a fucking care in the world except for the thing he was staring at in that moment.

Her.

A lit cigarette dangled from his fingertips as he blew out a heady cloud of grey smoke, and flashed her a smile that had her insides turning into knots.

Fuck him for doing that to her.

Instead of thinking about the way this guy made her feel—all the good and awful things—she chose to focus on the little boy holding tight to a toy truck as he stood next to his older brother's side.

"Hey, Diego," Lucia greeted. "Were you at daycare today?"

Diego smiled widely, and nodded. "I was. You wasn't there today."

"I worked in the kitchen today."

"Oh." Diego glanced up at Renzo, saying, "Is she gonna come, Ren?"

What?

Renzo patted Diego on the top of his head with a large hand, and passed Lucia a look. "Yet to be determined, buddy. So, are you busy, princess, or what?"

Lucia bristled.

Partly because of the nickname, and partly because she hadn't seen him since that morning he took off without as much as a goodbye in her direction. *Fuck.* He hadn't even looked at her as he left.

Lucia wasn't going to be any man's tissue to use and toss away when he was done with her, but especially not this man's. It didn't matter how much her stupid heart liked the way he was staring at her, or how those damn butterflies were back to make a mess out of her insides.

Did not matter one bit.

Maybe if she kept telling herself those things, she would start to believe them. God, she was a mess.

Lucia thought she might try for the subtle approach first, and go from there. "What, Ren, you didn't get what you wanted from me the first time? You need more?"

His gaze darkened as he looked her over, and then narrowed briefly. "You're pissed at me."

"You think?"

"Why?"

"You just took off!"

She hadn't meant for it to come out loud enough to scare off the birds resting along the powerlines, but there she was. Lucia watched the birds

89

scatter into the sky while the man a few feet away just chuckled like she had said something funny.

"Stop laughing at me," she snapped at him.

Renzo held up both hands, that cigarette of his dangling dangerously from his fingertips. "Sorry, princess."

"And stop calling me that, too."

"Kind of fits, doesn't it?"

Lucia didn't respond.

Renzo glanced down at his brother, and sighed.

"Listen, I had to be somewhere that morning, and if I hadn't got up and gone when I did, I would have missed my pick-up time for something I needed to run across the city. I would have been out that cash, and I needed it to pay my sister's expenses for the rest of the month, okay?"

It took Lucia a second, but she softened her stance. "I could have taken you, if you asked."

Renzo cleared his throat. "No."

That was it; that was all.

Just a quiet, simple *no*.

"But—"

"I handle my business, yeah?" Renzo shrugged a shoulder. "I didn't think to explain. I just had to handle my shit, and go. I don't really have to consider other people except myself, and my siblings. So, if you're expecting something like that from me, then you should also expect to be disappointed occasionally."

Huh.

The words slipped out of Lucia's mouth before she could think to stop them. "So, next time maybe explain before you just take off like that?"

A sly, sexy grin spread across Renzo's features, and his tongue peeked out to wet his lips as he nodded. "I will do that next time."

"Will you come with us, Lucia?" Diego asked suddenly, reminding her all at once that he was there, too, even if he was such a quiet kid. "Renzo said you would."

She looked to Renzo. "To where?"

"My sister has a thing," he said like it wasn't a big deal. "Figured maybe you'd like to do something—haven't seen you in a hot minute, you know?"

Lucia smiled.

She couldn't help it.

"Am I driving, or ...?"

Renzo laughed. "I'd rather take the bus, unless that's going to hurt your sensibilities, princess."

"Fuck you, Ren."

"Yeah, maybe later. We'll see how it goes, you know."

Ass.
And she liked it.
Entirely too much.

TEN

One seat ahead of Renzo, Diego leaned closer to the window to peer outside. Nothing interested that kid more than people, for whatever reason. Any kind of people. He loved to people watch, but he also enjoyed engaging others. Renzo wasn't sure what that would mean for Diego's future, but hopefully something good.

Smiling back at his brother, Diego asked, "Did you see the dog, Ren?"

He hadn't. He was too busy to be staring out the window between keeping an eye on his brother, and watching Lucia at the same time. Diego looked too happy to tell him he'd missed whatever dog had caught his eye *this* time.

"Yeah," Renzo replied, grinning.

Diego went back to the window with a nod. Satisfied for the moment that his younger brother was distracted and fine, Renzo went back to Lucia.

"Almost there," he murmured to Lucia.

Next to him, she nodded absently. Her attention was on something else entirely, though. The damn phone in her hand that hadn't stopped buzzing from almost the very second they stepped on the bus. Something was up—Renzo knew it even if she wasn't saying that was the case. She wasn't answering the calls or texts, and she'd put the phone on vibrate so now it was only mildly annoying … but it still hadn't stopped.

Her family, maybe?

She didn't talk about them a lot, if at all. But he wasn't so stupid that he didn't know enough about them to *wonder*. He was a lot of things, but he didn't have his head stuck in the sand, either.

Lucia *finally* looked up to meet his gaze, and she smiled like nothing was wrong in her world. He didn't know how true that was, but for the moment, he was willing to let her pretend.

"You good?" he asked.

Her pretty hazel eyes lit up like her smile. "Why wouldn't I be, Ren?"

"Seem distracted, that's all."

Lucia shrugged. "No place else I would rather be right now."

She offered that statement so freely and sweetly that he had no doubt she was telling him the truth. That didn't mean something still wasn't going on that he didn't know about. *That* was what concerned him.

Renzo really didn't need to be getting himself in some kind of shit because he got mixed up with the wrong woman. He knew just enough about the Marcellos to know they weren't the type of people to let things go.

That concerned him.

"You're not skipping out on anybody?" he asked, testing the waters.

Lucia flashed her teeth in a smile, and laughed. The quiet noise drew the attention of several other people on the bus, including Diego who quickly went back to his window-watching, but Renzo paid them no mind.

He figured right then, he had other shit to focus on. Like figuring out if there was a giant pile of steaming shit coming his way, and deciding whether or not it might be worth it to step in it for this girl.

She's here with you, isn't she?

His mind was a killer sometimes. Always reminding him of things he would rather leave to the wayside until he worked something out for himself.

That was a good point, though.

Lucia was there with him which meant, even if she was blowing someone else off, or her family wasn't happy … she was right where she wanted to be. That thought just made his chest tight in ways he couldn't explain.

"Well?" he pressed when he realized she hadn't answered him. "Did you skip out on plans with someone else for this?"

Lucia shrugged. "Not really."

Great.

"*Not really* isn't a no, Lucia," Renzo said, chuckling.

She gave him a look from the side, and just shook her head. "There wasn't anything specific going on tonight with my family or friends, so no, I didn't skip out on anybody. And even if I had, so what? Plans change all the time, right?"

It was that exact moment that her phone decided to start buzzing again in her hand. Renzo didn't miss the way her gaze dropped to check the screen, or how she was quick to reject the call with a simple wipe of her finger along the red phone icon that came up. She wasn't quite fast enough that he didn't catch whose name was on the screen, though.

Daddy, it read.

Damn.

"Lucian is your father, right?" Renzo asked quietly.

Lucia's head snapped back up fast. "What?"

"That's your dad's name. Lucian, right?"

"I was named after him, actually."

Renzo nodded. "I figured that's where the Lucia came from."

"Do you know my dad?"

Who didn't?

"I know *of* him," Renzo offered.

Which wasn't a lie. Any person who worked the streets under the Marcello organization, be it an errand runner, a drug dealer, a loan shark, or fucking muscle making sure everybody stayed in line and within their territory knew who the Marcellos were, and the people controlling the family.

It took Renzo a couple of years before he truly understood what the Marcellos were—not just powerful, rich people with a tendency for crime, but *mafia*. He heard the whispers, and as the saying went, there was always a grain of truth in every rumor. That alone was enough to tell him to be careful where the Marcellos were concerned.

Simple as that.

He did his job, and stayed off their radar at the same time. That allowed him to get on just fine, and kept them far away from his business. He dealt their drugs, managed his guys, never stole a dime, and always got paid on time. That was how he did business, and kept the people supplying him on their own side of the city.

Renzo wasn't out here wanting more. This was good enough for him. He didn't need any kind of trouble.

Lucia smiled slightly, and looked away at the same time. "I think knowing of my father, and *really* knowing the man might be two entirely different things."

Renzo agreed.

Partially.

"I think," he countered, "that the man I would get to know, if put in his path, is not the same man you know. To be fair."

"That could be t—"

Lucia's words were cut off by the buzzing of her phone. *Again.* This time, she wasn't as quick to reject the call, and Renzo saw that, once again, her father's contact lit up the screen.

Well, then …

"They're not going to send the dogs out looking for us," Renzo said, only half-joking, "right?"

There.

He asked.

What more could he do?

Lucia's teeth abused her bottom lip as she flipped her phone over and over in her hands for a moment. Then, she pressed the button on the side until the phone blinked out entirely before she shoved it into her purse at her feet.

Her gaze turned on him again, and he was struck silent by the intensity he found staring back from her. "I want to be here, Ren."

It sounded simple.

True.

"I know," he returned easily.

"It's other people who might not want me to be doing this. They also don't get a say."

Well, that was a matter of opinion. He really didn't need that kind of trouble, either. At the same time, he liked Lucia right where she was, too—at the moment, that meant she was with him.

"We're almost there," he said, changing the subject entirely.

Renzo would deal with whatever this was another time. If her family—or her father—had an issue with him, then he would just have to deal with it when the time came. If it ever even did come, he supposed.

Who knew if it would?

Lucia picked up on his desire to drop the conversation, and peered out the window. "One more stop, actually."

Renzo smirked. "You know exactly which school my sister is in, don't you?"

She shrugged and winked.

"You did say a private school for the arts in Brooklyn. There's only one of those. I have a friend who attended but graduated last year. This time of year is when they do their annual gallery and shows. It draws quite a crowd. People trying to get a glimpse at the next great artist."

Renzo made a noise that came out like a dark scoff. "Mmm, who they won't give a shit about until they've worked themselves to the bone, are left poor, and are dead in the ground. Only then will they care to spend way too much money for things like paint on a canvas that makes a pretty picture."

Lucia gave him a look.

"What?" he asked. "Where is the lie?"

"There isn't a lie," she murmured, "but there is more to art than just being an artist. None of that matters, though. Don't tell your sister what you just told me, Renzo. Why crush her dreams because you're a realist with a bitter streak, and she just wants to make beautiful things for people to enjoy?"

Huh.

"Yeah," Renzo said quietly, turning back to keep an eye on Diego again. "You're right. I won't."

• • •

Diego bounced on the balls of his feet as Rose finished chatting with one of her instructors twenty feet away. Renzo had to practically grab Diego by the back of his jacket just to keep the boy from running to his sister.

"Wait a second, now," Renzo said.

Lucia laughed. "He's excited."

"Yeah, he always is whenever he comes to see Rose."

Diego loved his sister like nobody knew. A lot like the way he loved Renzo, too. It was sweet, in a child-like kind of way.

Right now, though, they couldn't interrupt Rose's time. They were lucky enough to get an invitation to the event to see their sister's work hanging on the gallery walls, but they weren't supposed to drag Rose away from the people who had come in to judge the different pieces of art. At least, not until she was finished with her hour of being the speaker on the floor.

That hour was almost up, but she still had a minute or so to go.

"Did you see that abstract painting of hers in the far room?" Lucia asked.

Renzo glanced over at her, but found she was staring in the direction she spoke about. "I did see it."

"It was amazing, Ren."

"Yeah, Rose has always been pretty talented when you give her something to color on."

Her head snapped around, and she gave him a look. "Come on, this is a bit more than *just* coloring on paper."

He chuckled, and shrugged. "She's always going to be the little sister I used to steal crayons and paper for, so she could draw something pretty just to tape it up on whatever wall we could find, you know?"

Lucia quieted then, and nodded. Renzo hadn't really realized how easily he offered that information about his life, and his sister, but it was out there now. It wasn't like he could take it back, or anything.

He wasn't sure he wanted to, either.

"She must be so grateful for all of this," Lucia noted, peering around the gallery.

"She stopped saying thank you a few months back."

Lucia cocked a brow.

Renzo shrugged. "To be fair, I told her that if she didn't stop thanking me, I was going to stop bringing her money."

That wasn't a lie, either.

Lucia let out a sigh. "That's awful, Ren."

"What's awful is her thinking she doesn't deserve this, Lucia. Or that the only reason she's here is because I pay her lodging and other expenses. Truth is, she's here because she deserves to be here, and she worked hard to get noticed. She got the scholarship——I just made it *work*."

And he didn't want to be thanked for that because if he didn't do it for Rose, who would? Certainly not their mother who, half of the time, didn't even live in their reality. And it certainly wouldn't be their useless, deadbeat of a father.

Fuck up might be a better term.

Nonetheless, it was still true. Neither of their parents had ever shown even an ounce of interest, appreciation, or otherwise for Rose's accomplishments. In fact, their mother had the audacity to ask Renzo if he could pay three thousand a month for Rose, then why couldn't he spot her money every once in a while, too.

As for their father?

Shit, Rose was attending the private school for a good year before that asshole even knew about it. *Total fuck up.*

"Rose!"

Diego's shout brought Renzo back from his bitter thoughts quickly enough. Which was fine with him because he didn't want or need to be spending any more emotional energy on his deadbeat parents than he already did on a daily fucking basis.

He found his sister coming their way with a wide smile, and all he felt in that moment was pride. Rose looked like she was on top of the word with her hair done in soft waves, her face made up in neutral tones of makeup, and a pretty dress that made her look slightly older than her seventeen years.

Like she'd won the fucking lottery.

Maybe she had.

"Look at you," Renzo said.

Rose was already kneeling down to hug Diego, but just as quickly, she picked up their little brother and stood to face Renzo. "What about the way I look?"

Renzo smiled. "Nothing—you look good. *Happy.* Any news, then?"

"Well, I passed the practical, the presentation, and I'm pretty sure the verbal, but I have to wait for confirmation."

"So, a good night, then?"

Rose nodded. "A great night, Ren."

"Good."

He had a million and one other things he wanted to say, too. Like how much his sister deserved this, and that it was no wonder she earned her high marks and praise with how hard she constantly worked. He wanted to tell her that every single piece of art he saw with her name on a small plaque at the bottom made him feel a pride she would never be able to understand. Oh, he was sure she felt that pride, too, but in a different way. She'd made it, after all. He was just getting to watch her benefit from it.

That was good, too, though.

Rose's smile softened as Renzo stayed quiet—he wasn't the talking type. Not when it came to emotions, and shit like that. Not that his sister seemed to mind. Without a word, she came forward—still holding Diego—and wrapped Renzo in a tight hug. He hugged his sister back.

"Thanks," Rose whispered.

"Yeah, no worries."

Then, with a conspiratorial edge to her tone, his sister said, "Care to introduce me to your *friend?* I saw her waiting with you over here. Pretty sure I saw you holding her hand when you first came in, too."

Renzo laughed because *fuck*, his sister was sly as hell. Letting Rose go from his embrace, he nodded, and turned to Lucia. It was only then that he realized how quiet Lucia had been through the entire exchange.

Her warm gaze met his, and she smiled in *that* way. Sweet, and soft. Like she didn't want to take away from his moment, and she was fine with waiting in the wings until he was done with his siblings. He appreciated that, really.

"Rose, this is Lucia Marcello," Renzo said, offering his hand for Lucia to take. She did, and inched closer to his sister. "Lucia, this is Rose."

Rose set Diego to his feet on the floor, and put out a hand to shake Lucia's. Diego bounced at his sister's heels, and chattered on about all the pictures he had gotten to see while they waited for Rose to be done with her hour. He didn't seem to mind that no one was talking back to him, though.

"Nice to meet you, Lucia," Rose said.

Lucia nodded. "And you, too. Your abstracts are amazing."

A hint of pink tinged Rose's cheeks. "Thanks." Then, his sister gave him a look from the side before winking at Lucia, adding, "You know, I don't think I've ever met one of my brother's girlfriends."

Renzo stiffened.

Lucia blinked, but recovered quickly enough. "Is that what he is, then? My *boyfriend?* We haven't really put titles on it."

Rose let out a laugh. "He should probably figure that out, then, shouldn't he?"

It was not lost on Renzo how the two conversed like he wasn't standing right there. Even if they were teasing him a little, he didn't miss the truth to the words, either.

"Maybe he should," Lucia returned.

She said that to his sister, but she grinned at him.

Fucking woman.

He liked it, though.

A lot.

• • •

The quiet, dimly lit street didn't faze Diego a bit as he darted ahead of his brother and Lucia to jump over a large crack in the sidewalk.

"There's another," Lucia called to him.

Diego pumped a small fist in the air, and then ran forward to jump over that crack, too. This game of his continued on until the bus stop was in sight, and he decided that using the benches as a jungle gym would be more fun.

Renzo only smiled.

What else could he do?

Better for the kid to get his energy out now rather than later. Or, that was Renzo's opinion, anyway.

"You're quiet," Lucia noted.

He glanced down at her. She just beamed back up at him as if to deny what she said wasn't the truth. But it was true—he had been quiet ever since they left the art school's gallery, and said goodbye to Rose on the street in front of her apartment.

"Thinking," Renzo admitted.

"Do you do that often?"

He didn't miss the teasing note in her tone at all.

"Sometimes, yeah."

Lucia glanced down at the sidewalk, saying, "You know, I was just joking about what I said, right? At the gallery with your sister, I mean. There doesn't have to be any titles on whatever this is, Ren."

Yeah, he figured that out.

Didn't change the way his mind kept running over it, though.

Renzo brushed his hand along Lucia's lower back as they closed in on the bus stop, and their walk slowed. Without a word, he found her hand with his own, and wove their fingers together tightly enough that he knew she wasn't going anywhere.

No, he didn't like *titles*.

He wasn't even sure what this was.

He still liked it.

That was going to have to be enough.

Standing next to the small shelter the bus stop provided, Renzo tugged Lucia into his chest, wrapped his arms around her neck, and pressed a kiss to the top of her head. Diego was otherwise occupied with seeing if he could manage to jump from one bench to another, so he didn't seem to be paying them any attention.

Tipping her head back so those waves of her soft hair fell down around her shoulders, hazel eyes glittered up as they met his. "What was *that* for?"

Renzo shrugged. "Felt like doing it."

"Hmm."

"Don't overthink it, or anything."

Lucia grinned. "I won't. You're kind of amazing, you know that, right?"

Renzo blinked.

What?

"How am I—"

"You just are," she interjected softly, her hand coming up so that her fingertips could brush along the seam of his lips with a gentle touch that had sparks flying over his nerves. How could a *touch* do that? He wasn't sure, but he liked it. "You're always thinking about them, aren't you? Diego, and Rose. You get up every day for them, and what they need."

"Someone has to do it."

"And they love you for it."

"I guess so," Renzo returned. "Nobody else is looking out for them, though. Rose, she can handle herself if she needs to now, but I make sure she's able to put her focus where it counts."

"And Diego?"

Renzo glanced his little brother's way, but Diego was still busy with the benches. "Don't even know who his dad is, you know? Could be anyone within a ten-mile block of where we were living at the time that was willing to give Carmen a room for that night, or supply her habit for a day or two. I was so fucking pissed."

Lucia's fingertips drifted over his clenching jaw. "About what?"

"That she was pregnant again. I fucking *hated* him just for being there. Wasn't even his fault, you know, but I did. I hated him for it. The whole time she was pregnant, it just kept getting worse and worse. Like I was dying inside. She couldn't even stay clean for his pregnancy like she had for ours. She wasn't using as bad as what she had before she got pregnant, but it was enough to get her day to day without getting sick."

Her hand on his chest clenched into a tight first against his shirt, but Renzo barely even changed his tone as he spoke about something else he didn't like to talk about. Maybe he was fucking numb to it now, or he was just broken and couldn't feel anything at all.

Who knew what the issue was?

Not him.

"I just figured ..." Renzo drifted off with a sigh, staring at his little brother again. Diego, who loved him to death and never questioned it. Diego, who was entirely innocent and never asked for anything from anybody. Diego, who never even asked to be *here*. "I figured he'd be another mouth to feed. I was almost sixteen when he was born. Kind of realized he didn't have anybody either, and it wasn't really him I was pissed off at."

Lucia let her fingers drift through the longer bits of his hair that had fallen in front of his eyes. "But you love him."

"Loved him the second he was born. I was there—outside the room. Fed him first. Stayed up with him the whole night when she first brought him home."

Lucia's brow furrowed. "Where was your mom?"

"Getting high."

Story of my life.

"And you know," Renzo said in an exhale, "he didn't ask for her, either. Just like the rest of us."

"Wait ... if she was using when she was pregnant, does that mean he was born—"

Renzo openly frowned as he interjected, "He shook so bad, and cried so loudly. It got better after the first week, but it took another week before he could sleep for even an hour at a time. But he still jerked in his sleep. Scared the fucking hell out of me—I'd stay awake and just watch him because I didn't know any better. I thought he was going to stop breathing."

"Ren."

He was stuck staring at his brother, and remembering that first month of life. He hadn't known anything about babies—not how to feed, change, or care for them at all. But he learned a hell of a lot about love from Diego.

He figured out it was absolutely possible for him to love something in a world full of things that he hated.

"*Renzo.*"

His gaze drifted back to Lucia's pretty features. No pity stared back at him, and for that, he was most grateful.

"She had him in a clinic provided by a shelter she was using. They were already at fucking capacity and overflowing. More women coming in who couldn't afford a hospital bill." Renzo let out a dead laugh, so full of bitterness and anger. "It was a shift change when the talk of drawing blood came up, so a nurse mentioned drug screening. All *standard.* The shift change happened, another nurse came in talking about discharging Carmen and Diego because they needed the bed."

Lucia blinked, and understanding dawning on her face. "The blood screening never happened."

"He could have died going through withdrawals because she was too selfish to stop using. And fuck, maybe if they'd gotten that screening in, he'd be ... somewhere better. Given to a family that could have given him a good life, or—"

"You're the best place for him," Lucia said sharply, making Renzo meet her gaze again. "He wants to be with you."

Did that make it the best place for Diego, though?

Renzo didn't know, but he wasn't willing to find out, either. Diego was staying with him until the kid was old enough to take care of himself, and even then, Renzo would be watching his back. Simple as that.

"It's not even about you at all, is it?" she asked. "It's all for them when it comes to you."

Renzo smirked up at the inky sky. "There's no worth in *me*, Lucia. Why would I get up for me? More important people are waiting."

Her smile drifted away, then. Like she was seeing him all over again for the first time, but in a whole new way.

"Don't say that," she murmured. "You have worth. You're worth something to *them*."

He supposed.

He'd never really looked at it like that.

"And me, too," she added quickly. "You're worth something to me, too, Renzo."

The words were barely out of her mouth before he was kissing her. A fast, hard kiss that he was sure took her breath away because it sure as fuck took his away, too. All he wanted to do was wrap his arms around her, keep her close, and hide this girl away from the rest of the world. She couldn't possibly be real, right? All the shit he thought he knew about Lucia, she kept blowing right out of the water.

It was bad for him.

It was *good* for him, too.

Renzo found their kiss was like a familiar dance, now. Teasing lips gliding over his, and a tongue that always needed to seek out just a taste. Her hands fisted into his jacket, and she kept him close even as he forced himself to break away.

"Lucia, is you gonna come have spaghetti with us?" Diego asked, pushing in between the two like he didn't know what was going on. He probably didn't—poor kid. Peering up at them both, Diego smiled. "She is, right?"

Lucia wet her lips, meeting Renzo's gaze. "Spaghetti, huh?"

"Yeah, his favorite."

"Mine, too."

"You don't want to miss out, do you?" he asked.

Strangely, he found himself wishing she would say no as much as he wanted her to say yes. He wished she would say no because no matter what, there was still a part of him that felt like they just didn't fit. Oil and water at the end of it all. His world was not hers, and her life was not meant for people like him.

And yet, he needed her to say yes because he wanted her.

Renzo had never wanted someone before.

Not like he wanted Lucia Marcello.

"Definitely not missing out," she said, leaning up to catch his mouth in a kiss again. "But I'm making the sauce. We'll stop at a store. They'll have what I need."

Renzo laughed.

What else could he do?

"Whatever you want, babe."

ELEVEN

"Kindergarten is gonna be *awesome*," Diego crowed, stuffing a whole meatball into his mouth as soon as he finished.

Lucia pressed her lips together to keep from laughing at the kid. "Oh?"

Diego nodded, and sauce dripped down from his mouth over his chin. It went right down to the collar of his yellow T-shirt, and made a mess there, too. Not that Diego seemed to mind at all. "Yep!"

"Jesus." Renzo chuckled as he reached for napkins that Lucia already had ready for him to take from her outstretched hand. He made quick work of wiping the mess up, but as Lucia suspected, a stain remained on Diego's shirt. "Well, that's done with."

The kid paid his older brother no mind. He was too busy regaling Lucia with all his stories about kindergarten, how he'd met his teacher, and all the things he was going to get to do next year when he attended. Lucia couldn't help but notice how Renzo sat quietly through his little brother's stories. At the small kitchen table—it only had three chairs to fit around it—the three were quite cozy in the tiny kitchen, but she liked that. Usually, she sat at tables so large for family dinners that people had to get up and bring food down to somebody if they wanted something.

The smell of spices clung to the air. There was no way in hell Lucia was having spaghetti without adding all the secret spices her grandmother used to make the meatballs and sauce something more than just food to put in your mouth. With a little extra love, regular spaghetti became an *experience*.

"And how do you feel about that?" Lucia asked.

It took Renzo a second to realize she'd been talking to him. His head popped up from where he was spinning spaghetti around a fork, and he cocked a brow. "About what?"

"Him starting school."

"Fine," Renzo replied.

"*Really*, just fine?" Lucia passed Diego a look, but the boy was fully concentrating on cutting a meatball in half because he apparently didn't want to try to shove another whole one in his mouth. "You're basically his only caregiver. Every day, right?"

"So?"

"I mean … moms sometimes get emotional when they send their kids off to school. I just wondered if you might feel a little sad to see him go."

Renzo blinked, and Lucia laughed at the expression that flitted over his features. It was a mix of a lot of things, and nothing she could really put her finger on. At the same time, she thought that surprised expression looked damn good on him. It wasn't very often Lucia could catch Renzo off guard, but somehow, she had managed to do it tonight.

"I'm not his *mom*," Renzo said.

"Mom's gone," Diego muttered absently before popping a half of a meatball into his mouth. "Right, Ren?"

A heaviness came to sit directly on Lucia's chest in that second. When had their mom taken off again? Sure, Renzo didn't owe Lucia anything when it came to his life. He didn't have to tell her a damn thing if he didn't want to. But that wasn't really the point, either.

Diego seemed entirely unbothered as he sat next to Lucia at the table, announcing his mother was gone. Just like that—*gone*. It kind of pissed Lucia off, too. Not at Diego or Renzo, but rather, their mother. What kind of woman just didn't care about her kids at all? What kind of woman gave birth to kids she had no desire to look after? One that chose drugs time and time again instead of her kids?

Lucia wasn't the type to judge. She always tried to find the silver lining in bad situations. Something to paint the blackness of life with a little bit of color. When she found Renzo's mother drunk, or high—hell, maybe it was both—she thought to help the woman. Because clearly, Carmen had needed help.

Right then, Lucia only felt a growing resentment and bitterness toward the woman she'd tried to help. Oh, sure, the anger was there, too. But the other bit felt more important, she supposed, because she could empathize with Renzo. She finally got it—really, truly understood—why Renzo spoke with such coldness every time his mother came up in conversation.

Lucia would never consider speaking about her mother with the same cold detachment Renzo used regarding his mother, but she also knew ... it wasn't at all the same. Her mother had never abandoned her; Jordyn loved her children wholly, and fully. Always their loudest, and first supporter at the beginning and end of each day. All they had ever known was love when it came to their mom, and even their dad.

Renzo never had that.

Neither had Diego, or Rose.

Sure, Lucia had realized those things before, but it was as she sat there with Renzo and Diego that it finally really hit her, and what it meant. She could hear about their struggles—she could even *see* them first hand. Yet, she would never fully understand what it meant because that wasn't her life. She had been given the privilege and beauty of a good life, two great parents, and a whole family that also acted as a support system for her.

From her grandparents, to her uncles, aunts, and cousins.

The Marcellos were one unit.

105

"You went quiet," Renzo noted.

She peered over at him, and watched as he popped a half of a meatball into his mouth before shooting her a wink. He didn't seem bothered at all by his little brother outing the fact their mother was MIA. Like this was something he was used to—her coming, going, or not giving a fuck about them at all. Maybe that was what hurt Lucia the very most.

Renzo was amazing.

He didn't know it, but he was.

He deserved better—and so did his siblings—than what his mother was giving him. And his father, too, likely. Because where was that man?

Who knew?

"When did she take off?" Lucia asked.

Renzo cleared his throat, and took a moment to set his fork down before wiping his mouth with a napkin. He chewed and swallowed his food before meeting her gaze once more. "Whenever she was released from the hospital, I guess."

"You guess?"

He shrugged, so flippant and distant from it all. Maybe that was just the way he protected himself, Lucia wasn't really sure, but it still hurt her heart for him all the same.

"Yeah, I mean … that night you tried to help, she was here and *out of it.* It got really bad—she started throwing up, and choked a bit. I did what I usually do in that case, and called for an ambulance. I called the hospital twice. Once the next day to make sure she was …" Renzo trailed off, and passed his little brother a look. Diego was fully engrossed in his food, but Lucia knew that didn't mean anything. A kid could pretend like they weren't hearing anything, but in truth, they likely heard everything. "Hey, you done, buddy?"

Despite playing with his food, Diego hadn't put any spaghetti in his mouth in a few minutes. Most of his plate was empty, too. He'd loved it, which just made Lucia smile.

All good Italians loved their food when it was pasta, and some kind of sauce. It didn't matter what walk of life they came from, that would never change.

"Yeah," Diego said.

Renzo nodded. "All right, go strip down in the bathroom. Looks like you need a bath. I'll come back in a few and run the water for you."

"Okay!"

Diego pushed the chair out from the table, and dropped down to the floor. He gave Lucia a wide, toothy smile, saying, "Thanks, it was good."

"Next time, I'll make you something new."

"Promise?"

Renzo cleared his throat, but Lucia didn't know why or for what. She just ignored him.

"Absolutely, pinky promise," Lucia told Diego.

"Awesome."

Soon, the boy's footsteps echoed down the hallway toward the front of the apartment as he headed for the bathroom. Renzo leaned back in his chair, folded his arms over his chest, and eyed Lucia in that silent, contemplative way of his that usually had her feeling all kinds of things she didn't understand.

This time was no exception.

"What?" she asked.

Renzo shrugged one shoulder. "You're just going to keep coming back, huh?"

She blinked.

He didn't move a muscle.

Didn't he know?

"There's no place I would rather be, Ren."

"Yeah," he said gruffly, "I guess not."

Then, from the bathroom, Diego shouted out, "I'm ready, Ren!"

Renzo gave her a look, leaned over the table to press a fast kiss to Lucia's temple, and drifted out of the room without a look back. She supposed their conversation about his mother was done ... for now, anyway.

She couldn't say she was disappointed. She bet that woman already took up far too much time in Renzo's head to fuck with his emotions. He didn't deserve that, either. None of it.

• • •

Lucia wiped the wetness from the bathroom floor with the towel Renzo had left on the edge of the tub probably after drying off Diego. She hadn't gone in with the boy when he took his bath—instead, she opted to stay in the kitchen and clean up the mess. She cooked, sure, and while the rules in her family were usually those who didn't cook needed to clean ... well, she figured Ren probably had enough shit to do. He didn't need to be cleaning up her mess of pots and dishes.

Besides, she needed something to do while she waited. Lucia wasn't going anywhere. Not yet.

Dropping the wet towel over the edge of an off-white laundry hamper, she turned to find Renzo standing in the bathroom doorway. The sight of him there struck her hard in the chest. Like for the moment, she couldn't even *breathe*. She didn't know why—maybe it was the way his dark eyes

107

traveled over her so unashamed and *curious*. Like he enjoyed what he was seeing, and he wanted far more of it. Or maybe it was the fact she didn't know how long he had been standing there watching her to begin with.

"What are you doing?" she asked him.

Renzo's mouth quirked at the corners—a hint of a smirk, maybe. Goddamn him for looking so good even when he wasn't doing anything at all. There was just something about his face. All those hard lines, and soul-searching eyes. Dark like sin, and looking right at her. Haunted, she thought. Sometimes, when he didn't know she was looking at him, Lucia thought he looked oh, so haunted.

Life had made him that way.

Yet, he still tied her in knots.

Like right now.

"I could ask you the same thing," he said, smiling slyly. "You cleaned the kitchen, too. What are you doing in here picking up shit?"

Lucia wiped her hands across her pants to remove the dampness from the towel she'd been using to clean up the water mess. "I mean, do you want to do all this before you go to bed? I sure as hell wouldn't."

"But you don't have—"

"I know. I wanted to."

She expected him to come back with something else to say his life and business wasn't her responsibility to worry about. That just seemed to be Renzo's way, didn't it? If he felt like she was getting to close, he was quick to push her away. Yeah, she'd gotten him figured out, now.

So, maybe it surprised her a bit—although, it wasn't a bad surprise—when he nodded, and turned in the doorway with a wave of his hand. "Come on, then."

Lucia trailed behind him through the hallway until the two of them were standing in the living room. He yanked an opened can of soda up from the coffee table in front of a couch that did not look like the one that had been here the last time. The clean, brown microfiber was vastly different from the frayed, worn out light blue one that had sat there before.

"New couch?"

Renzo took a long swig from the can, and set it back down to the table. "Couldn't clean the other one of Carmen's mess, so I just said fuck it, and grabbed this one."

She noted the pillow and blanket folded up on the end. "And you're sleeping on it, too, apparently."

"I usually do when she's not around using it."

Lucia frowned, and couldn't help but wonder … where in the hell did he sleep when his mother was around? This apartment was only a one bedroom. She didn't know how big Diego's room was, but was that where

Renzo slept usually?

Renzo's quiet chuckles brought Lucia out of her thoughts. She found him smirking at her in *that way*. It was as sexy as it was fucking annoying. She had come to find that look of his meant he knew something she didn't, and he found it funny.

"What?"

"Your wheels are spinning," he murmured, reaching out to press the pad of his thumb against her forehead. Right on the spot above her eyes. His thumb stroked her skin like he was trying to smooth out the lines she'd made while thinking. Lucia couldn't help but smile. "When you're thinking too hard about something, you get a little knot right here, you know."

"Do I?"

"Every single time, baby."

Huh.

"I was just wondering where you slept when your mom is here."

That question made Renzo stiffen, and his gaze drifted away from her. She could tell right then that whatever the answer was, he clearly didn't want to give it to her. Renzo's best defense was to simply ignore a question when he didn't want to answer one. She expected him to deflect her question to something else, but once again, he surprised her.

"Wherever the hell I can," he said quietly, "but Diego's room is too small for a second bed, and I'm not getting in his little twin, either."

"So ..."

"The floor, a chair ... the tub. I just need to close my eyes once in a while, Lucia. I don't really care where in the fuck I do it."

The tub.

Renzo gestured at the couch, adding, "I haven't seen Carmen since they took her in the ambulance. I called the hospital about seventy-two hours after she was taken in to see when they were going to release her. I guess she signed herself out after the forty-eight-hour mark. They couldn't stop her, then. She's not been back."

That heaviness was back in Lucia's heart again.

So was the bitterness and anger.

"She hasn't called?"

"If she's even got a phone," Renzo said, "she's using it to pick up men, or to call in someone to supply her habit. She doesn't use it to call us, but that's fine, too."

"But—"

"She only upsets him," Renzo interjected firmly, giving her a look that told Lucia he wasn't willing to fight the point. It was what it was. "Diego, I mean. Whenever she calls fucked up, it upsets him. When she shows up, and then takes off again, it upsets him. When she's here and she's causing chaos, it upsets him."

"And you."

Renzo let out a heavy sigh. "I'm used to it now."

But wasn't that kind of fucking terrible, too? He shouldn't have to be *used* to it. He shouldn't be numb to any of this because it shouldn't be happening at all.

Yet, it was.

Lucia kept her thoughts to herself.

"It does upset me when Diego gets upset," Renzo muttered, "but at the same time, he loves Carmen. He's still at an age where ignorant innocence takes importance over the self-preservation of his own emotions. So, even though she keeps hurting him, he still misses her when she's gone. He still asks me where she is. He loves her; like I did when I was just a kid who had to depend on her even though she proved over and over again that she was never going to look out for me."

Lucia fidgeted with the sleeve of her shirt, whispering, "And that's why you let her keep coming back, isn't it? That's why you don't shut her out from him. Because—"

"He still thinks he needs her, yeah." Renzo cleared his throat, and picked up the can of soda to finish it off in one long gulp. Nodding his head toward the kitchen, he asked, "Was there any of that left?"

Lucia grinned. "A bit. Why?"

"I might want more."

"There's more."

"Good."

Lucia followed Renzo into the kitchen, and waited as he dropped the can into a small green pail.

She set herself up on the edge of the counter, content to watch Renzo make himself another plate of food. Her mother had always told her that the way to a man's heart was absolutely through his stomach. Men were easier to deal with when they weren't hungry, and that was definitely true with Renzo.

Trying to get her mind off the fact that she really liked the sight of him enjoying her food, Lucia toyed with the small bottle of honey that had been left out on the counter. It was shaped like a small bear, but it gave her something to do with her hands. Not that it helped all that much. She still ended up staring at him like an idiot.

She couldn't help it.

Who would?

Of course, her staring didn't go unnoticed by him. Passing her a glance, he quirked an eyebrow. "What?"

Lucia grinned. "I'm not doing anything."

"You're over there staring and smiling. Why?"

"I can't stare at you, or smile?"

"Well—"

"I can't like what I'm looking at?"

His tongue peeked out to wet his bottom lip as he shot her a smirk. Setting the plate of food aside, he made his way over with a gleam in his eye that promised fun.

It'd been a while, she thought. Maybe too long since the last time she'd had him between her thighs. Now seemed like a good time to remember exactly what it felt like for him to be losing control while he was fucking her.

Yeah, why not?

"And do you?" Renzo asked, setting himself between her widened legs.

"What?"

"Like what you see, Lucia. Do you?"

"Oh, are you fishing for compliments now?"

Renzo chuckled, and leaned in to press a quick kiss to her lips. That kiss wasn't nearly enough, though. She pushed back against him to get more, edging closer to the end of the counter all the while. She wanted to feel him pressed all over there—to get him hard between her thighs where she had no doubt she was already wet.

Hell, all she had to do was *look at him*, and she was wet.

His tongue tangled with hers, reminding her that no, for the moment, she didn't need to worry about life or anything else when the two of them were like this. All she needed to focus on was the way his hips flexed forward, and just how good the ridge of his erection felt rubbing against the thin cotton of her panties when her dress slid up around her hips. Those warm hands of his found her throat, keeping her in place as a thick groan fell from his lips.

It was almost funny how she felt like a fucking teenage girl getting her first taste of pleasure in those moments. Like the first time she realized that if she rubbed something between her thighs in just the right way, it felt *really fucking good*. She couldn't remember the last time she had gotten caught up in feeling that sensation, but she missed it.

Renzo seemed all too happy to keep kissing her like he was and indulging the way she wrapped her thighs around his waist to get him closer. *God, yeah.* She wanted more of that.

"Could you come like this?" she heard him ask. "Just rubbing that sweet pussy on me, Lucia? Could you?"

She let out a ragged breath. "Yeah, I think I could."

Already, her thighs were shaking.

That coiling tension was thick in her belly.

111

Oh, yeah.

She could definitely come like this.

And then she felt it.

Sticky.

Wet.

Her concentration was broke just like that, and the teasing promise of an orgasm was gone as she realized what had happened.

"Shit," Lucia laughed, pulling away.

The top on the bottle of honey had come off, and she spilled a good tablespoon on her hand and wrist. She didn't even get the chance to reach for the dishrag hanging off the side of the sink before Renzo caught her wrist in his hand, and pulled it to his mouth. His tongue snaked out first, tasting and teasing. And then his lips wrapped around the sticky sweet mess to lap the rest of it up, too.

Something hot shot through her body.

It made her needy, and so fucking weak.

His gaze stayed locked on hers as he cleaned the honey with his mouth, and all she could think about was how sinful he looked like that, and why couldn't she breathe right again?

The very second all that honey was gone, he came for her again. Strong hands skimming up her thighs, and yanking her dress higher. Those panties of hers were pulled down her legs so fast, she barely even felt them brushing against her skin. She couldn't get into his pants fast enough, couldn't get them down around his hips quickly enough to satisfy her want for him.

But she did.

Somehow.

"Yeah, shit, like that," Renzo grunted. "Love your hands on me, you know."

He watched the way Lucia stroked his cock once she had him free of his boxer-briefs. There was something inherently wicked about the way his features shadowed as he stared down between them. Or maybe it was beautiful, and not wicked at all. His thumb stroked the wetness smeared on her thighs, coming closer to her pussy with each swipe, while she continued jerking him off. He was heavy in her palms, but soft, too. All those veins in his cock pulsing against her fingertips.

"Want me to fuck you?"

Lucia nodded, wetting her lips, and watching him through lowered lashes.

"I like *words*, Lucia."

Of course, he did.

Even when she struggled to find them.

112

"I want you to *fuck me*," she whispered.

The words were barely out of her mouth before he kissed her again. Harder, and deeper than before. Stroking those flames that had already been blazing out of control inside her body as his lips worked roughly against hers. Vicious and harsh, his kiss left her gasping. She heard the foil wrapper crackle, and watched his hands work that latex down his length before he was fitting himself between her thighs, and pushing in deep.

Lucia got it, then.

She understood exactly why Renzo had looked the way he did when he was staring at her pussy while she jerked him off. The sight of him sliding through the lips of her sex until he was seated fully inside her, their bodies were tight together, and she couldn't draw in a proper breath was … intoxicating.

His fingertips stroked her jaw, and then her lips.

It felt like electricity snapping her nerves *alive*.

"Oh, my God," she mumbled.

"Mmm."

That was all she got from him, that quiet agreement as his hips shifted, he pulled back out to show just how wet his cock was with her, and then slammed back in hard enough to push her back a bit on the counter.

"Fucking *hold on*," Renzo muttered.

She did.

To him.

She was still caught in watching the way his cock pulsed and looked covered in her when her gaze darted up to find he wasn't seeing the same thing she was.

He couldn't.

He was too busy watching her.

Those russet eyes of his locked on hers, and Lucia was *gone*. High, blissed, and crawling closer to the edge with every flex of his hips.

"You gonna come for me?"

"So hard, Ren."

He gritted his teeth, and she bared hers.

"You gonna come *with* me?"

Fuck.

"*Yeah.*"

Her words weren't even really words now. Just whispered punctuated by hard gasps of air as pleasure swam through her bloodstream. She could feel the tension in his back with every thrust. The way he tightened, and released. His hands still hadn't left her throat, and she let him tip her head back, so he could fit his mouth on the hollow of her throat.

He sucked.

Bit.

She fucking flew.

He came then, too. She felt it in the way his dick jerked inside her, and his shoulders loosened. He groaned against her skin, and all she could do was sigh.

"Not so hungry now," she heard him murmur.

Lucia laughed breathlessly. "Just tired, I think."

"Yeah ... shit, yeah. The couch, then?"

"Do I get to use you as a pillow?"

Renzo's laughter was far louder than hers as he pulled her in for a soft, trembling kiss. "Yeah, I'll be your fucking pillow. Whatever you want, Lucia."

• • •

It was a constant, loud banging in the back of Lucia's dream-filled mind that first made her open her eyes. The banging continued even as she wiped the sleep from her eyes, and realized exactly where she was.

Still with Renzo.

On top of him, as a matter of fact.

He shifted under Lucia, his face still a mask of relaxation in his sleep. One of his arms kept a firm hold around her waist, while his other had been shoved under the pillow beneath his head to give him extra support. For a second, Lucia took the minute she had to enjoy the sight of him like this. Unbothered, and quiet. His mind filled with dreams instead of everything else she suspected he was always needing to worry about.

Did life ever really let this man enjoy that he was alive?

She didn't think so.

She couldn't help but trace Renzo's lax lips with her fingertips before memorizing the shape of his cheekbones by touch, too. It was only the slow curve of his lips that told her he wasn't sleeping at all.

"Morning," he said, cracking his dark eyes open. He looked directly at her, making her breath catch. "You're a nice sight to wake up to. Especially when you're on top of me, you know. In case you can't feel it, I definitely like it."

Oh, she could certainly feel just how much he liked having her right where she was. The man just woke up hard, and she happened to be in the perfect position to feel his length pressing against her aching pussy. She was probably wet, too. It didn't matter that she had gotten to enjoy him the night before—she just wanted *more.*

That's what Renzo did to her.

Lucia *might* have been a little embarrassed over that fact on another day, but today was not it. She wasn't going to be ashamed of the fact she wanted Renzo—wanted to fuck him ... just *wanted* him.

"What was that noise?" he asked.

Lucia pressed a kiss to the underside of his jaw. "What, the banging?"

"Mmm, yeah. The banging." His hands slid under the thin blanket to grab tight to her ass. His fingertips dug in, surely leaving behind pink marks that she would love to stare at each time she undressed in front of a mirror. "Shit, I want to tell you to keep doing that, but someone is gonna get up really soon, and we shouldn't be—"

Renzo's words cut off when that banging in question picked up again. Only this time, it was accompanied by a female's voice shouting along with it. It took Lucia a second to realize who it was practically trying to put their fist through the apartment door. It was the sheet of dark anger that slid over Renzo's features that only confirmed it for her, really.

"Open the fucking door, Renzo! You can't keep me from seeing Diego!"

"Jesus Christ," Renzo snarled under his breath. Lucia was quick to climb off of him, and search for her discarded clothes from the night before as he pulled on a pair of jeans, but didn't bother with anything else. She didn't even have time to admire the sight of him shirtless before he headed for the apartment door. "Right, she's back for *Diego*. Fucking bitch."

"Ren," Lucia hissed, her gaze darting to the hallway where she was sure if Diego wasn't awake, he soon would be because of the noise. "Don't say that about her where he can hear. I know it's true—she's *terrible*. But he loves her, doesn't he? Don't let him hear you say awful things about her; it'll hurt *him*."

He met her gaze over his shoulder, and nodded quickly. She made fast work of pulling on the rest of her clothes, and he waited until she was fully dressed before yanking open the door. Not that it mattered, really. She figured she probably still looked like she had spent the night wrapped up in a man given the state of her hair when she tried to run her fingers through the waves to smooth out the strands.

And her makeup?

Probably ruined, too.

Lucia still couldn't find it in herself to regret it.

How could she?

"What, are you bringing *whores* into your apartment now, Renzo?"

Lucia came back to reality with a harshness that felt like a slap to her face. Renzo's mother came down the hallway with a sneer already affixed to her face, and it only became worse when Lucia met the woman's gaze. At least, she thought, Carmen Zulla looked a hell of a lot better than the last time Lucia laid eyes on the woman. She didn't look so goddamn close to death.

Shame, really.

In that moment, death might be preferable to Carmen than the way Renzo was glaring at her like he was seriously considering killing her right where she stood.

"Shut your mouth," Renzo snapped. Then, to Lucia, he tried to smile, but it didn't come out as true. "You should head out, baby. I've ... got some work to do today, anyway. I'm sure someone is wondering where you are and all."

"*Baby?*" Carmen's screech and high-pitched laugh felt like nails raking down a chalkboard. "Please tell me you're not throwing money or something at *that*, Renzo. You won't even give me anything and—"

"Because you deserve *fuck all*," Renzo said, hate coloring his words. "Lucia, please ..."

He trailed off with a wave toward the door. The last thing Lucia wanted to do was leave him there with his awful fucking mother to battle her alone, and deal with the aftermath when Diego finally woke up, but she could tell he also didn't want her there, either. She didn't think he was trying to protect her from seeing the awful parts of his life, though.

Maybe ... he was just trying to protect her from the vileness of one woman in his life.

"Number's in your phone," Renzo said as Lucia passed him by, his hand coming up to snag her wrist in his tight grasp. "Call me, Lucia."

She nodded, and gave him a quick kiss. That only served to have his mother ranting again. This time, though, Carmen's words didn't bother Lucia all that much. She barely even heard the insults the woman hurled at her back.

They weren't worth it.

Neither was Carmen.

"I'll call," Lucia promised.

"You better."

• • •

Lucia saw her father leaning against her car long before she even stepped foot on the shelter's parking lot. She really hadn't thought much about what she was going to say or do to explain where she had gone missing to for an entire evening and night. She'd stopped even looking at her father's messages, and didn't bother to pick up any of his calls.

Besides, he said it himself, didn't he? He had people *watching* her. Surely, Lucian knew exactly where Lucia had been the night before if his people were any good at doing their job. Or, if they hadn't lost her again.

"Morning," Lucia greeted, hitting the unlock button on the fob for her car. "You—this—couldn't wait until I got home, Daddy? At least let me get some food into me before you go on another rant about who I can or can't spend my time with. Makes your hypocrisy a little easier to swallow, maybe."

Lucian made a thick noise in the back of his throat. She could tell—without a doubt—her careless attitude bothered him more than anything else ever would. "*Lucia.*"

She gave him a look from the side. "Yes?"

"Do you know how fucking worried I was about you last night?"

"Because I went to a gallery in Brooklyn, and then stayed the night with someone? Why would you be worried—"

"I told you—that young man is bad news!" Her father's shout echoed over the quiet parking lot. Lucia was unmoved. "You know *nothing* about that boy, Lucia. Not how he grew up, or the things he's seen. All you know is the fact he looks half decent, and is paying you a bit of attention. That's *it*. And what about when something bad happens, huh? What are you going to do then? Go on and tell me. I've apparently got time to stay up all night getting updates on where you are, worrying myself fucking sick over you, and then make my way over here this morning instead of waking your mother up like I do every morning. So yeah, go and tell me, I will wait."

Lucia blinked. "Daddy, stop."

"You don't know anything—"

"You keep saying that like you know it's true. But I bet I know a hell of a lot more about him than you do. Or, I actually made the effort to learn things about him while you only got to see what you could pull on him. Deny it."

Lucian didn't.

Lucia wondered …

"You know I'm not Liliana, right?"

Her father's jaw stiffened at that question. She bet he was clenching his teeth so hard, his molars were aching. Years ago, her oldest sister had gotten involved with a man who nearly killed her when he beat her up in the back of a limo. At the time, Lucia had been way too young to really understand the kind of impact that must have had on her sister, and even her father … Lucian was so close to his children, but especially his daughters. She didn't think that was easy on her dad. Not at all.

"Did you feel like you failed her back then?" she asked quietly.

Her father's gaze blazed. "Every single day."

"This isn't the same thing. That's not who Renzo is, and—"

"Liliana would have said the same thing back then, Lucia. She didn't know either. Not until it was too late." Lucian scrubbed a hand down his

117

jaw, and peered down the lonely looking street. "That man was also nothing that Renzo is—he had money, contacts … clout behind his name. He wasn't the kind of man you saw and thought, *abuser.*"

"But you do for Renzo."

Her father's gaze snapped back to her. "Lucia—"

"You look at him, you know he sells drugs—but you don't care why—and you see his life, and think … he's a terrible person; he must be a horrible man. He's not."

"I don't want to find out if that's what he is, Lucia. And I *do not* want to wait around for you to find out that's what he is, either. I may not know everything about him, or his life, but what I know is enough to tell you to stay the hell away. His father—a fuck up of a man—has a serious gambling problem that he likes to aid with a bottle of liquor. Do you know how many times he's been brought in on charges of domestic violence? He's got a rap sheet longer than you are tall, *dolcezza*. Boys don't wake up one day and hit girls. They *learn* it."

Lucia was still unaffected. "He's not like that."

She was going to keep saying it until her father heard her.

"You're to stay away from him. That's the end of it."

"Your feelings are clouding up your judgment, Daddy."

"They are not."

"They *are.*"

Lucian's jaw clenched again. "I made myself clear, didn't I? He's not the type that I want you to be mixed up with. You're going to force my hand, Lucia, and you may not like what I do, but I will do it if it means keeping you away from that young man."

"What does that mean?"

Her father simply gestured at her car, and stepped away from the vehicle at the same time. "I will see you at home."

TWELVE

"I don't mind waiting for you, Ren," Rose said. "You should be back soon, right?"

Renzo pulled the phone away from his ear to do a quick check of the time. "Probably not," he replied when he put it back to his ear. "I've got a drop off to make, and that's going to take a while."

By drop off, he meant the drugs he was currently taking to his guys, so they would be well supplied for the next little while. His sister didn't like all those details, and so he didn't offer them to Rose. She'd worry too much, and then he would have to listen to that as well. Renzo didn't have the time for any of that today. The faster he got this shit into the right hands on the street, the quicker he could get back to Rose and Diego.

"You know, you're going to have to head back to your place soon."

"I'm fine here for a couple more days to help you with Diego," Rose said.

"Diego is fine," Renzo argued. "He's got a spot in the daycare as long as I get him there early enough, and a chick down the block who can watch him otherwise, so—"

"He hates her."

That wasn't a lie.

Well, hate was a strong word. The woman had a couple of her own kids, and they were little brats, to be honest. Always picking a fight with Diego who was just too nice for his own good. He much preferred to go to the shelter daycare if he couldn't go out with Renzo ... which most days, he couldn't. It just wasn't safe.

"I have Diego figured out," Renzo said, wanting to get his sister back on track for her life. She was always willing to put shit on hold for him and Diego, but Rose didn't need to be doing that at all. He had his shit handled. "You need to get back to school before you miss a whole damn week of classes, and it starts showing on your grades."

Rose sighed.

Renzo just laughed.

"You're impossible to talk to, do you know that?" his sister asked.

"I have heard that a few times, yes."

Renzo wasn't even bothering to pay attention to what was ahead of him on the street. At dusk, it was very unlikely someone was going to jump out and try something with him. Not when he mostly used alleyways for the majority of his travels. He was almost to the meeting spot with his guys now, though, so it wouldn't be much longer before he didn't have the drugs on him at all.

And even if someone did try some shit with him, the gun at his back would keep him safe regardless. As long as he had time to *pull* it.

"Listen, don't wait for me to get back. I know what time the movie starts, and I won't make it back in time. He'll miss forty minutes of it, at least. Take the money I left on the counter, get him to the movie, and take him somewhere to eat after. I'll be home by the time you get back, and he'll have just as much fun with telling me all about the movie."

"But—"

"*Rose.*"

"Fine," his sister grumbled. "He asked about her again today. Wanted to know if Carmen was coming back, or if she called. I didn't know what to tell him, so I said nothing. Distracted him with something else."

Renzo's lips twitched, threatening to turn into a scowl if he didn't fix his fucking face and get in control of his emotions. He really didn't want to go into a meet with his guys being pissed off, not when there were already enough rumors about his life on the streets as it happened to be. He didn't want to give them something else to talk about and make them believe he wasn't on his best game.

"Distracting him is the best thing you can do when you don't want to answer."

"Oh, I wanted to answer … I also knew it wouldn't be a kind answer. He's little—he doesn't understand."

Renzo rubbed at the spot on the back of his neck as he slipped into the last alleyway that would bring him around to the spot just across the way from the corner store's parking lot where his guys were waiting for their pick up. He'd realized that Lucia had a point the other morning when she told him not to slander his mother anywhere near Diego. It wouldn't do anything good for his brother, but it would make him angry and confused.

The last thing Renzo wanted to do was turn Diego into *him*.

Because that's all he was, too.

Angry and fucking confused.

"I told her to stay the hell away," Renzo muttered, "so let's hope she does that."

"Yeah, *hope.*" Rose made a quiet noise. "And until you really do have Diego figured out, and stuff slows down, I can afford a couple more days off school."

"No, you can't."

"Ren—"

"Take him to the movies, all right? We'll chat when I get home. Later."

He didn't give his sister the chance to argue with him further. Instead, he just hung up the phone before she could get started again. There was no point in arguing with Rose over the phone. Like him, she was too stubborn for her own good, and once she set her mind on something … well, that was it. Renzo was going to have to try another direction to make his sister understand he *was* fine, he did have Diego handled, and she needed to get back to school.

End of.

"Figured you'd be around these parts tonight, Renzo."

Halfway down the alley, and Renzo hadn't even thought to look up from the ground once as he chatted with his sister. Maybe he was getting too cocky on these streets—too *stupid*. Maybe he was overconfident in his belief that nobody was going to purposely try to cause him any kind of shit because they knew him well enough to *know* better.

Tightening one hand around the messenger bag strap hooked over his shoulder, and slipping his other up under the back of his coat to get a good grip on the butt of the handgun tucked into his jeans, Renzo found the man who called his name. He recognized the voice, of course, but it wasn't like this man to hang around in alleyways *just because*. His usual motive was to drop off Renzo's shit—when it was him doing the drop-offs—and go on his way until it came time to collect payment … if he was the one who wanted to collect the payment, that was.

Johnathan Marcello.

Lucia's fucking brother.

"John," Renzo said, coming to a stop a good ten feet away from the man.

There was a rule he'd once heard—seven feet. A person needed at least seven feet of distance between them and someone else in a bad situation to make it better for them. Seven feet to make a better choice, or move fast enough to save their skin.

Just seven feet.

Renzo gave himself a couple of extra feet just in case.

John fingered a Zippo lighter, and flicked the top open and closed. Then, he pulled a cigarette out from its place tucked behind his ear and lit it up. Taking a hard drag from the smoke, he eyed Renzo from the side. His gaze did a slow travel, like he was weighing his options, or maybe trying to size Renzo up.

It made him fucking edgy.

John had a couple of inches on him, but that was it. Size-wise, they were about the same. Lean, but muscular. Able to take a good punch, or throw a mighty one.

He heard enough shit about John on the streets to know the man wasn't to be messed with. Rumor was that he just got out of prison after serving a

121

couple of years for going on a tear, pulling a gun on someone, and beating the hell out of a few cops during the process. People had a lot of things to say about John when someone had the balls to ask. They called him crazy … said he had no fucking control when he was pissed.

Renzo didn't know exactly how true any of that was, but there was always a bit of truth to every rumor. Add onto it that John was a supplier for Renzo, and while these were *his* streets, they were also fucking John's.

Simple as that.

"I hear you're stepping out of line," John murmured, wetting his lips as he stared at the cherry red tip of the cigarette. "How true is that, now?"

"Stepping out of line how?"

John gave him a look that said, *foolish boy.* "Don't play dumb, Ren."

"I don't know—"

"My *sister.* Lucia. Seems you've been hanging around her a lot lately. Going wherever … *doing whatever.*"

Renzo arched a brow. "That a problem?"

"My father seems to think it is."

"That sounds like something he should probably handle, then, doesn't it?"

"Renzo."

He didn't know what did it—maybe the tone of John's voice, so patronizing and cold—but Renzo tightened his hand on the gun at his back just in case he was going to need to use it. Fuck, he didn't want to. At least, not on *this* man. It would do him no good to kill a fucking *mafioso.* Beyond that, this was Lucia's brother.

Her brother.

"You're not seeing things very clearly, are you?" John asked. "That, or you just don't give a shit. There are bigger rules at play here. Ones I don't expect you to understand. Your attention on Lucia isn't appreciated … that's all there is to it. So, either you're blind, or you're just too stupid to care. Either way, I am here to warn you before someone else comes looking for you on these streets to do it. Trust that you want *my* warning, and not theirs. Listen to me, and you're going to be fine."

"And what's the warning, then?"

He figured he already knew.

His answer was already picked out, too.

"Stay the fuck away from my sister, Renzo," John said, pushing off the alleyway and closing about five feet of distance between them in a blink. Just like that, the seven feet rule was gone, and Renzo had to make a choice to act, or not. He hesitated … just long enough for John to take a drag from his cigarette, and toss it to the ground. "Stay away from her, or you'll be lucky to walk these streets again. Do you hear me? I'm trying to help you out here."

Renzo let go of the gun at his back, suddenly unconcerned about having to use it. That's all this was—one big fucking *show*.

Nothing was going to happen.

Not today.

"Well, do you understand?" John asked.

Renzo smirked. "How about fucking *no?*"

• • •

Renzo's first inclination when he saw Lucia sitting on the steps of his apartment building laughing with the other people who usually loitered around the front was to ask her what in the hell she thought she was doing. But he didn't. Instead, he hung back a bit, and watched her interact with people who had only given her some kind of grief any other time she showed up at his place.

He was too far away to hear what they were saying while he leaned against a car, and lit up a smoke. Not that it mattered. Watching was just about as good as hearing, and he could step in if he needed.

Lucia pointed a finger at the man to her left in response to something he said, and the girl with dreadlocks at her left threw her head back with a hard laugh. Someone in the apartment building opened their window, and music filtered out. A loud, fast beat that immediately had the people on the steps dancing where they sat.

Even Lucia.

Renzo grinned.

He was coming to learn that absolutely *nothing* about this woman was what it seemed. She was more than capable of making friends wherever she went. She wasn't a wilting wallflower, either. If someone gave her shit, she could hand it right back, and with a smile, too. She might have been wearing a silk dress and heels with those goddamn red soles again, but once someone let her in, they quickly realized she could fit in anywhere.

Or maybe it was just him that had to learn that fact.

"Ren!"

He wasn't sure who it was that called his name because he was still a little busy staring at Lucia as she moved her hips and swayed her shoulders to the beat of the music filtering out from the apartment up above. Although, as soon as someone called his name, that ended her dance.

He didn't like that at all.

Her smile lit up his whole fucking day, though. He'd been going non-stop—barely got in a couple of hours the night before, really. The sun wasn't even up fully, and he was already out of the apartment, and gone again to do something for someone else. He'd had to run a package all the way down to Hell's Kitchen, and then take a message back again. All the while, checking in with his guys, and doing a couple of deals on the way for customers that called on him when they wanted an eight ball.

Lucia smiled at the girl to her left, and nodded when something was said. She didn't linger with the people on the steps for any longer than she had to once she realized he was there, though. Not soon enough for his liking, she came down the steps, and crossed half of the parking lot to come stand in front of him.

Already, he was reaching for her.

Renzo felt a hell of a lot better when he had his arm wrapped around the back of Lucia's neck, and he could drag her closer. Her soft laughter filled his mind as he dropped a kiss to the top of her head, and tightened his hold. Her arms snaked around his waist to hug him back, and the rest of the shit in his head that had bothered him over the last day just drifted away.

Gone.

Instantly.

"What are you doing here, huh?" he asked.

Lucia tipped her head back, and grinned in that sweet way of hers as her teeth cut into her bottom lip. "What, you don't want to see me?"

"You know I do."

Of course, he did.

He always wanted to see her.

Shit was always getting in the way, though.

"You didn't think to call?" he half-joked. "I would have made sure to be here when you showed up, Lucia."

She shrugged, and kind of nodded a bit at the people back on the stairs. "Yeah, but I had company so it's all good."

He quirked a brow. "That so?"

"I made friends, Ren."

He chuckled because really, what else could he fucking do at this point? When someone told this woman not to do something, she turned around and did it with a smile just because she could. Besides, he wasn't going to tell her *not* to make friends.

"Those are good friends to make," he murmured. "They'll always keep an eye out for you as long as you keep an eye out for them. That's the deal—got it?"

Lucia met his gaze knowingly. "Got it, Ren. They keep calling me princess, though."

He laughed.

He couldn't even help it.

Lucia smacked him on the chest with an opened palm. It stung, but all he did was rub the spot with his fingertips to soothe the ache. All the while, still laughing.

"Stop laughing! It's not even funny."

No, it *really* was.

"You kind of are a princess," he muttered.

"Shut up."

Instead of shutting up like she told him to, he just kissed her instead. The second his mouth found her silky lips, the rest of the world ceased to exist. All he could think about was getting a taste of her, and nothing else mattered. He was fucking hungry, and his lips working against hers was the only thing that might satisfy him. He nipped at her bottom lip, and pulled away before he really wanted to, but at the same time, he also didn't want an audience.

Not that it made a difference.

A shout came from the people on the steps, anyway. Renzo rolled his eyes, and gave Lucia a look.

"What?"

He shook his head, and wet his lips. "Nothing, baby. Absolutely nothing."

• • •

Renzo dropped the bag of takeaway on the counter, wishing he'd grabbed more food for Lucia. "Were you at the shelter today?"

She nodded, propping herself up on the edge of the counter to watch him pull items out of the bag. "Came over after my shift was done. Where's Diego?"

"Took a trip with Rose to Brooklyn today. Where was your car, then?"

That question made her look away from him, and that was Renzo's first sign that something was up. Maybe, if he was a smarter man, he wouldn't push the topic, and just let it drop. But he wasn't very smart lately, apparently, and so he asked.

"What was that about?"

"What?" Lucia asked innocently, her eyes going wide.

Too innocent, really.

Renzo peeled the wrapper off a cheeseburger, and pointed at Lucia at the same time. "That right there—you won't look at me. What's up with the car?"

She sighed. "Nothing, really. Just ..."

"*Lucia.*"

She pressed her lips together in an effort to keep from smiling, and still failed. Maybe she just wasn't that good of a liar, but he thought it was cute as hell. And probably not very good for her.

"My dad, actually," she finally admitted.

Renzo's arm froze as he held out the cheeseburger for her to take from him. "What?"

"My dad." Lucia shrugged, and snagged the food from his grasp. Before taking a bite, she was quick to add, "He decided to take my car away because apparently, he thinks I'm a fucking idiot who doesn't know how to use a cab, subway, or a bus ... or that I don't have friends to call to take me places when I want to go."

Renzo blinked.

They took away her car?

She was *eighteen.*

Lucia seemed to read his expression, and the thoughts running through his head. "Yeah, I know, right. But he bought it, so he can take it. Or that's his reasoning. I didn't even bother to argue."

"But why?"

"Why didn't I argue?"

"Why did he take it in the first place?"

Lucia cleared her throat, and set the burger down on the wrapper. Wiping her hands down on the skirt of her dress, she didn't even seem a bit bothered that those tiny greasy fingerprints were probably going to ruin the silk. "He wants to make a point, I think. To me."

"But *why.*"

This time, it wasn't even a question. Renzo meant for it to come out like it did because he wasn't stupid—she was avoiding the question. He wondered if ...

"Because he doesn't want me around you," she murmured quickly.

Yeah, there it was.

Exactly what he thought.

Renzo popped a couple of fries into his mouth, leaned against the counter, and stared at her for a while. Neither of them said anything, but he was fine with that. He needed a second to think, and there was something about Lucia that always put him in a different headspace when she was talking. He was much more interested in listening to her speak than caring about what was running through his head.

"They're pretty determined to keep you away from me, huh?" he asked.

Lucia arched a brow, and those pretty pink lips of hers curved sinfully. "Yet, here I am."

Yes, here she was.

With him.

"For now," he returned.

Because he did wonder how long this was going to last. He didn't think her family was the type to put up with nonsense very long before they just said fuck it, and did what needed to be done. Renzo wouldn't say that scared him, really. As long as Lucia wanted to be here with him doing this … whatever this was between them … then that's exactly what she was going to do.

He didn't give a shit about them.

"Your brother came to see me yesterday, too," Renzo said. "Cornered me in an alley and warned me … not that it did any fucking good, but yeah."

Lucia stiffened on the counter, and her hazel gaze narrowed. "John?"

"How many brothers do you have?"

Because Renzo wasn't really sure.

"Two sisters, Cella and Liliana. One brother … just John."

Renzo nodded. "Yeah, well, him."

"Huh."

Something dark colored her tone, but Renzo didn't have the chance to think on it for very long. It was the ringing of his phone inside the messenger bag on the counter that took him away from her just long enough to pick up the call. He didn't even bother to check the ID before answering with, "Yeah, Renzo here."

"Ren, man … I need you to come get this cash out of my hands," Noah said.

Renzo's brow furrowed. "I just did the exchange with you for the week yesterday."

"I know, but I hit a party last night. You know I don't like having this much cash on hand or at my place. Didn't you have to grab something from Perry, anyway?"

Sighing, he scrubbed a hand down his face. "It can't wait until tomorrow?"

He would much rather spend his time here with Lucia instead of heading out on the streets again. He already knew Noah's answer before the guy even spoke. He really didn't like to carry around a lot of cash—he got paranoid about it. Renzo blamed that on the fact the man smoked the wrong strain of weed, and wouldn't listen when he was told to cut the fuck back.

But that was none of his business.

"Perry's doing work at the shop tonight, stripping a car," Renzo said. "You know where—I can meet you there."

"Sounds good."

Noah hung up without a goodbye, but Renzo wasn't even offended about it, really. Lucia smiled at him from her perch on the counter. She

127

looked entirely too sweet and good sitting there in her silk wrap dress with her hair down in free waves, and her face clean of makeup. Entirely too innocent for him, except the gleam in her eye told him she wasn't innocent at all.

He knew that first hand.

"Work?" she asked.

Renzo shrugged, "What else?"

"Can I come, then? I've got all night."

He should have told her no. It wasn't like her family needed another reason to hate his stupid ass, or to try and keep her away from him. Even if he was ready to fight whoever the fuck thought they could try to come in on him for keeping this girl at his side, he was quite aware that it wasn't smart of him to poke the goddamn bear.

Because that's what the Marcellos were.

A nasty, mean bear sleeping happily in its cave. And he was the fucking fool with a stick poking them right in the ass.

"Well?" Lucia asked.

He should have told her no.

She looked way too good to refuse, though.

"Yeah, baby," he said, grabbing his bag, and then helping her down from the counter. "You can come—grab the food, though."

Lucia laughed. "Whatever you want, Ren."

Maybe that was part of the problem. She was all too willing to go along with whatever he wanted, and he was perfectly fine with letting her do exactly that, too. Maybe that was what would get them in the most trouble.

Only time would tell.

THIRTEEN

Lucia hung back from Renzo as they entered what he called the *shop*. She didn't think the run-down warehouse looked anything like a shop. At least, not from the outside. He'd vaguely explained that they worked on cars inside the shop, but he didn't give her much else to go on.

She knew why now.

Lucia understood perfectly well what was happening once they were inside the building, and she had a clear view of the men working. Sparks flew and danced across the cracked cement floor from a lit torch as it was brought down through metal. She was quick to turn her eyes away from the bright light. Car parts were being packed in plain brown cardboard boxes filled with packing peanuts. Every single part from lights, to a smaller box for an emblem.

A Rolls-Royce, by the looks of it.

A *Phantom*.

That was, by no means, a cheap car. And without sounding like a spoiled, rich little bitch, Lucia highly doubted anyone in this warehouse could afford to go out and buy a Rolls-Royce Phantom.

She took in the sight of the unknown guys packing away a car they'd clearly just chopped down, and said nothing. Yeah, she knew what they were doing. It wasn't very fucking hard to figure out.

Renzo's fingers tightened around hers, and he tugged gently on her arm to bring her attention back to him for a second. "You good?"

She nodded. "Absolutely."

A little curious about whose car that might be, though. She suspected there were only so many Phantoms in the city. It wouldn't be very hard to track down the owner.

"Sometimes they get requests," Renzo muttered, drawing Lucia to his side as they had to pass the torch-wielding duo cutting the chassis apart. He kept her just far enough away from the sparks that none would catch her shoes or clothes. "You know what I mean?"

"Not really."

His lips came up to graze her ear as the noise level picked up a bit in the warehouse. "Most times, they're just boosting whatever they know is going to be easy to resell on the market without it coming up as stolen after they remove all the identifiers and change paperwork. But *sometimes* ... they get a request. Someone knows they're not going to get their next few payments in, or whatever. They're paying insurance, so if it gets stolen ..."

Lucia blinked. "It's all paid for."

"Exactly."

She heard what he was saying, then. The Phantom was a request by someone.

Huh.

She hadn't even thought to ask Renzo what they were doing here—did he do this sometimes, too? Not that it mattered, really. A couple of the guys working stopped their business to glance up, and watch the two pass. Renzo nodded at one, but Lucia didn't bother. She didn't know them at all.

Once they were just beyond the guys working, Renzo directed Lucia to a row of crates with soda cans tossed into a box in front of them. Wordlessly, his hands grabbed her waist, and she let out a laugh as he picked her up like she weighed nothing at all before sitting her down on the crates. All at once, the noise of the warehouse and guys drifted away as Renzo inched closer to her, and his hands grabbed her thighs tightly. A gentle squeeze of his palms was all it took for her to be entirely distracted, and a little too hot.

What was it about this man that did it for her?

She wasn't sure.

She just liked it.

Renzo's gaze held hers as he leaned close, and pressed a fast kiss to her lips. His thumbs stroked her thighs as he murmured, "Stay put, and don't wander. I'll only be a few minutes. Got it?"

She pursed her lips. "I'll think about it."

His laughter came out dark, and heady. She loved the way he looked when he laughed—so carefree, and unbothered. It was the only time—except maybe during sex—when he seemed truly free. Especially in his happiness.

"You stay put," he murmured, kissing her once more.

Lucia nodded.

Where was she going to go, anyway?

Renzo patted her cheek with the palm of his hand, and then turned away. Lucia watched his back disappear deeper into the warehouse where she could see a couple of guys waiting for him. Who they were, she didn't know. Renzo was already shrugging off the messenger bag that was a constant companion on his shoulder whenever she was around. She never thought to peek inside the bag, and frankly, he never left it alone where someone could get a look at the contents, anyway.

Not that she wanted to.

That was his business.

The exchange was so quick that she almost missed it, really. Renzo pulled something from his bag to hand to the taller of the two. She couldn't quite see what it was he handed over, though. Then, the shorter of the two passed over an envelope that was sizeable in its thickness. Renzo was quick to shove it in the bag, close it up, and shrug it back over his shoulder. Widening his arms, he got a nod from the two guys, and he replied in kind.

It didn't exactly seem like the conversation was over, though, because the three continued standing in their semi-circle even after they exchanged their stuff. Sure, she couldn't hear their conversation at all, but Lucia didn't need to, either. Not to recognize what she was seeing, anyway.

Maybe it was the way Renzo stood ...

Or how he directed their conversation ...

She'd grown up around men who led—she recognized one when she saw one. Renzo was absolutely the leader of his ... crew. Was that even what he called it?

Lucia was so caught up in watching the exchange at the back of the warehouse that she didn't even notice the guy coming up to her until he was sitting beside her on the crates. He shoved the welder's mask high on his face, exposing handsome features. A few streaks of ash had been smudged along his jaw, and cheek. His eyes—a bright blue—looked her over with interest, but she wasn't.

Interested, that was.

Not at all.

"And who are you?" he asked. "Haven't seen you around before."

She doubted these guys had women in here very often, if at all, to be honest. Unless they had a woman working on the cars, this just wasn't a girl's scene.

"Lucia," she said simply, "I came with Renzo."

That was all she gave the guy, mostly hoping he would get the hint that she wasn't up for conversation, and make his way back to his work. He didn't get the hint at all.

Leaning in closer to Lucia, the guy smiled. "My name's Karl, but everybody just calls me Diesel."

Fascinating.

Lucia kept her mouth shut as to not make the guy think she was interested in having a conversation with him, but her silence didn't seem to bother him a bit. He just continued talking like he was the only one between them who might have anything interesting to say. "I fucking knew he was keeping something on the low. Are you the same one that parked the nice car in front of his apartment building, then?"

Lucia blinked.

Who was this fucking guy?

Then, he got *closer.*

Too close, really.

Lucia leaned back, and it wasn't subtle, either. It was clear she was putting more distance between them, but that didn't faze Diesel, either. His hand found her thigh before Lucia even knew what was happening.

"You're fucking wasting time with Ren, girl," he said, grinning. "You're too pretty for a guy like him, anyway. Get what I—"

Her gaze narrowed, and disbelief swept through her system. The anger that followed right behind it was just as swift, and destructive. Lucia didn't even think whether or not it might cause a problem for Renzo when she outright slapped Diesel's hand away from her body. The sound *echoed*.

How had it gotten so quiet in the warehouse?

"Don't *touch* me," she murmured.

He opened his mouth to speak, but Lucia had already jumped down from the crates. Spinning on her heels to head for Renzo on the other side of the warehouse, she came up short in her first step at the sight of him standing right there. At first, by the hard, cold expression on Renzo's face, she thought he might be pissed at *her*.

But just as quickly, those dark eyes of his drifted past Lucia to the man still sitting on the crates. Renzo arched a brow, and strolled closer, and shoved his hands in his pockets at the same time.

As he came up to her side, one of his hands lifted, and he stroked her cheek with two fingers. "You good?"

"It's fine," she promised.

It wasn't. The guy *really* overstepped his boundaries like a lot of guys did, but she was okay. She just wanted to get the hell out of there, now.

"Give me a second," he told her.

"Ren," she whispered.

A plea, maybe. A request to just let it go so they could leave. It was the simple shake of his head that told her, no, he absolutely would not be letting it go.

"No harm done," Diesel said, throwing his hands up with a playful smile. "I was just testing her, Ren."

"Yeah?"

"Yeah."

Renzo nodded, and came to a stop right in front of Diesel. He glanced to the side like he found something interesting to stare at in the corner of the warehouse before his gaze cut back to the guy on the crates. "Didn't know you were working here with Perry, too."

"Gives me extra cash."

"I bet."

His words were tight, and so was his jaw. Like he was holding something back, but it was about to spill out like lava shooting from a fucking volcano.

"Listen," Diesel said, pushing down from the crates to land on his feet, "just thought you'd wanna know what she was like when you weren't looking, you know?"

Renzo let out a short laugh, his head tipping down a bit as he muttered, "I fucking know exactly what she's like when I'm not looking. I don't need *shit* from you when it comes to her."

"Ren—"

Before the guy could even finish whatever bullshit he was about to spew, Renzo struck out at him. Renzo caught Diesel by his face and throat with both hands. It was but a blink, and he had smashed the other man back into the crates, busting them apart and taking Diesel to the floor with a loud *bang*.

The noise from the others working stopped altogether. Someone shouted, but Lucia wasn't hearing them at all. She moved forward—not because Renzo needed help as he picked Diesel up, and slammed him into the floor again, but because she didn't want trouble for *them*.

She didn't even get close to him.

One of the guys Renzo had been talking to earlier pulled her back with a dry laugh, and his large form blocked her from moving closer to the mess a few feet away. His large hands came up to make it clear he didn't want to put his hands on her, but he would if she tried moving past him again. "Hey, I'm Perry. And you're not going over there."

The other guy from earlier came up on her other side, shrugging like this wasn't anything new. "He's always trying to fuck with Ren, you know? Pushing his buttons, and trying to get away with more shit than the rest of us. He'd have fewer problems with Ren if he'd just do what he was told like the rest of us."

Wait, Diesel was a part of the guys Renzo was running, too?

"Look at me, yeah?"

Lucia knew those words weren't meant for her, but she still peered around Perry's large linebacker-like form to look at Renzo. Still leaning over Diesel on the floor, his hands hadn't left the man's throat or face. If anything, he'd just dug in his fingers because the guy's face was red and he didn't look like he was willing to fight his way up from the ground. Peeking out from the back of Renzo's jeans where his jacket had ridden up his back was the sight of something Lucia was all too accustomed to seeing, but had never saw *him* handling one.

A gun.

She sucked in a shaky breath.

Maybe it was because she'd never seen Renzo get really angry before, or rather … he never had a reason to show violence with her around, but she found this shocking. How quickly he could go from smiling and easy-natured to a man willing to beat a guy into the ground because he stepped out of line.

Lucia couldn't decide whether she liked it, or it scared her.

Both, actually.

It was both.

"You get your fucking ass back to work," Renzo hissed at Diesel, "and I don't want to hear another goddamn word out of your mouth, either. And don't you *ever* put your fucking dirty hands on what's mine again. You got me?"

Lucia blinked.

What's mine ...

"Got it, Ren," Diesel rasped from the ground.

Renzo let him go, and turned to Lucia with a nod to the side. "Let's go, baby."

She didn't say a word.

She just went.

• • •

"No, there's no fucking *discussion* here, Rose," Renzo grumbled into the phone. It'd started ringing damn near to the second that they slipped out the back of the warehouse. "He's coming back tomorrow, and you're going back to school." He was silent for a moment before adding, "I get it, but he's taken care of. Like always. Stop worrying about it. Got it?"

Lucia didn't hear his sister's reply, but she figured Renzo got the response he wanted when he nodded, smiled, and then said goodbye. Hanging up the phone, he slipped it into his pocket like nothing was wrong. Like he hadn't just been seconds away from beating the hell out of a guy just a minute ago.

They were walking alongside the warehouse when Lucia finally found her ability to speak again. "You know, you didn't have to do—"

She didn't even get the words out before Renzo grabbed her wrist, and spun her around fast. So fast that everything around her was nothing more than a blur in her vision. The empty, dark alley echoed with the noise of Lucia's back hitting the wall. It didn't hurt, but the sudden movement was such a shock that all she could do was drag in a sharp gasp, and freeze when Renzo's hands came up to lay flat on either side of her head.

He came so close to her, then.

So fucking close.

All she could see were his russet eyes, and the way they practically nailed her to the wall. Those hands of his—soft to the touch, and able to heat her up in no time at all—cupped her cheeks and jaw. He tipped her head back, and came closer still, his weight pressing against hers and keeping her pinned in place.

Not that she minded.

Not at all.

Not when he looked like *that*.

Intense.

Sure.

Dangerous.

Her heart raced, and her nerves felt like they were on fire. All because he was close, and yet, she wanted him closer still. Strange how that worked.

"Yes, I absolutely did have to do that," he murmured, his lips so close to hers that they grazed her mouth with every word he spoke. "Because there's a lot of shit I am willing to deal with from stupid fucks who want to test me, but you are not *ever* going to be one, Lucia. This time, it's someone thinking they can get too close to you while I'm standing right there. Putting their fucking hands *on you*—he's lucky I didn't rip his fucking esophagus out of his goddamn throat right then and there for doing that. But next time? Next time, if I didn't make my point clear, it might be something else."

She blinked, and sucked in a ragged breath when his palms slipped down her throat. Those teasing fingers of his tapped a sweet beat along her pulse point. His gaze followed the same path, still dark and heady and *wanting*, she thought. He wanted her, and fuck her if she didn't want him, too.

She shouldn't.

That should have scared her.

Sent her running, maybe.

Lucia was fine right where she was.

"Next time," he added, his lips ghosting over her jawline, making her shiver, "it might be something *worse*. Now, it won't be anything at all."

"Okay," she whispered.

Renzo hummed under his breath. "*Just* okay?"

"Give me a little warning next time when you want to go on a jealous rampage, I guess?"

His laughter was a balm to her soul. Dark, thick, and wonderful.

"I wasn't jealous," he said, but his gaze wouldn't lift to meet hers again. He so fucking was—she could hear it in the way his tone heated and turned just gruff enough that the sound alone was enough to make her *crazy*. "I can't be jealous of someone else over something they don't have, Lucia."

She blinked.

It took her a second, and then two.

"See, I've kind of decided on that," he murmured, his russet fire meeting her hazel storm, "or didn't you know?"

135

She did.

She still wanted him to say it, though.

"Know what, Ren?"

"*You're mine.*"

His words were punctuated by a kiss that *bruised.* God, she loved his kisses when they were rough, and demanding. Loved the way he could own her with a kiss. She didn't even think he knew it was possible.

Renzo's hands dipped under the skirt of her silk dress find what he wanted between her thighs. No fucking surprise, she was already wet and ready for whatever he wanted to do for her. And maybe that was the part that should have made her ashamed—she *always* seemed to want him.

It didn't matter they were in a back alley.

It didn't matter someone might see them.

None of that factored in to what Lucia wanted at that moment at all. She only cared about the way Renzo's fingers felt rubbing fast circles around her throbbing clit, and how his other hand wrapped into her hair while his teeth scraped across her bottom lip.

"Fucking here, then?" he asked gruffly.

His tone was so dark.

Full of sex and promises.

"Right here," she agreed.

He was down on his knees before she had even blinked, and he yanked her dress higher as he went lower. Her panties went down with him. *Oh, God.* She only caught part of his sly smirk as he glanced up, and the gleam in his eye before he buried his face between her thighs.

That first flick of his tongue was pure heaven.

That first second, she couldn't *breathe.*

His fingers dug into the soft skin of her thighs, pushing her legs open even wider as her hips rolled against his mouth. Her fingers tangled into his hair, determined to hold him *right there* until she came apart. It was his heady groan that really did it for her, though. The way he sounded his approval of the taste of her loudly, and *often.* With every flick of his tongue beating against her clit, she came a little closer to that edge.

And then all at once, with the slide of his fingers into her clenching pussy, she came undone. Her shout of his name echoed in the alleyway. She was pretty fucking sure her knees buckled, too, but he was right there to catch her before she could fall.

Not that it made much difference.

He stood fast, turned her around, and put her hands to the wall. She heard him shifting behind her, dropping his pants, and rustling foil before she felt his fingers sliding between her thighs again with his latex-covered cock pressing against her wetness, too. He slid his length against her sex, over and over. Until she was backing into him to try and get more.

"*Fucking crazy*," she heard him mutter. "You make me crazy, Lucia."

Him, too.

He did that for her, too.

He gave her no warning as he pushed inside. One hard, long thrust that sent her flying up on her toes. His words were a dark whisper in her ear as he pounded into her from behind, relentless and rough. The sounds of their fucking echoed. Skin on skin, his gruff words, and her gasping cries.

Harder, and *more,* and *please.*

It all slipped from her lips so easily. Too easily. She couldn't get enough. It didn't matter that it was dirty, or that she'd be sore in the morning. She just wanted more of him.

"What are you fucking doing to me, huh?" he asked, his fingers squeezing the back of her neck hard enough to leave bruises behind. "*What,* Lucia?"

What was she doing to him?

What was he doing to her?

This wasn't her.

This girl in this alley.

This recklessness …

These feelings making her do stupid things …

All of him.

This wasn't her.

Or it hadn't been.

God knew she liked this version of her a lot better. She liked herself more when she was with him.

FOURTEEN

"But I don't wanna spend the night—"

Renzo barely caught himself from sighing out loud. He didn't want to upset Diego any more than he already was, and it wasn't the kid's fault that he didn't understand what was going on. All he knew was that for the next couple of days, Renzo wouldn't be around, and Diego wouldn't be sleeping in his own bed. Nothing else mattered to the kid—not the *whys*, like the fact Renzo had the chance to do a quick job for somebody that included boosting five specifically requested vehicles, and shredding them down in a matter of a couple of days.

The pay, though?

Ten-K.

Ten thousand for a couple of days' worth of work.

How could he pass that up?

Truth be told, Renzo didn't pick up these kinds of jobs very often. Sure, his name was passed around between a few guys who ran chop shops if they needed an extra pair of hands, and shit worked out on Renzo's side of things—like Diego—so that he could take the job. But mostly, he didn't take them because he couldn't.

But this one?

He'd be stupid to overlook it.

"I don't wanna, Ren!"

Diego's voice had raised a couple of octaves which told Renzo his little brother was about three seconds away from a goddamn meltdown. They really didn't have time for this today, even if he did understand what the problem was for Diego. Thing was ... Renzo being available to do the job was contingent on the fact he made sure Diego was handled for the day. Then, the chick that watched him during the evening hours would pick him up later that day, keep him for the night, watch him all day tomorrow, and Renzo would be back before bedtime to grab him.

Simple.

Diego didn't like that idea *at all.*

"Ren!"

Stopping their walk on the side of the street, Renzo bent down to rest on one knee so that he could be face to face with his little brother. Diego looked like three and a half feet of angry four-year-old in those seconds. He'd come to learn that kids could really be dramatic when they wanted to be. It could be something small they didn't like, but it might feel like their whole life was burning down around them because of it. Renzo didn't want to diminish how his brother felt, but this wasn't something he could bend on, either.

Everybody had to make sacrifices to make shit work.

That's how life was.

And if all else failed, Renzo knew bribery was a good trick when it came to kids. That was probably a big no-no, but frankly, he just needed to get the goddamn job done, and he would deal with his brother later.

"Hey," Renzo said, cupping his brother's little face in his, "you look at me, Diego."

Watery brown eyes drifted to his, but Diego was still scowling in that way of his that said he was not ready to give up this fight just yet. Already, Renzo knew they were getting down to the last few minutes when he would be able to get Diego a spot in at the shelter daycare, and if they wasted any more time, he was going to miss his chance. Then, all his plans would be fucked. There was no way he could take his brother with him for this kind of work.

No fucking way.

"It's a night and a day," Renzo told Diego, shrugging to make it seem like it wasn't a big deal. But it was—he knew it was. While he didn't want to pass this up, he also didn't want to trust someone else to keep an eye on his brother while he was gone, too. What choice did he have? "I will be back before you know it. And then we'll go do whatever you want, yeah? Trampoline park—movies. Whatever, Diego. But I need you to be good, and not fight me on this anymore."

Diego's lips twitched as he whispered, "Ma leaves all the time, too. She's back right now, but she'll go again, too."

Was that what it was, then? Unfortunately, their mother had shown back up a couple of nights ago. Renzo had a good mind to keep the bitch right out in the cold—even if it was the end of August—where she belonged, but then he looked at Diego ... he let Carmen in for his brother, gave her a place to sleep, and kept his money and drugs well hidden until she was gone again.

Because that was the thing.

She would go again.

She always fucking did.

Renzo sighed. "I'm not like Ma, you know that."

"But—"

"I won't *ever* be like Ma."

He'd decided that long ago. It was why he never drank anything stronger than a beer—and only on very few occasions—and the exact reason why he never put anything into his body stronger than cigarettes or weed, when he was feeling up to it. He sold drugs to make a living, all the while watching drugs kill his mother and take her away from them …. he didn't need the hypocrisy or the irony of it all shoved back in his face about the whole thing.

He wouldn't be the next one sucking on a pipe because his body wouldn't survive without it. Drugs would *not* be the thing that took Diego away from him. That poison wasn't going to be the one thing that made him fail for his sister, and anyone else who fucking counted on him. He was not like his mother.

Never would be.

Diego sniffled, and shuffled his foot along the pavement. "You *promise* you'll come back?"

Jesus.

"Cross my heart," Renzo murmured, leaning forward to give his brother a kiss to his forehead. "Now, you good?"

Diego let out a sigh that sounded anything but good or confident, but still said, "Yeah, I guess so."

"All right, then." Renzo stood, and offered his hand to Diego. "We better hurry up, or you'll miss your spot today."

Once the two of them were walking down the sidewalk again, Diego glanced up at him. "Do you think Lucia will be there today?"

He smirked a bit, meeting his brother's eye and winking. Diego liked Lucia just as much as Renzo did, but not in the same kind of ways or for the same kind of reasons.

"I don't know, *maybe.*"

Fact was, he knew Lucia would be there and she was working in the daycare today. At least, that's what her text said when he messaged her earlier. Which meant that would make this day slightly better for Diego once he figured it out. He wouldn't complain as much if Lucia was there to keep an eye on him, and distract him for a few hours.

How he reacted when Misty came to pick him up later would be anyone's guess. Right now, Renzo wasn't even thinking about that. He just needed to focus on getting through the next couple of days.

Soon, the daycare entrance was in view, and Diego walked a little lighter at Renzo's side. He knew seeing the place would help the kid. Despite how nervous he was for Renzo to be gone, he couldn't help but love this place. Smiling a bit, Renzo held his brother's hand tighter just in case the kid decided to dart ahead of him.

Behind the colorful paint on the windows, Renzo was pretty sure he caught sight of a familiar face—Lucia—but he didn't get the chance to think on it for long. They didn't even make it to the door before Laurie pushed it open, and stood on the stoop. Renzo didn't know what it was that put him on edge, but the woman's posture sure as fuck didn't help when she widened her stance and crossed her arms over her chest.

He cocked a brow. "Something wrong?"

"Morning," she greeted to him, and then to Diego, "Hi, buddy."

Diego beamed, and waved at the woman who ran the shelter. Renzo almost wanted to tug on his brother's hand, a silent command to be quiet simply because something felt off. He didn't have a reason to feel that way, really. Frankly … Laurie had given them a hand out more times than Renzo cared to count. He liked Laurie because she gave a shit about their community. She didn't care for the whispers she heard about Renzo, and what he did for a living, but she cared enough about Diego and his well-being that she was willing to turn a blind eye to what she didn't like about the rest.

There were times when shit would have been a lot worse had this woman not opened up a spot for Diego at this place. Not that it mattered when she spoke her next words.

"We won't be able to take Diego at the daycare any longer, Ren," Laurie said firmly.

Renzo blinked.

What?

Beside him, Diego just looked confused as he stared between his brother, and Laurie. "Why not? I be good when I come. Like Ren tells me to, right, Ren?"

His hand tightened around his brother's again, but it felt like the heaviest weight had come to rest down upon his shoulders in that moment. "You're always great, buddy." His gaze cut to Laurie again when he asked, "I called yesterday and made sure there was still a spot open for him if I brought him in time, didn't I?"

Laurie wouldn't meet his stare. "Things changed, that's all. I'm sure you under—"

"No, I really don't fucking *understand*," Renzo snapped.

"There's no reason to get angry and use foul—"

"Oh, fuck off with that."

Laurie stiffened on the steps, and her defensive posture was back in a blink. "The decision is final, Renzo. You'll have to leave the property as soon as possible, and without making a scene, or I will have the front desk phone the police."

Wow.

The last thing he ever did was cause a damn scene.

"Something wrong?"

Renzo hadn't even noticed Lucia coming out of the shelter until she spoke. He'd been too focused on keeping his anger in check, really. He didn't want to blow up, and have his little brother see it. Diego saw enough shit like that from their mother, he didn't need Renzo acting like a fool, too.

"No, go back inside, please," Laurie said to Lucia.

She didn't even listen to the woman, and instead, pushed past her in the entrance to come out further. Stopping directly between Renzo and Laurie, Lucia looked like Switzerland in the middle of a war. The only one who wasn't really ready to go to war, yet stuck directly in the middle, anyway.

She looked to Renzo with her caring gaze, and concern writing lines across her pretty features. This wasn't her fight, really. He didn't want her to get in the middle of it, and hurt her position at the shelter. She genuinely loved the job, and the people inside of it. It wasn't lost on him how he'd once thought this woman was nothing more than a trust fund baby with privilege stamped on her ass who wouldn't ever be able to appreciate the struggle of someone else.

Mainly, that she wouldn't be able to appreciate *his* struggle.

How fucking wrong he'd been.

About all of it, but mostly her.

Renzo had been oh, so wrong about her.

"Ren?" Lucia asked quietly. "What's wrong?"

He shook his head, not wanting her to get into it. "It's fine. I have to head out, or I'm going to miss out on work today. I'll give you a call—"

"Okay, I'll take Diego in, then."

Lucia held her hand out to Diego, but the boy hesitated in leaving Renzo's side. Instead, he shot a wary look at Laurie on the step, and whispered to Lucia, "Mrs. Laurie says I'm not allowed in the daycare anymore."

Renzo swore time slowed down. It was like life came around to laugh in his face, and give him every minute detail of Lucia's expression and reaction as she realized why they were standing out there, and exactly what was going on that he hadn't been willing to tell her. She was quiet for a second as her sweet mouth turned into a frown, and her hazel eyes blazed with an emotion he didn't recognize.

"Why?" she asked Diego.

His little brother shrugged. "Don't know."

Lucia turned to Laurie. "Why?"

The woman sighed. "For reasons that I am not required to share with you, or anyone else. The shelter has the right to refuse anyone access to the daycare—it's our policy. We don't need to explain it."

"Or you don't want to," Lucia countered.

Renzo didn't know what it was, but something about the way Laurie's throat jumped and her gaze darted away from Lucia felt ... *wrong*. Lucia saw it, too, if the way she stepped toward the woman with a finger pointed was any indication.

"Please tell me," Lucia started to say, "that this has nothing to do with me, or my father."

Laurie still wouldn't look their way. She seemed far more content to stare at the wall of the entrance where a few strips of paint were starting to chip, and fall to the ground.

Her silence was answer enough.

Was this what John meant, then, when he cornered Renzo a while back? This was how the Marcellos played dirty when it came to teaching somebody a lesson—they just fucked with their lives in such a way that it backed a person into the corner?

"What," Lucia asked the woman, "did he stop by, and threaten to drop whatever donations he was making to the place if you kept Renzo away from me, then?"

Laurie's jaw stiffened, but she stayed quiet. A silent answer, as far as he was concerned.

"Are you fucking *serious*?" Lucia hissed.

"He didn't threaten to *drop* anything," Laurie countered, "he offered to triple it."

Renzo's surprise came out in a harsh noise from the back of his throat. Just how much money *was* Lucian Marcello throwing at this place that Laurie would be willing to block one single person from using the daycare? It kind of stunned him, but then again … he wasn't surprised at all.

"I have to go," Renzo said, turning while pulling on Diego's hand at the same time. "I don't have time to stand here and talk about this stupid shit. Not today."

"Ren, wait," Lucia called at his back.

"Lucia, you have a job to do inside. Please, go back to doing—"

"Fuck you, I quit. And you can let my father know it, too."

Renzo was a good thirty feet down the street before Lucia finally caught up with him. He was a lot of things in those moments—feeling a lot of shit that he really didn't want to deal with. But above all else, he just felt fucking defeated and *pissed.*

"Where am I gonna go, Ren?" Diego asked, peering up at him.

Lucia grabbed him by his wrist at the same time, tugging hard enough to make him stop and swing to face her. "I'm sorry."

That was the first thing she wanted to say?

Renzo didn't know why.

"It's not your fault, but I *really* don't have time today. I need to get Diego a place to stay for the day, and then let the woman know who's going to watch him for the night and tomorrow where she can pick him up later. So, I'll call you when I get a minute, okay? Go back to the shelter, Lucia.

They love you there. You like working there. Don't quit for—"

"No," she murmured. "Absolutely *not*."

He blinked.

She just stood firm.

Then, she glanced down at Diego who looked like he was three seconds away from bursting into tears. "What if I took him? Like, for the whole time. You could just ... pick him up from me. I can text you where I'll be staying because I am *not* going home. Not if that means I have to see my father."

"I don't need you to do shit, Lucia," Renzo muttered.

Pride was a bitch.

So was defeat.

She smiled just a little. That sweet, soft smile he loved so fucking much. The same one she graced him with when he woke up with her beside him. Fuck, he loved that goddamn smile.

He loved a lot of things about Lucia.

He was pretty sure he loved her, too.

"I didn't ask if you needed me to do something for you," she replied, "I asked if I could take him."

Renzo sighed, and scrubbed a hand down his face. This really wasn't his day, and he was stuck between a rock and a hard place. "Listen, you can't take him back to my apartment. Carmen showed up, and I don't trust him to be there with her when I'm not. You know what I mean?"

Lucia nodded. "I wasn't planning on going there anyway. I was thinking ... a hotel, actually."

Diego peered up at his older brother. "Can I go with Lucia, can I, Ren?"

He didn't have a choice but to say yes.

Not that it mattered.

There wasn't anyone else he would trust his brother with like he could with Lucia. It wasn't anything specific that she did, or anything particular about her that made him feel that way—it was everything she did and all the things she was put together.

"All right," Renzo said. He let go of his brother's hand, and Diego darted to Lucia, grabbing her outstretched fingers tightly with his own. "I'll call you when I get a minute."

He moved forward, and caught Lucia's lips with his own in a kiss that set his fucking soul *on fire*. He couldn't linger, even though he felt the curve of her mouth against his, and the way she answered his kiss with a teasing flick of her tongue ... but damn, he wished he could stay.

He just didn't have the time.

Renzo didn't look back as he headed down the street. He couldn't.

He'd go back, then.

Back to her.

• • •

Renzo stared up at the inky sky as he strolled down the street, and ignored the stinging in his hands. Other than a quick dip under lukewarm water with a shitty bar of soap someone had found in the barely useable bathroom inside the stuffy warehouse, he hadn't properly washed his hands in two days. Which meant they were stained with grease, oil, and *dirt*. Way too much fucking dirt.

He hadn't known very damn much about cars before this job started, but he knew far more than he wanted to now. He sure as hell didn't know how to fix one, but he now knew how to take one apart and cut the rest of it up.

Maybe he understood why Perry and Diesel—that stupid fuck—took on a side hustle in a chop shop, although he doubted they were getting paid what he just did for their work.

Flexing his hands at his sides, his skin stung like nothing else. All the little crisscross cuts and scrapes that covered his knuckles and palms opened up again, and screamed with discomfort. He felt it, sure, but he couldn't find a reason to complain about it. Not when he had just shy of ten thousand dollars in small bills inside his messenger bag, and a whole lot of relief in his heart.

Well worth it.

At the moment, he didn't even care to think about where that money was going to go, or all the things it could do for him, and his siblings. He could figure all that out later.

Right after he dealt with more important things first.

Checking his phone, Renzo scrolled to Lucia's last text. A picture of Diego jumping on a bed that looked like it would take twenty of him just to fill it up. She'd kept him updated over the span of a couple of days. Where they went, and the things they did. She sent pictures, too, just because. Diego looked like he had the time of his fucking little life.

Nothing else mattered.

Scrolling up through the texts, he checked the name of the hotel where Lucia had set them up for a couple of days just to make sure he was at the right place. The gold lettering along the front of the entrance made Renzo quirk a brow, but hey, it was her money. Or … her father's. The girl could spend it whatever damn way she wanted.

Especially after what that man did.

Entering the hotel, Renzo ignored the look the woman at the front desk passed him. He was far more interested in the woman coming out of the bank of elevators, and the boy holding tight to her hand at her side.

Lucia and Diego.

He grinned when his brother caught sight of him, dropped Lucia's hand, and darted forward with a loud holler. He dropped his messenger bag to the ground, uncaring that for once, he wasn't holding it despite the contents. He didn't think this fancy fucking place was the kind of business that harbored someone who was going to steal his shit.

Renzo caught Diego with both arms, and stood, lifting the boy right off the floor in a tight hug. Diego's little arms wrapped around Renzo's neck, and squeezed hard enough to take his breath away.

Damn.

"Missed you, buddy," Renzo murmured, stroking his brother's hair. "Did you have fun with Lucia?"

Diego leaned back, and grinned to show off his pearly white teeth. "We did *everything.*"

Renzo arched a brow. "Really?"

"She let me jump on the bed, too."

"Yeah, I saw that."

Renzo put Diego back on his feet to the floor as Lucia came closer. She wore that same smile he loved so fucking much, but he could tell there was something wrong at the same time. "Hey."

Once she was close enough for him to grab, he did just that. Pulling her in for a tight hug, he pressed a kiss to the top of her head. Lucia hugged his middle, and lingered for a beat longer than she usually would before she let him go.

"What's wrong?" he asked, catching her cheek in his hand so he could force her to look at him. "And don't tell me nothing—I can see it, baby."

She shrugged. "Just family."

Renzo's gaze drifted to his brother who was entertaining himself by asking the girl at the front desk a million and one questions. He didn't know what kind of pull Lucia's family had, but he suspected it was enough that they knew where she was at all times, and exactly how to get to her should they need to. That concerned him a bit.

"No one showed up here, right?"

Lucia shook her head. "No, but I got enough messages to know when I get home ... well, never mind. That's for me to handle, I guess. Did you get everything done?"

Renzo grinned. "Yeah, I did. Thanks to you."

He snagged her wrist in his hand, and let his thumb drift over her pulse point. There was something about the beat of this girl's heart that settled him. Like all he needed to do was feel her heart beating its smooth, steady rhythm, and nothing else mattered at all. All was good in his world. Strange how that worked.

Tugging Lucia close to him again, her hands splayed across his chest, and she smiled. Things seemed more beautiful when she was smiling, even if he could see she was doing it for his sake. Dropping a quick kiss to her mouth once, and then twice, Renzo settled on letting her have her lies … for now.

"Everything is great," she told him. "Let me know if I can help again … I don't mind, Diego is wonderful. And he really missed you."

Sure. But he wondered …

Just by the look on Lucia's face …

Was it great?

• • •

"Don't drop your bag, Diego," Renzo said, laughing as the boy's backpack started to slip from his arms as they climbed the last flight of stairs in their apartment building. "Here, let me—"

"I gots it," Diego muttered strongly, shifting the bag back up to its rightful position. It couldn't be that heavy, really. A couple of changes of clothes, and a toy or two that Diego had wanted to take with him while Renzo was gone. Nothing major. Peering up at his brother, Diego nodded. "See, I did it myself."

Mmhmm.

He'd done it all himself. And Renzo would not point out how for most of their trip home, he had been the one who carried Diego on his back because the kid didn't want to walk. Or rather, he was too tired to walk.

"Good job, buddy."

Renzo didn't need to be told to see it—Diego was damn tired, and ready for a nap. He suspected Lucia had kept the kid entertained and moving non-stop since he'd been gone. Probably to keep Diego distracted enough that he wasn't worried about where his brother was, or if he was coming back.

He appreciated it.

"Will Lucia watch me again?" Diego asked, taking those last couple of steps slowly.

Renzo was already opening the doorway to the hallway leading to their apartment when he replied, "Maybe, we'll see."

"Okay, I like her."

Yeah, he knew that.

No doubt.

"Who's that, Ren?"

Renzo turned in the doorway as his brother passed him by to see who

Diego was talking about. There was a lot of shady characters that came in and out of their apartment building on a regular basis. Sometimes, they'd see a face once, and never see them again. That was just fine with him, because those were usually the people he didn't *want* to see again.

Not that he was any better, he supposed.

To some, he was bad people, too.

The man leaning against the wall directly next to Renzo's apartment door, however, was a whole different breed. Never once had he laid eyes on Lucian Marcello. They'd never crossed paths, or had a need to, for that matter. Renzo liked that just fine. But just because he never had a face to face with the man didn't mean he wouldn't recognize him when Lucian was standing just a few feet away.

Maybe it was because the man's eyes matched his daughter's. A bright hazel, with secrets hiding in the depths. Or maybe it was because he was an older version of his son—tall, intimidating, and dangerous in more ways than one.

It could have also been because Renzo saw the man's face flashed on the news a few times throughout his life. All the Marcellos had made their rounds in the system—courts, or otherwise.

It didn't matter.

Renzo recognized him.

Quickly, he snatched the back of his brother's backpack, and pulled Diego behind him. His brother tripped over his feet, but all Renzo cared about was getting Diego out of Lucian's view. He didn't know what the man was here for, but he didn't think it was anything good, either.

"Ren?" Diego whispered behind him, hugging his legs.

He reached back, and patted a hand against his brother's head. He figured … his best bet was not to let this man think he had bothered him in any way by randomly showing up where he lived. Like that wasn't threatening enough, really. If a fucking *customer* showed up at Ren's place, he would beat the person within an inch of their life, so they never even thought about doing it again.

He didn't think this would work out well for him if he tried that on Lucian.

Lucian smiled a slow, cold grin as he pushed away from the wall, and fixed the cuff on his suit jacket. Maybe it was the man's posture, or the very expensive clothing and jewelry he wore, but the guy just screamed *money*. More than even his daughter did in her designer dresses and red-soled heels.

"Hope you don't mind me dropping by, Renzo," Lucian murmured, glancing up to meet Renzo's gaze as he strolled closer. "Or do you prefer *Ren?*"

Renzo's gaze narrowed. "I'd prefer if you left, actually."

"Soon, soon." Lucian shrugged. "No worries—this place isn't really my scene."

No fucking doubt.

Renzo chose to keep his mouth shut.

Not that Lucian cared.

He came to a stop just a couple of feet away from Renzo. Too fucking close, really. If he was intimidating several feet away, he was incredibly imposing being this close. Renzo refused to show it, though.

"If you're here to tell me to stay away from your daughter—"

Lucian barked out a laugh. "Yes, I am here to tell you exactly that. And to explain a few things while I'm at it. Seems you don't understand my reach, young man, or you just don't care."

Renzo refused to even blink with this man standing in front of him. "Go with the last one."

"Funny—you're a stupid one, then."

"I—"

"Quiet," Lucian murmured. "I know what my daughter did for you these past couple of days, and I know *exactly* where you were and what you were doing. See, I also know where you work on a daily basis, who works for you ... who is supplying you." The man leaned sideways a bit to smile down at Diego, but Renzo inched sideways to block his brother again. "And him ... I even know his doctor's name when he gets sick, and you need to take him in. I know the names of your sister's teachers, and the address where she lives when she's not coming back here to help you every once in a while."

Renzo's jaw stiffened. "Your point?"

"I made your life a little bit harder, didn't I?" Lucian asked. "By taking away one thing—the daycare—you needed to fix it. Scramble to make it better. You fixed it this time around, but what would I take away next, young man? How much do I need to take away from you before you finally get the hint?"

Jesus Christ.

"Your sister?" Lucian asked, continuing on even when Renzo stayed silent. "Your apartment ... or how about the way you keep it all afloat, hmm? What if I took away your ability to make money, and survive?"

Renzo tipped his chin up, fire in his heart and hate swimming in his blood. "You could try. My ability to get my hands on shit to sell isn't dependent on the Marcellos, Lucian. You're one supplier of many. Try something else."

That was a lie.

It would be *damn hard* for him to work something else out, but he would do it.

"I'm sure," Lucian said, stuffing his hands into his pockets. "Here's the thing … you have no business with my daughter. And while I am usually fine to let my children do their own thing, not in this case, Renzo. See, I don't know you, but what I do know, I don't fucking *like*. I don't want my daughter mixed up in you, your business, or your life. I don't want her getting caught up in something I can't save her from. You're a wild card—I don't know what number you're going to show when I flip you over, and I can't have that. Not when it's my daughter's safety that's being gambled."

Was that what it was about?

He thought Renzo was bad for her? That he was going to hurt her?

"I would never hurt Lucia."

He couldn't.

Not when he loved her.

Lucian's cold expression didn't change. "So you say. Do understand that if you continue to see my daughter, this is only going to get worse for you. Don't be confused on whether or not this is something you should take seriously—it's a promise, young man. Do you hear me?"

Renzo said nothing.

It wasn't as simple as just *staying away* because someone told him to. How was he supposed to walk away from the only woman that managed to somehow climb over his walls, and make herself at home in his shitty fucking life and heart? He couldn't just walk away from Lucia. That was never going to happen.

Lucian smiled again. "Oh, and your mother—I assume that's who she was—left a while ago. Said she didn't know when she would be back. Quite a mess, that one."

Yeah, *fuck*.

That one stung a little.

"Go to hell," Renzo muttered.

Lucian chuckled. "Men like us, Renzo, are already living there. It's death that finally brings us heaven. I'm sure you understand."

FIFTEEN

Renzo hadn't been gone from the hotel for more than five minutes before a black car pulled up in front, and a familiar face exited the vehicle. He never came inside the hotel, but rather, stood just beyond the doorways like a looming figure waiting for her. Which was strange considering her uncle, Giovanni, was anything but looming, really. Always laid back, and fun ... he was the easiest person to deal with in their family.

She'd gone outside to greet him, and he quickly explained he was there to take her home. Just like that. No room for argument, and he was not taking no for an answer. She had known this was coming. The random texts from her father gave her a good lead up to the fact someone would be coming to get her when it was time. Like they just knew what she was doing—he let her have her moment, but now it was over.

Now—almost home—her uncle finally decided to speak from the driver's seat. "You're worrying your father, Lucia. You know that, don't you?"

"How?"

She didn't miss the way her uncle's brow dipped in the rearview mirror. She'd chosen to get in the back seat instead of the front because she figured that would leave her closed off to a conversation. Clearly, that was wrong.

"How?" Giovanni asked.

"That's what I asked. How am I worrying him?"

"Because—"

"Because I have a life?" she questioned quietly, staring at the passing trees on the highway. It was easier, she felt, to look at anything else but her uncle as she talked. She didn't want to be angry with Giovanni. It wasn't his fault for all of this, or the way she was feeling about her father. "Because I'm interested in someone he doesn't approve of, but let's be fair to Renzo ... Daddy's not even *tried* to know who he is, anyway. Or is he worried because—"

"All of that and more," her uncle muttered heavily. "But mostly because your behavior is not like you, Lucia. Defiance, going off without a word, and forgetting where you came from."

Lucia's brow furrowed. She watched the confusion light up her features in the reflection of the glass. And then as quickly as that confusion came, it was replaced by something else entirely. The scoff bubbled up hard in her chest—it was *painful* as it came out of her mouth, and echoed in the quiet car. She turned, but already found that her uncle was staring at her in the

151

rearview mirror, waiting. That was the thing about Giovanni … he *expected* people to do things that were out of character, but especially when backed into a corner or under strange circumstances. He didn't expect people to be unfeeling robots, but rather, emotional beings.

He could handle emotional people.

Not so much frozen statues of nothingness.

"Forget where I came from?" Lucia asked, the sarcasm thick in her tone.

"That's what I said."

"I have spent the last while working in a place that I doubt you have ever even stepped foot inside, Uncle Gio. I have fed people who told me *thank you* because that would be their only meal for the day. I was given the honor of watching children who were born poor and already oppressed because that's the situation society has made for them. Yet they still smiled at me every day because at least while they're young, they don't know that everyone around them is going to make good and damn sure they are always poor and oppressed."

Lucia made another disgusted noise—although, not for those people, but rather her family—and sat back in the seat with her arms folded over her chest. "And do you know what I did, then?"

"I don't, sorry."

She nodded.

Not surprised.

"I went home every day to a home that would comfortably fit five of those families. To parents who have more money in their bank accounts than most of those people will ever see in their lifetimes. I came home to people who never neglected or abused me, or left me to fend for myself."

Sighing, she added, "I slept in Egyptian cotton—some of them are lucky if they have cardboard to make the ground softer. I know where each meal of mine is coming from. I can drop five thousand on a pair of shoes, and it won't even make a dent in my trust fund. I can go to any college I want because my surname affords me that—I didn't even need the fucking grades for it. *Hell,* my father was able to get me in for the second semester in California despite their classes being full just because he had enough *money* to get me on the list."

"Lucia—"

"And I had the *privilege* of meeting Renzo," Lucia continued, ignoring her uncle altogether. "And it is a privilege, Uncle Gio, because despite everything I was seeing at the shelter, I still felt removed from it because I didn't have to deal with those things at home. He made it *real,* and he taught me to look beyond what you see on the surface. There is more to people than their money, status, or lack of it. He's someone who isn't like me at all, and doesn't care about *my* life because he's too busy trying to survive in his own. But yeah, you go ahead and tell me about how I forgot where I came from. I can't fucking forget."

How could she?

"I can't forget," Lucia repeated, "because my reality will never be his, and we both know it. So fuck you, and Daddy, and anyone else who wants to tell me what I *forgot*."

Yeah.

Fuck all of them.

"Lucia."

"*What?*"

She wished she wasn't one of those people who cried when they got mad, but here she was. It made her look weak, like she was ruled by emotions, when all she wanted to do was just fade away. Using the back of her hand, she swiped away the tears but refused to meet her uncle's gaze in the rearview mirror even though she could practically feel him begging for her to do exactly that.

She expected her uncle to lecture her on their life, and tell her to suck it up. Or even to tell her that, despite what she wanted to do, her father was still her father, and she needed to respect his choices and decisions even when all they did were hurt her or someone she loved.

Because she did.

Love Renzo.

Entirely.

Her uncle surprised her.

"Give Lucian time," Giovanni murmured as he took the exit ramp off the highway that would soon lead them to her family's home. "I think part of your father has, for a moment, forgotten where he's come from, but beyond that ... he's scared. Lucian has never done well when he's scared of something. History shows us he overreacts, makes bad decisions, and tends to become un-fucking-bearable."

Lucia couldn't help it. She let out a small, bitter laugh. "That's putting it mildly."

Giovanni shrugged his broad shoulders. "But not a lie."

"Hmm."

"So, he's scared," her uncle continued quieter, "because one daughter is starting her own life, and another has already left him ... mind you, after nearly being killed by a man who professed to love her. But she is gone now, in her own life with her husband, too. And John—well, let's not get into your brother because that is a whole other topic, Lucia. But that just leaves you. The youngest of the bunch. His last child. And he's terrified that you might leave, too, or he might not be able to protect you ... but mostly that you're going to leave him behind."

"You say that like it should excuse the things he's said, or done."

"Not excuse. *Explain*."

"It doesn't really help, though," she said, going back to staring out the window.

"No, I imagine it doesn't."

Thankfully, her uncle quieted for the rest of the trip home. He did follow her inside her parents' home once they arrived, although without saying very much to her. She found her mother waiting inside.

Jordyn Marcello was an enigma. She'd not been brought up privileged like the man she married, or the family that welcomed her with open arms. Her life hadn't been easy—Lucia heard those stories, too. Maybe that was why, once her mother had kids of her own to love and raise, Lucia couldn't even remember Jordyn raising a hand or her voice to them over the years. She protected them with everything she was—so fierce, and full of love. She did whatever she had to do for them like a mother should.

But right then, her mother just looked sad.

And disappointed.

"I called you," Jordyn said softly. "Three times, these past couple of days. At least, you chose a hotel where I could check in even if I couldn't check in with you."

Yes, because despite the fact Lucia refused to come home, and decided instead to keep an eye on Diego for Renzo, it really didn't matter. All it would take was a quick check of her accounts or cards, and her family would know exactly where to find her. Or even, a simple call to her enforcers.

There was no hiding.

So, she hadn't.

Giovanni hung back in the hallway as Lucia kicked off her shoes, and dropped her bag in the corner. "I needed some time, Ma. Sorry."

"But why—"

Lucia's head snapped up, and her gaze narrowed in on her mother. "*Why?*"

Jordyn didn't seem at all fazed by Lucia's angry question. In fact, her mother stayed leaning against the wall like this whole night was just something else for her to deal with. Not like it was an actual problem.

That was the thing …

For Lucia, this was a huge problem.

Her father … the shit he did, that was a problem.

"How is the young man?" her mother asked. "Renzo, I heard his name was. I guess he's quite good at what he does. Your brother let me in on that. Your father told me some other things. So, how is he?"

Lucia blinked.

She could have settled on a lot of things to say, but only one thing felt appropriate for how she felt about Renzo. "He's great."

Renzo was so much more than just *great*. He was everything Lucia had never needed to be. He had the kind of strength she could only wish to have. He was fucking amazing.

Jordyn nodded once. "You could try to see things from your father's perspective when it comes to the young man, Lucia. Walk a mile in his shoes, so to speak. You could at least—"

"At least, what, Ma?" Lucia interjected sharply. "Pretend like Daddy doesn't think Renzo is trash? Act like he didn't take away the only thing that really helps Renzo out by getting his little brother kicked out of the daycare where I help out? And for what, because he's *involved with me?* Fuck that."

"Lucia, language."

"What, like everybody else around here doesn't swear all the damn time?"

A throat cleared behind Lucia, and it took her a half of a second to realize it was not her uncle. She spun on her heel to find her father shrugging off his suit jacket before he hung it up on the waiting hook designated to him. She wished it didn't have to be like it was, but just *looking* at her father sent her anger flaring even hotter.

"How could you do that to him, Daddy?" she demanded.

Giovanni cleared his throat, and gave Lucian a look who pretended like he didn't even see it. Her father took his time fishing the keys, phone, and wallet out of his jacket pockets before he loosened the tie around his neck. Nodding in the general direction of her mother, Lucian demanded, "You apologize to your mother for speaking to her like that. If you have a problem with me, then you take it up with *me*, Lucia. You do not, however, speak to your mother like that. Not in this house."

Lucia's shoulders stiffened, but she still said, "Sorry, Ma."

"It's fine," Jordyn said softly. "I'll just … Gio, would you like a coffee, or something?"

"Put some whiskey in it for me?"

"And I won't tell Kim."

Giovanni laughed. "You've got a deal."

The hallway felt pregnant with a loaded silence until the footsteps of her mother and uncle faded into the kitchen. She desperately wanted to look at anything *but* her father in those moments. Still, she tipped her chin up, and met her father's cool gaze down the hall.

"You quit the shelter," her father stated.

It wasn't even a question.

No surprise he already *knew*.

"I love that place," Lucia whispered, "and you ruined it for me by doing that to Renzo."

"The daycare was a warning," Lucian murmured, tipping one hand over like it meant nothing. "For him, and not for you. But you ... you are so stubborn, like your mother, and—"

"More like you, I think."

The ghost of a smile curved Lucian's lips at the corners, but as quickly as it was there, it was gone, too. "Maybe more like me than I want to admit, Lucia. Nonetheless, it was a warning not meant for you."

"And yet, I still heard it, Daddy. *I* answered it, didn't I?"

She didn't miss the clench of her father's jaw.

Then, her father waved a hand as if to brush it all off. "Doesn't matter. I am sure after tonight, Renzo will make the right choice where you are concerned. I believe he now knows just how serious I can get when I make a statement clear."

Lucia frowned. "What does that mean?"

"It's not for you to worry about."

Her father strolled down the hallway, tension following him the whole way. She had no doubt that this was going to be her life for the unforeseeable future. Tension, arguments, sadness, and pain.

"But," Lucian added with a tick of his finger over his shoulder, "safely assume he won't be around to see you, if he's a smart young man. I believe he is."

Rage filtered through Lucia's system.

Fuck him.

"Why can't you just let it go?" she called at his back.

Her father didn't even turn around. "Because he's not for you. He never will be."

"That's not for you decide!"

"But I did, didn't I?"

No.

She did.

• • •

Yeah, I'll be there in an hour, Lucia typed back to her sister, Cella. She figured since she hadn't spent a lot of time with her family lately, that she should at least try to spend time with the family members who weren't pissing her off. Like her older sister. John, the sibling she was most close to despite their age difference, kept calling and texting, but Lucia ignored every one of them.

He had *no business* approaching Renzo like he did. Lucia was not in the mood to play nice with her brother, no matter what he wanted. Maybe, when she wasn't so angry with him anymore, she might pick up one of his calls or reply to his text messages. Just to tell him to fuck off, of course.

Right now, she didn't even have the desire to do that.

"Lucia?" her mother called from the kitchen as she passed it by. "Don't you want breakfast?"

Not particularly.

"No thanks, Ma."

"But—"

"I'm good. Heading out to see Cella."

"Well ... okay."

Breakfast meant spending time with her father when he finally rolled out of bed. It had been a couple of days since she came back home, and despite all her father's efforts, they just weren't talking. She made sure of it. The tension in their home was thick enough to smother a person with all the bitterness and words left unspoken that was weighing it down.

Lucia wished she cared.

Except she didn't.

At all.

Because for every single day that passed without contact from Renzo, she was left feeling more and more bitter with her father. She didn't try to reach out to Renzo, to be fair, but that was because she was waiting for him. Had her father—whatever he did—scared him off for good? Was he making a choice about her because he felt like he had to?

Then, so be it.

It still hurt, though.

God.

Like an ache deep in her chest that no matter what she tried to do, she just couldn't ignore. It was there when she went to sleep, and lingered long after she woke up. She would become accustomed to it just long enough for her to forget about it before it came back around to kill her again.

Still, she didn't call.

"Are you sure—"

Lucia swung the front door opened, and stepped outside before her mother could even finish her question. She didn't need to hear it, anyway. *Yes,* she was sure that she didn't want to spend even one more minute than she had to in her father's presence. It would only lead to the two of them arguing again, and she just wasn't in the mood today.

Glancing one last time at the screen of her phone, Lucia shoved the device into her pocket, and glanced up. It took her a second to realize what she was seeing at the end of her driveway, and exactly what it meant.

A second for her heart to start beating out of control, and feel like it was going to *burst.* A second for her to catch air in her lungs when he smirked, and winked from his position leaning against an older, restored Mustang with beautiful lines and a bright, fiery red paint job. A second for her own smile to grow wide before she darted off the steps, and closer to the man who was currently holding her entire soul in his hands, but probably didn't even know it.

Renzo.

He looked like sex on a stick in his black jeans, leather jacket, and a plain white T-shirt. With his scuffed up combat boots hooked one over the other, and his arms folded over his chest, he seemed as though he didn't have a single problem in the world. Certainly not because he was standing where he was … where he absolutely shouldn't be right in front of her fucking *house.*

No doubt, the enforcer leaning over the hood to talk to Renzo was telling him exactly that, too. He didn't even pay the guy any mind, just waved a hand, but kept his gaze on Lucia all the while.

She heard the last bit of the man's statement to Renzo, though.

"If you're smart, you'll get the fuck out of here, man."

Renzo didn't even reply. He was too busy pushing off the hood of the Mustang with arms wide open to catch an oncoming Lucia. His arms wrapped around her like *bars,* but damn, she'd never wanted to be locked in more than she did with Renzo. Nothing would make her happier, honestly.

His lips moved against the line of her hair as he said, "Morning, baby."

She grinned, tipped her head back, and found those familiar eyes of his drifting over her face like he was taking her in all over again. "What are you doing *here?*"

Blasé, far too sexy for his own good, and a little too cocky, Renzo shrugged one shoulder. "Last couple of days were busy, and I finally got a day to relax a bit. Wanted to spend it with you."

Lucia arched a brow, and passed a look to the enforcer who was still lingering a little too close for her liking. Never mind the fact he was digging in his pocket, likely for a cell phone to call somebody. Probably her father who very rarely woke his ass up out of bed before eight, but usually closer to nine.

They needed to get out of here.

And *quickly.*

"Besides," Renzo added, nodding his strong chin in the direction of her house, "asked around, got your address easily enough … figured, might as well make it clear I wasn't going anywhere."

Oh, God.

She liked that as much as it terrified her.

"I'm sorry for … whatever happened," she murmured.

Renzo's thumb came up to press against the seam of her lips. His silent way of telling her to *hush*. He raised his brow, and then winked. "Diego went with Rose to get some things he needs. I'm not good at the whole … shopping bit."

Lucia laughed. "Wouldn't have guessed it."

Her teasing only prompted him to squeeze her waist roughly enough to take her breath away, but shit, she liked it. She always liked what this man did to her—loved it, really.

"Yeah, we got a problem, you know."

Lucia glanced to the side to see the enforcer walking away from them. "We should get out of here."

"Probably," Renzo agreed. "I was thinking … the beach."

"It's the first of September."

"Which is the perfect time to go, watch the waves, and not be bothered by other people."

He had a good point.

The enforcer turned back around to face them with his mouth already open to say something else that would fall on deaf ears.

"Get in the car," she told him, laughing. "*Now.*"

Renzo had just slipped into the driver's side when the enforcer neared the vehicle again. Not that it mattered. Tires screeched as he backed out of the driveway. Lucia simply waved goodbye to the man who had probably been told to keep her from leaving. Then, she texted her sister.

Change of plans, Cella. Another day.

She had better things to do today.

• • •

Lucia leaned back against Renzo's chest, and wordlessly, his arms snaked over her shoulders to hug her closer. Sitting on the hood of the Mustang, using the windshield as a backrest, he'd covered them with a multicolored quilt he'd pulled from the car. *Just in case*, apparently. It wasn't that cold for September, but she wasn't going to tell him to get rid of the blanket. It kept them hidden away from the rest of the world, not that there was that many people on the beach.

It didn't matter.

She liked this.

Warm.

Tucked in.

Close.

Him.

"Where'd you get the car, anyway?" she asked.

"A friend. Let me borrow it for the day." Renzo chuckled, his head

159

dipping down so he could kiss the back of her neck. It sent shivers racing through her system like nothing else. A heat followed the same path. "For a fee, of course. Everybody wants something for nothing, but you still end up paying for it, right?"

She glanced over her shoulder at him, but he leaned in fast and caught her lips with his own in a slow, burning kiss. She was quick to part her lips for him, inviting him deeper. There was nothing quite like the way Renzo kissed, she thought. Controlled, yet wild. Slow, but overwhelming all the same.

All too soon, he was pulling away.

Lucia couldn't have that.

Rolling over to her knees, she faced him. She used his body as a pillow of sorts, resting her chin on the backs of her hands sitting on his hard stomach as she peered up at him. He was quick to readjust the blankets, covering her back, and his legs, but leaving her head exposed.

"You were right, you know," she murmured.

"About what?"

"The beach is nicer when there's less people around."

He grinned. "I know. This is Diego's favorite time to come and build sandcastles."

There it was again.

That *love*.

His tone thickened with it.

Sweetened, even.

It never failed when it came to his brother.

"And I thought you would like it, too," he said quieter, his gaze meeting hers again. "Or I hoped so, anyway."

She heard it, then too.

Love sweetened his tone for her.

Renzo placed his arms behind his head, and stared up at the sky. "What time do you need to go back tonight?"

"I'm not going back tonight, Ren."

His gaze dropped to her again. "No?"

"Nope."

She was soaking up every moment she could with him. This was where she wanted to be. Only with *him*.

Renzo smiled in that lazy, sexy way of his that had her heartrate picking up all over again. "Good. I thought maybe you would stay with me, so just in case, I have one more surprise for today."

"Oh?"

"Yeah, baby."

"You didn't have to … do anything for me. Just show up."

Prove you don't care about what they say.

"You know, the car, whatever other surprises you have," she said, pushing up to rest on her knees and leaning in close enough that their noses were touching. "None of it. I don't need any of that from you."

Something she couldn't place flashed in his eyes as they dropped to her mouth. "Ever?"

"It's not about *things* for me, Ren. It's about us."

She was the one to kiss him that time. Harder, and faster than he kissed her. She wanted another taste of him because she just couldn't get enough.

"Still yours, right?" she whispered against his lips.

Renzo smiled. "Can't be anyone else's, can you?"

Not at all.

That was the thing ...

The words slipped out easily, then.

Three little words she thought might not make a difference to what she already knew, but at the same time, would probably change *everything*.

"I love you."

His hands on her waist tightened. "Do you?"

"Like crazy. Stupidly, apparently. That's what people keep saying."

"But you still do."

"How can I not? I don't care what they say, anyway. They know I don't care—maybe that's what scares them the most."

She didn't expect him to say it back even if she thought she knew what he might say. She didn't say it just to make him tell her the same thing. She said it because it was *true*. That was all that mattered to her. That she said it; he heard it; it was *true*.

Renzo kissed her again, his tongue flicking out to strike against the seam of her lips before he murmured, "It doesn't matter what they think. It only matters what you want, Lucia, and if you want to be here, then nobody is ever going to take you away from me. Do you know why?"

"Why, Ren?"

"Because, girl ... I love you more than you know, Lucia. It's never gonna be enough, but I do."

He was wrong.

So *very* wrong.

It was always going to be enough.

It was okay that he believed he wasn't enough for her, though. She didn't mind taking the time to prove him differently. He'd taken the time to see who she really was, after all. She already saw him, too.

He just needed to see himself.

SIXTEEN

"You got a hotel room?" Lucia asked him, giving him one of those sweet smiles. "You know you didn't have to—"

"But I wanted to."

It wasn't like him to drop six-hundred a night on a hotel room because usually, he didn't have that kind of cash to drop *anywhere*. He was careful with money because he had to be, no excuses. If it was just him depending on the money he made, then that would be one thing. But it wasn't just him. He needed to take care of his siblings, too.

Renzo handed the keycard over for the room, and let Lucia open it up for them. The room probably wasn't up to her level of taste, but he knew it wouldn't make a fucking difference to her, either. Just the fact that he'd done anything at all for her made Lucia happy. She was easy to please like that, and he loved that about her, really.

Inside the room, which was roomy enough with a king-size bed, a small sitting and eating area, plus a large attached bathroom—yeah, he'd checked it out earlier—Lucia dropped her things over the side of the couch, and spun a small circle. The room wasn't fancy, but it was nice, and comfortable. Which was all he needed to make his night better, especially because Lucia was there with him.

"Way better than going home tonight, Ren."

He chuckled, and fished his cell phone out of his pocket. "Check it out, if you want. I have to make a phone call."

She bit her bottom lip, grinning. "I think I need to wash the sand off, actually."

"Shower is in there," he said, gesturing at the one room with the door closed.

Sweetly, she asked, "Are you going to *join* me, then?"

It took him a second.

He blinked.

Glancing up at her, Renzo said, "I will if you want me to."

That smile of hers turned sexy in a blink. All too suggestive, really. He loved it. "Make your phone call. I'll be in there when you're ready."

"You got it, Lucia."

Renzo waited until she had closed the bathroom door with a wink over her shoulder before he dialed a familiar number and put the cell phone to his ear. His sister picked up on the third right.

"Ren, hey."

Shifting on his feet, and putting his back to the bathroom door to keep his thoughts from drifting *there* for the moment, he asked, "How's Diego?"

"Fine. Why do you always think he melts down when he spends a night with me?"

"I don't always think—"

"Yes, you do."

Fine.

But it was mostly because he knew how much Diego depended on him for practically everything. He had woken up to Renzo basically every single day of his little life. Renzo put him to bed, for Christ's sake. Taught him how to use the bathroom, and how to properly hold a spoon. And yeah, sometimes, Diego panicked when his brother wasn't around.

So did Renzo.

"He is fine," Rose promised. "Loved all his new clothes, and even got a couple of toys."

Renzo smiled. "Good."

"And speaking of money ..."

"What about it?"

"Did my landlord get it right when she said you paid my expenses up until the end of the year, Ren?"

Ah, yeah.

Lucian Marcello made a threat, and Renzo answered accordingly to keep his family safe and secure as much as he could. He had some money saved up that he didn't like to touch unless absolutely needed. Mostly, he pretended like that money didn't even exist, really. Add onto the ten thousand he'd made on the car boosting job, and he made sure his rent, his sister's expenses, plus a safe daycare for Diego was paid for up until the end of the year. He had an envelope for Rose to use for other things like food, and whatever else she might need over the coming months, too, plus, he knew during her gallery exam that she'd sold some pieces which would help her out a lot.

So yeah, fuck Lucian.

Even if the guy *did* try to screw up Renzo's ability to make money, they were safe for a few months. At least until the end of the year. That would give Renzo far more than enough time to figure something out.

Hell, go *straight*, even.

Get his work off the streets, and into something legal. Not that any money he made from a regular job—considering he didn't even have his high school diploma—was going to be enough to take care of his sister's schooling and expenses. It wouldn't even come close. Sure, it would take care of his needs, and Diego, too, but not Rose.

Which meant ...

Fuck.

He was still going to be selling drugs, and doing whatever else he needed to do to make sure his sister stayed right where she was. Making something of herself, and not screwed like they were.

Didn't matter.

Renzo would *always* do what he had to. But at least until the new year, he had his shit figured out, and taken care of. Including his sister and brother. Lucian could screw him over all he wanted, but Renzo was going to be *fine*. He'd have all the time in the world to work something else out if he needed to.

Simple as that.

"Yeah, you heard the landlord right," Renzo told his sister. "And I've got extra for you, too, as a just in case, or whatever."

"Ren—"

"And don't bother to ask where it came from, either. Because you know it's none of your business, Rose."

"You know if you get caught," his sister murmured, "then we're all going to be—"

"Except I won't get caught, so drop it."

Rose sighed. "You won't even entertain the idea that—"

"Nope."

"Impossible. You are absolutely impossible, Renzo."

"I like to think of myself as resilient."

He had to be, didn't he?

He had to be so they didn't have to be.

"I'll be around to pick him up tomorrow, but if he asks for me tonight, just call," Renzo said.

"I don't think he will. He did fine the last time he was with me."

"That was then."

This was now.

He left that unspoken.

"All right, Ren. What are you doing tonight, anyway?"

He grinned, and glanced over his shoulder to peek at the closed bathroom door. "Hanging out with Lucia."

Forever the perpetual seventeen-year-old girl, his sister made a high-pitch squealing noise that might have burst his eardrums had he not pulled the phone away in time. He just shook his head when Rose started going off on the phone.

"I will talk to you tomorrow," he told her.

Without a goodbye, although he suspected his sister didn't really give a shit either way, Renzo hung up the phone. Dropping it to the foot of the bed, he already had his shirt and jacket tugged off *and* his jeans undone by the time he reached the bathroom door. Behind it, he could hear the water running, and a soft humming, too.

He listened for a moment.

Waiting.

Turning the knob and opening the door to step inside the bathroom, he heard it again. Clear as day, and sweet as could fucking be.

She sang in the shower.

He stood there, watching through the frosted glass of a shower that was big enough to hold at least five people comfortably as Lucia danced behind the glass, and sang a song that was *way* too popular on the radio.

It wasn't really the singing.

Or the song.

It was just her.

And the crazy thought that filtered through his mind of, *I'd like to hear her doing that every single day, not just today.*

"Hey." Lucia popped her head out of the shower, and eyed him with a sexy grin. "Coming in, or ...?"

God.

How could she even ask that like he might refuse or something? There was no way he was ever going to tell this woman no when she offered something like that to him while naked, wet, and ... yeah, Renzo was so fucked.

Renzo stumbled over his own damn feet in an effort to get what remained of his clothes off so he could jump in that huge shower with Lucia, and find the heaven waiting for him between her beautiful, creamy thighs. Her laughter only spurred him on to move a little faster when he growled, "Keep laughing at me, and I'll give you something to fill that pretty mouth of yours full, Lucia."

Sweetly, she asked behind the glass, "Promise?"

Yep.

He groaned.

So fucked.

He didn't even think about the condom in his pants—he was always keeping one on him because he couldn't seem to keep his hands off of Lucia whenever she was around—and slipped into the shower. Hot water hit his back, but he didn't even feel it. He was too busy coming for the woman backed against the far wall that had tiles replicating rocks. Above her head, three large showerheads poured down, and she grinned at him.

"Took you long enough."

"*Tease,*" he muttered.

"I know, I'm terrible."

Yes, yes she was.

But in the best ways.

Renzo closed the distance between them in a blink, his lips crashing down on Lucia's as her hands came up to grab tight to his face. Her wet body tucked in close to his, warming him in a way the water would never be able to. Already, his fucking cock was hard, and jutting out between them.

He didn't have to keep his promise to fill her mouth full. She did that for both of them when she dropped to her knees, grabbed the base of his dick in one hand, and took him in her mouth.

"Holy fuck," he groaned, his head falling back.

But as much as he wanted to enjoy the feeling of her mouth on his cock while he squeezed his eyes shut and got lost, he really wanted to *watch* her do it, too. Renzo stared down, captivated by the sight of his cock slipping between Lucia's grinning lips. Her tongue laid flat to the underside of his cock, her cheeks hollowed, and she sucked him hard.

"So fucking beautiful," he murmured. "Are you gonna swallow all of me, too?"

She winked.

Yep, fucked.

He'd certainly like that—watching her swallow his come—but what he really wanted was just to be inside her. It almost killed him to pull her off his cock, but he did, standing her up so he could get another taste of her mouth. Lucia's leg hooked around his thigh, and she rolled her hips, letting his cock slide through her slick folds.

All it took was a shift of his hips, and hooking her other leg around his hips, and he was sliding home inside her pussy.

Finding heaven.

Inside her again.

Right where he wanted to be the very most.

Lucia's soft sigh matched his own. Relief, he knew. All he felt when he was inside her was the sweetest kind of relief. He never got that from anything else. Life was always fucking him over in one way or the other.

But not with her.

Never with her.

She kissed him again.

The rest of the world disappeared.

• • •

Renzo decided Lucia looked best when she was wearing nothing but his white T-shirt, and her skin. Even if she was trying to get away from him after throwing popcorn and hitting him *right in the face.*

Goddamn woman.

166

"Get back here right now," Renzo muttered.

Lucia's teasing laughter colored up the hotel room as she jumped on the bed, and just out of his grasp. She tossed him a sexy smile over her shoulder, and threw *another* piece of popcorn at him. He managed to duck this one at least. He took the time to enjoy the sight of her standing on the bed in his clothes, her bare legs smooth, golden and silky. Every single time she moved, he got the nicest peek of her ass and the heaven between her thighs.

Because yeah, she wasn't even wearing panties.

She was nothing but fun and sin like this. His good time, ride or fucking *die*. It kind of hit him right in the chest all at once. Sure, he knew it. He fucking *said it*. He loved this girl like nobody could ever possibly know. No one would ever understand the way just looking at her made his chest tight, and his heart fucking explode.

Sure.

He knew it.

He said it.

But it was that moment right there when Renzo really understood what it all meant to him. That he would do anything for this girl. Die for this fucking girl. Love her to the ends of the earth and back if that's what she needed from him. He would do it. All of it. And he would never even question it.

God.

Somebody loved him.

Someone was looking out for him.

Maybe that was the gift of Lucia Marcello. Maybe she was his reward for everything that had happened in his life up until this point. She was the thing he was given to make up for literally *everything* else.

Lucia smiled down at him. "What?"

Renzo laughed. "What?"

"Nothing. You just went still, and … stared at me."

"I can't stare at you, princess?"

She rolled her eyes, and threw a whole handful of popcorn at him that time. Renzo didn't even try to duck the mess coming his way. The popcorn sprinkled over his head and shoulders before falling to the floor. They'd made a mess with the whole popcorn fight, but that was fine. He didn't mind picking it up. Especially if she helped, and that meant he got to stare at her pretty ass every time she bent over to pick stuff up.

Yeah, shit.

His mind went back there *quick*.

"You're doing it again," Lucia said in a sing-song way. "Staring at me like that, I mean."

Renzo shrugged. "I was just thinking about how much I love you, actually."

Lucia blinked. Her shoulders relaxed, and her grip on the bowl of popcorn softened just enough to give him an opening. He took the chance without thinking, jumping onto the bed before she even realized what he was doing. Yanking the bowl out of her grasp with one hand, and locking his arm around her waist with the other, Lucia's laughter echoed in the room as he took them both down to the bed. It made an even bigger mess, sure. Popcorn *everywhere*.

He didn't regret it at all.

Not when he had her tight body under him, moving in the very best way. He hadn't bothered to pull his clothes back on after their shower. Besides, she took his shirt anyway, and he didn't see the point in getting dressed. Not when he was liable to spend the rest of his night trying to keep Lucia out of her clothes.

His head tipped down, and he caught her mouth in a bruising kiss. Those hands of hers slipped down his chest as her thighs wrapped tightly around his waist, dragging him even closer. The sensations of her nails dragging lines down his skin while her naked sex ground against his hardening cock made him crazy.

So fucking insane.

It never failed to amaze him how every touch from this woman felt like the first time. Each kiss, every stroke of her hands across his body, and the way she felt under him. Her sounds were music. Beautiful, and addicting. If there was a silk he wouldn't mind paying for, it was the softness of her body under his hands.

He'd die to feel that all the time.

"*Please, please.*"

Her words whispered along his skin as his mouth found her throat. She tasted like candy and salt and *sex*. Him, too. She tasted like he'd been all fucking over her. Because he had.

Those fucking hands of hers slipped under his boxer-briefs, and found his length. His teeth found her pulse point at the same time she squeezed his cock, and stroked him from base to tip. All the while, she kept rolling her hips, and making those noises he just couldn't get enough of.

So responsive.

So beautiful.

Perfect.

Every inch of her was absolutely perfect for him.

He was two seconds away from burying himself exactly where he wanted to be the most—between her damn thighs again—when a noise in the background drew him back to reality with a harsh yank. Like a damn hand around his throat that practically ripped him away from Lucia.

"Fuck," he groaned, pressing his forehead against her chest.

Her hands let him go, but skimmed up his bare back at the same time. "It's fine," she said, laughing. "Go answer the phone."

He could have ignored it, except that ringtone meant it was his sister. And the only reason why Rose would be calling was for Diego. No way could Renzo ignore that.

"Yeah, shit, I better."

Thankfully, Lucia didn't make any effort to pull him back to her as he pushed away, and clamored off the bed to find his phone. That didn't mean it was easy, though. All he had to do was peek over his shoulder and see her spread out on the bed with her pussy on display, glistening wet, and ready for him, and he wanted to crawl right back there.

Fuck the call.

But no.

He couldn't do that.

It took him entirely too long to find the goddamn phone shoved under his forgotten jeans on the floor. How the phone had even made it to there when he'd put it on the bed earlier, he didn't know. He supposed that was a testament to the mess he and Lucia had made in their popcorn battle.

By the time he did find the phone, it had stopped ringing. Renzo was quick to call his sister back, and Rose picked up before the second ring.

"Sorry," Rose said in a heavy breath, "I didn't want to call."

"I told you to, though."

His sister's laugh sounded bleak, but in the background, he could hear Diego wailing, "You said, Rose, you said so!"

"He was *fine*," his sister muttered, "and then I mentioned—just to make him feel okay—that if we needed to, we could take him back to you. He took that to mean he was going back home tonight, or you were coming here. When I tried to explain that, no, you were not coming unless he needed you to—"

"He had a meltdown," Renzo filled in.

"Yeah. Shit, I'm sorry, Ren."

He didn't blame his sister.

Diego could be fickle like that. He wanted what he wanted, and nine times out of ten, what the kid wanted was his big brother.

Pinching the bridge of his nose with his fingertips, he turned to glance at Lucia. Instead of laying back spread-eagle on the bed, she had sat up and crossed her legs one over the other. It was a shame, really. He couldn't see the heaven between her thighs anymore, and she was frowning.

Shit.

He did not want to ruin their day and night, but—

"Diego?" Lucia mouthed.

Renzo nodded.

She shrugged, and offered him a small smile. "You should go get him."

He gave her a look.

She just laughed.

"Go get him. It's okay. We can put a movie on, order food up, and he'll have a great time."

He would.

The kid loved Lucia.

Renzo was just now understanding—because he'd known for a while—how much Lucia cared about Diego, too. She didn't look like she felt that her time with him was ruined. She didn't care at all that the rest of their day and night would be spent keeping Diego entertained.

And hell ...

Maybe he loved her for that even more.

"Ren?" his sister asked, bringing him back to the call.

He checked the clock on the bedside table. Already, it was well into the afternoon. By the time he made it to Brooklyn, and got back with Diego, it would probably be supper time or a little later.

"Tell him I'll be there in an hour, maybe a little more," Renzo said.

"Did you hear that, Diego?"

Apparently, she'd had him on speakerphone because Diego's wailing stopped, the kid sniffled, and said, "Okay, Ren."

That was that.

He said goodbye, and hung up the phone. He made quick work of shrugging on his jeans, and by the time he got to Lucia, she was already pulling off his shirt, and handing it over to him.

Damn.

He tried not to ogle her tits.

And failed like a fucker.

"I *will* be dressed by the time you get back," she warned as he slipped on his shirt.

"Do you want to come with me?"

She eyed the mess on the floor. "I should clean this up, shouldn't I?"

"I'll help, if you—"

"I can do it."

"Should have gotten a two-bedroom suite, I think."

Just in case.

He'd remember that next time.

Lucia reached out, fisted his shirt and yanked him in for a burning kiss. Then, she murmured against his lips, "Go get your brother. And don't worry about me. I'm not going *anywhere.*"

Good to know.

Not that he ever doubted her.

• • •

Diego skipped ahead of Renzo with his blue backpack jumping on his shoulders with every step. It was very possible that the kid was more excited about seeing Lucia than he was about the fact his brother had come to get him. Renzo wasn't willing to admit that, though.

"Can I get pizza, too?" Diego asked over his shoulder.

Renzo chuckled, and nodded. "You sure can."

Whatever this kid wanted, Renzo would give him. Or at the very least, *try*. It was the least he could do for Diego, considering everything else the kid had to deal with.

"Be careful with my bag, Ren," Diego said as seriously as he could manage in his four-year-old squeaky voice. "I got *the best* car."

Yeah, Renzo saw it.

In the box.

In a million little pieces.

That he would have to put together.

He didn't mind, though. That model car would keep Diego occupied for *days*. And it gave Renzo the chance to spend quality time with his little brother, too.

Definitely worth it.

Renzo smiled. "I won't break your new toys."

"Good."

"The door with the seven on it," Renzo told Diego as he was coming up to the room in question. "Just go right in—Lucia's in there waiting for you."

Diego pumped a tiny fist in the air, let out a holler, and picked up his pace. Renzo would have jogged to catch up with his brother, but he figured the kid was fine. As he told Diego, the room was unlocked. Diego slipped inside, but left the door open.

"Lucia!"

"You don't need to yell for her, it's one damn room, Diego."

"*Lucia!*"

Why was he yelling?

Kids were strange creatures.

Renzo figured out exactly why Diego had been yelling for Lucia when he entered the hotel room, and found it empty. Clean, with no popcorn on the floor like he'd left it. The bed made, not messed from the two of them rolling around in the sheets. He blinked, and took in the space again.

Her things were gone.

She was gone.

The bathroom door was left wide open.

Diego turned around to face Renzo with a frown. "Where's Lucia?"

He would have answered his brother, but something on the bedside table caught his eye. He dropped the bags he was carrying, and crossed the room. Plucking the handwritten note up that looked like it had been scrawled on a writing pad, and ripped out, his rage blew out of control.

Eleven words.

Two sentences.

One signature.

That's all the note was.

Yet, it still killed him inside. Killed him, and made him so fucking angry, too.

I warned you, didn't I, Renzo?
Stay away from my daughter.
—LM

SEVENTEEN

"Lucia, I hope you understand *why* your father is doing this," the enforcer droned on in the driver's seat like he might think Lucia was listening to him. She wasn't. "Do you know how it would look for your family if you were found in a hotel room with a guy? There's no reason for you to be getting involved with a young man who—"

"I'm sorry," Lucia murmured, continuing her staring contest with the window even as she spoke, "what are you paid to do again?"

"Excuse—"

"Because I don't think you're paid to talk to me at all."

Out of the corner of her eye, Lucia saw the man's shoulders tense from her comment. Yeah, she bet that one *sucked*. She wasn't some stupid little girl with her head stuck in the sand like a lot of people thought when they looked at her. She knew a hell of a lot more about her family and their business as a mafia than anyone really knew. Besides, no one ever hid the details when she thought to ask, too.

Enforcers weren't very high up on the food chain. And like *fuck* was Lucia going to allow an errand boy or muscle to lecture her on what she should or should not be doing. She doubted this man was a virgin, and she hadn't seen a ring on his finger, either. No way was he going to chide her on behavior when she seriously doubted he was innocent.

He couldn't be.

Look what he did for a living.

"Your father was right," the man muttered, "you're not like yourself lately, Lucia."

She laughed, and went back to staring out the window. The passing buildings leading into upper Manhattan were a far nicer sight than the enforcer glaring at her in the rearview mirror. "Is that all he says about me? Shame."

The enforcer grunted, but otherwise, kept quiet.

She was grateful.

Lucia was not in the mood to get in a sparring match with anyone, let alone the man who practically threatened to break down her hotel room door if she didn't come out willingly. *By order of your father, Lucia.* Well, it was him and another man, but she didn't know where that guy went. She was taken with this man while the other one headed inside the hotel to grab her things. Or, that's what she was told.

She scoffed inwardly, and glowered at her reflection in the window. This was getting ridiculous, wasn't it?

Now, Lucian was just going to pull her out of every situation he didn't like? Forcibly remove her from places?

Okay.

If taking away her car didn't stop her from leaving whenever the hell she wanted, and doing whatever she wanted, then nothing would. Besides, her father forgot that Lucia had access to an entire trust fund that Lucian couldn't touch, too. Compliments of her biological grandfather before his murder. Once she had turned eighteen, all that money became hers to do with what she wanted, whenever she wanted.

What was it, twenty million, now?

Something like that.

If she wanted another vehicle that he didn't buy …. if she wanted *anything at all,* she could go get it herself. Lucian was living in the clouds if he thought stepping in and making things difficult for Lucia was going to stop her from seeing Renzo if she wanted to do just that. It wouldn't do anything but annoy her until she figured something else out.

"Almost at the restaurant," the enforcer muttered from the front.

Lucia had a good mind to tell him she didn't give a damn how close they were, but she opted to keep quiet. She probably pissed him off enough already without adding to it. Plus, it wasn't really his fault, and she knew that. He was just doing what he had been told where she was concerned. He was given an order, and he followed it through.

Resting back in the seat, Lucia's fingers itched to have her phone. At least then, she could call or text Renzo and let him know what happened. She bet Renzo was back at the hotel by now … probably wondering where in the hell she was, or why she took off.

Not that it mattered.

She didn't even have her phone.

They took it away.

And her, too.

They took her from Renzo, too.

That pissed her off far more.

"You know," the man droned on from the front again.

Why was he still talking?

"No, I don't know, and I don't care to know," Lucia grumbled.

Jesus, just let me stew in peace.

It wasn't hard.

The enforcer just chuckled. "Well, I'm going to tell you anyway, *principessa.*"

She used to love when people in her family called her a princess. It never held bad connotations, and instead, offered her a great deal of respect from everyone. She was a Marcello princess. One of a few—the youngest, and the most spoiled. Maybe that was because she was her parents' baby, or even for the simple fact she was the last *principessa della mafia* of her generation.

Who knew what it was, but it extended her great privilege.

Funny.

Now that privilege just felt like it was weighing her down.

"I will tell you," the enforcer continued on, "that in this life, it is far easier and you will get a great deal more by falling in line like the rest of us. Stepping out of line does nothing good for you, and gets you nowhere."

Lucia said nothing.

She'd stayed in line her whole life.

No more.

• • •

Lucia had to give the enforcer credit. He kept a *mostly* respectable distance behind her as he directed her into a familiar business. He still loomed there, sure, but at least he wasn't invading her personal space or talking again. All points in his favor for the moment.

Usually, Lucia loved this restaurant. Her father had owned it for longer than she had been alive, honestly. A lot of memories had been made at this place. Typically, she would be comforted by the dark stained, shiny wood and the chrome lighting overhead. Nostalgia would fill her to the brim each and every time she stepped foot in the place, reminding her of chasing after her father as a little girl, and playing with her older siblings during family dinners.

Not today, though.

Today, she felt none of that.

Peering back at the man behind her, Lucia asked, "Can I have my phone back now? We're here."

He shook his head. "Nope."

Fuck.

What was she—thirteen?

More frustrated than ever, Lucia tried to tamper her desire to blow up on anyone and anything close to her as she neared the private dining area. The same space her family dined in for years. More meetings happened here than anyone cared to admit. As her father rid himself of businesses over the years—liquidating assets he no longer had any interest in maintaining—this restaurant never changed hands. It was always his.

Coming up to the doorway, Lucia could already hear a group of familiar voices inside. Her uncles laughing about something, followed by the feminine tones of their wives agreeing. And her mother and father.

Lucia dragged in a hard breath, and willed her anger to at least lighten up a bit. If she went in there angry, who knew what might happen? Nothing good, she suspected.

It didn't matter, it seemed.

That anger and her contempt for the things her father kept doing to her and Renzo were now bred deep into her bones. The more she tried to ignore it, the worse it festered. Growing, and infecting.

"Go in," the enforcer murmured behind her, "they're expecting you."

Lucia scoffed. "I'm sure."

But she didn't have any desire to stand out there with the enforcer any longer, so she headed inside the private dining room. She was entirely unsurprised to find all her aunts, uncles, and her mother and father sitting at their usual table. Or rather, two tables pushed together and set up close to the window where they could watch the people outside, but the people couldn't see them because of the mirrored glass. She swore it was the only time these people put their backs to a window, really.

Instantly, her father's gaze landed on her in the doorway. Lucia didn't move even when her father fixed two buttons on his suit jacket, and nodded as if to silently welcome her to the table with the rest of them.

Nope.

She wasn't going over there at all.

"Lucia," her father said quietly.

Calmly, too.

Too calm, maybe.

Maybe it was his calm state that really pushed her over the edge. The kindness that stared back from her father like he didn't think he had done anything at all. Like he wasn't *hurting* her. All that anger she'd been trying to hold in felt like it was bubbling to her surface all over again. Violent, and raging. Like a soda bottle that had been shaken and shaken before the top just blew. No one would be safe when she finally let go.

It surprised her as much as it scared her. Lucia was not *angry*. Not like this. She wasn't this person, and yet, the man across the room made her exactly that. Whether he wanted to or not, this was what he had made her into, and he probably didn't even realize it. That, or he just didn't care because he was getting what he wanted.

How fucking *nice*.

"Do you want something from me?" Lucia asked her father. "Or am I free to leave?"

Lucian stood from the table, and gave Jordyn a look when Lucia's mother was about to stand, too. "I thought you might like to join your family for dinner. Or have you forgotten that you are a part of this family,

Lucia?"

The silence echoed—weighted, and hard to swallow. Like the ache in her heart that just wouldn't let up. She *adored* her father. More than he could ever possibly know, but he was ruining that each time he did something to hurt her regarding Renzo. Every step he took against them only pushed her further away. But he probably didn't even realize it.

She didn't care to look at the other people sitting at the table. She loved them, sure, but this was no longer about them. This was between her and her father. This was *them*, and his ridiculous need to keep interfering in her life. Something he had never done before now, but she still wasn't going to stand for it.

"If being a part of this family means every choice I make is chosen by *you*," Lucia said, shrugging, "then no, I'm good over on this side of the room."

That hit a nerve.

"Lucia!"

Her father's shout barely even stung.

"Sucks, doesn't it?" she asked, arching a brow in challenge.

Lucian stiffened on the stop. "Excuse me?"

"It sucks when someone you love does things to purposely hurt you. In this case, I said something I knew would hurt you. In your case, you keep trying to take away someone I—"

"We're not discussing that young man here. That is not why I had you brought here, Lucia."

She nodded, glanced to the windows at the side of the room, and let out a bitter laugh. "So, you're saying you purposely dragged me away from Renzo today just because I went with him this morning, and you don't approve, but I can't ask you why you did that or bring it up. That's really what you're telling me right now?"

"We can talk about it later."

"I'd rather talk now, Daddy."

"Fine."

Her father's sharp word had her glancing back at him fast. His clenching jaw, and blazing eyes told her that he was no longer playing around. Lucian wasn't fucking happy, and he was about to let her know it. She recognized that look.

Good.

Get it out, and get it over with.

She had no doubt that whatever her father planned to say was the exact same thing he'd been saying for weeks now. Renzo was no good for her. He was involved in things that she shouldn't be mixed up in. He might hurt her. He's dangerous. All things that mattered very little to Lucia at the end of the day because of just how hypocritical it sounded coming from *this* man in front of her.

The gall of a *mafioso* to lecture someone on the dangers of someone else in her life. Like her own father hadn't spent months in jail when she was a girl. Like he didn't carry a fucking gun around every day. Like their house wasn't paid for with dirty fucking Marcello money!

But her father surprised her.

Those were not the things he talked about at all.

"Fine, Lucia, you want to talk, then let's talk," her father said, folding his arms over his chest. "Let's talk about the last time you saw your sister … or how many calls and texts you've ignored from your brother. How about the last time you sat down at a table with your mother? Oh, me, I get … I understand entirely why you wouldn't want to sit down with me, but *her?* While we're *talking,* let's not forget to mention how last week, I had to send out your final paperwork for you to get started with the second semester at college in California like you *wanted to.* Or did you forget about that, too?"

Her father had progressively inched closer to her until he was just three feet away. All the while, Lucia never once moved or looked away from him. She couldn't because if she did, he would think he *won.* He wasn't winning.

"Or how about the shelter," Lucian added, widening his arms a bit and giving her a look. "You were so determined to work there during the month of August that you put off the first semester of college just so you could do it. For one single *month.* But what did you turn around and do, Lucia? *What?"*

She refused to answer him.

What would be the damn point?

"You *fucking quit,"* Lucian said darkly. "You quit for—"

"Because of what you did, not for him. If you're going to throw shit at me," Lucia told her father, "at least throw the right shit."

Lucian's jaw clenched again, and he dragged in a heavy breath. The same thing she did whenever she was overwhelmed, and needed a second to recoup. It wasn't lost on her how similar she was to her father at the end of the day. And maybe that was a huge part of the problem. She was so like her father that this moment right here was always bound to happen at one point or another.

"My driven, intelligent, independent, and *good* daughter went from having goals, and wants, and knowing exactly what she had planned for her life to …." Lucian gestured with his hand. Not directly at her, but rather, at the room. As if he were silently saying, *all of this, Lucia, you turned into all of this.* "You cared about your family, about school, and you had some sense of responsibility. But now? Now, you're defiant, combative, and you don't even know what you're doing anymore. You don't want me to blame Renzo

Zulla for the person staring back at me right now, but you've not given me a reason not to blame him, either."

Lucia blinked.

Unfeeling, and numb.

That was the thing about all of this. She felt nothing because the man across from her still thought he had no part in her behavior. He just assumed she was like she was because of Renzo, and not in reaction to the shit he was doing to her because of Renzo.

Not the same.

"You don't get it," she told her father, shaking her head. "You don't understand at—"

"Understand *what?*" her father snapped. "That during the span of a month, you've gone from having aspirations and goals to chasing some fucking *boy* all over the city? Tell me I am wrong. Tell me you've given college one ounce of your time and thoughts since you started seeing him. Tell me you've made an effort to go see your *pregnant* sister since meeting him. Go ahead, and tell me that since your brother got out of prison, you've tried to spend time with him. Or your mother, the rest of your family ... *me.* Apparently, I have all the time in the world today for your bullshit, Lucia, so please go ahead and tell me."

Lucian shrugged, adding with a wave, "I will wait, go ahead."

Lucia stayed quiet again.

Why?

Because her father wasn't entirely wrong. She hadn't given college much thought over the past month. She hadn't filled out those final papers, because apparently, he had. She hadn't started prepping to find a place in California like she was supposed to. Her time with her family dwindled down to nothing at all. And yes, a large part of it was because she had been entirely distracted with Renzo, but that wasn't *his* fault.

That was hers.

Not that she expected her father to understand.

Lucian sighed, and shook his head. "Here's the thing, Lucia. I need you to get back to where you were before. Before this month, and that ... man. I need you to put some effort back into your goals, and being who you are, not just an extension of someone else. And I will continue to make sure you do exactly that. Starting today, your phone is gone, along with anything else that isn't needed. You will go home today, and begin the process of readying for California, and starting the second semester of college. Things you wanted to do before—"

"It's not going to make a difference, you know," she murmured, keeping her calm tone although she didn't know how, really. "You can treat me like a child, punish me like one, too, but it still won't make a difference. I have

179

access to my own money. I am eighteen. And if I want to see Renzo, then I will. You can tell me to do whatever you want to tell me to do, but I am still going to love him whether you like it or not, Daddy."

Her piece said—because she really didn't have anything else to say—Lucia turned around, and headed for the exit of the private dining area. At her back, her father called, "I could ruin him, Lucia. Permanently remove the problem, if need be. It would take one phone call. Five seconds of my time, and three fucking words to do it. But I haven't for *you*. Do you understand that?"

She didn't answer her father.

She had nothing left to say.

"Lucia!"

"Lucian," she heard her uncle, Dante, say, "just let her go. Better for her to go and take a moment, than for you two to keep shouting at one another like this. That's not what you want to do."

"You don't fucking know what I—"

"I know exactly what you want to do, brother. I *know* very well. And it will not help, Lucian. It won't."

At the door, the enforcer from earlier stepped in her path. "I will take you home, Miss."

Lucia gave the man a look. "Oh?"

"And I will be escorting you wherever you need to go for the unforeseeable future, or until your father tells me otherwise."

"That so?"

"Yes."

Lucia nodded. "Well, fuck you, too, then."

"Lucia!"

That time, it was her mother.

The first time Jordyn even spoke.

Lucia still didn't turn around.

EIGHTEEN

Renzo stuffed his hands in his pockets, and ignored the buzzing of his phone. Like he didn't have enough problems to handle at the moment, he wasn't about to go and add more to the pile by picking up that fucking phone. He already knew what the calls would be about if he did pick it up, anyway.

Perry, Noah, and Diesel.

One, or all of them.

He didn't know what to tell his guys—his supply was gone. He couldn't get any more drugs for them to sell. He hadn't been able to make a proper connection to do a handoff in a *week*. He seriously suspected Lucian cut him off like he said he would, but he also didn't have any definitive proof that was the case. He just couldn't get anyone on the phone who supplied him. But there also wasn't any reason for Renzo to think Lucian hadn't followed through on his threats, either.

Well played, Marcello.

If only because now Renzo's guys were pissed. They had shit easy when it came to him. They never had to worry much about handling things like where their supply was coming from, or taking care of the cash. He always did that. From getting their shit, delivering it, to taking their money and making sure everybody got their fair and equal cut.

He did it all.

Now, they were scrambling.

Panicking.

Renzo had other shit to worry about. For once, they could take care of themselves. Stretch money for a week, or go out and find another crew to get their shit from to take to the streets. If, or when, Renzo got around to finding himself a new supplier, then he'd reach out to his guys and see if they needed or wanted to work with him again. If not, then fine. They were a dime a dozen.

That was the thing about these streets.

People willing to hustle were *everywhere*.

Whatever made money.

Just as soon as the phone started buzzing in his pocket again, Renzo let out a heavy sigh, and silenced the phone. Not that it mattered. No doubt, he was going to have a good fifty missed calls and texts by the time he got around to checking them. Not that a single one of them would be from the person he wanted to hear from the most.

Lucia.

Something painful slithered around his heart, and tightened to a painful point at the thought. Like a fist grabbing the organ tight, and refusing to let go.

A week.

One entire week.

No calls.

No texts.

Nothing.

It was like she dropped off the fucking radar. Every call he tried to make went to her voice mail. And then, her damn voice mail was full, too, so he couldn't leave anything there. All of his texts were going unanswered.

He didn't think that was purposeful on her part. He figured it was because someone wasn't giving her the option to get ahold of him at all. Someone like her father.

Renzo tried to play it cool. He tried to wait it out, and see what would happen. Maybe his girl would figure something out, and get a call through to him, or make her way over to his side of the city.

Something.

All he got was nothing.

And now he was just pissed.

But worried, too.

When one day turned into two, and then two turned into three ... without even a word from Lucia. That fucking terrified him for more reasons than he cared to think about. His whole life had been spent taking care of his siblings, and looking out for himself. Then, there walked in Lucia like she had always belonged in his life as she made herself at home there. He couldn't get her out if he fucking tried—not that he wanted to. Now, he had Lucia added onto that pile of things he needed to think about and consider, too.

Her father might have made a promise to do whatever he had to in order to keep Lucia away from Renzo, but that was the thing. Renzo made a promise, too. Not to Lucian, but to the only person who really needed to hear it from Renzo. He promised Lucia that nobody was going to take her away from him, and he fucking meant it.

Not her father.

Not anyone else.

Nobody.

She was his, and that's all there was to it.

End of.

It probably didn't help his mood that Diego kept asking about Lucia, but Renzo didn't have any answers. But he was about to fucking get some, one way or another.

That was his goal today.

Answers.

The thing about Renzo that people didn't understand was that just because he was quiet didn't mean he was fucking stupid. He was quiet because silence served him a hell of a lot better in the grand scheme of things. He was quiet because he knew that way, he would hear a lot more if he wasn't also talking.

Since he started working on the streets, and running errands for people connected to the Marcellos, he'd been listening. He knew names, places, and exactly where he could get information when he needed to. Or rather, he knew exactly who to go to in order to get what he needed or wanted.

It was a dangerous game to play, sure. Asking anything about the Marcellos, especially when it came to something personal like their family members or their daily business, only brought trouble for the person wanting information. A quick, usually violent, message would be sent to make sure the person knew to mind their own fucking business.

Renzo was willing to take that risk.

He had to.

Taking a left at the end of the block, Renzo came up on a familiar pizzeria that he'd visited on a few occasions. Well, truthfully, he'd met people in the back to do an exchange, or whatever the case may be. But he'd heard enough to know the place was owned by a close friend of a Marcello Capo. The guy let the family use the back rooms as a storage, when needed, and have their meetings if something else couldn't be worked out.

Bill was his name.

And because of his connections to the Marcello family, even if it was just through affiliation, Renzo assumed the guy either had information about the family, or he knew a way to get it. Which was exactly what Renzo needed today. Plus, if the guy had connections, he knew how this life worked. He likely wouldn't be willing to call the cops if Renzo made a bit of a scene to get what he wanted.

Or if he made some threats …

Inside the pizza joint, Renzo found the place wasn't very busy. He expected that given it was only a little past ten in the morning. Most people weren't all that interested in pizza in the morning, anyway. Soon, he expected the business would fill with the afternoon rush, but for now, this emptiness worked in his favor which was exactly why he chose to show up at this time. He dropped Diego off with a lady from the first floor of their apartment building who he knew needed some extra cash as she'd lost her job when her employer found out she was expecting her first child, and headed out before he'd even eaten breakfast.

Bypassing the tables, and the one server who was filling a guy's glass with water, Renzo headed for the kitchen area. No one even noticed him slipping into the back. He knew where to go to find the owner of the place, and it wasn't at the front. Whenever he visited the pizzeria, the owner was either in the back chatting with people, or shouting orders in the kitchen.

"Hey, you can't be in here!"

"Who the hell are you?"

Renzo ignored the two cooks wiping down the metal surfaces, and picked up his pace when one of them looked like they were going to come around the counter at him. They could fucking try it, and see how well it worked out for them.

By all means …

Siding his hand into the back of his jacket, Renzo palmed the butt of his gun as he entered the back hallway from the kitchen. He already had the gun out, and racked back when he found the owner of the joint sitting behind his desk in a cramped office. The place looked like a goddamn hurricane had blown through it what with the paperwork that was strewn everywhere. Renzo put his attention where it counted—on the man behind the desk.

"Bill, right?" Renzo asked.

The older, balding man with a middle far too round to be healthy glanced up from the phone in his hand. His eyes widened when they fell on the gun that was pointed directly at his face. Renzo had stared down the barrel of a gun more than once, and it was not a fun experience.

"R-Renzo?"

Renzo smiled a little. "Didn't think you would even remember my name given the handful of times I've been around this place, but hey, it's good that you know. I don't mind my name being passed around when you get it right. I need information, and you're the guy who can help me to get it."

Bill blinked, and his gaze drifted from the gun to Renzo. His hand twitched, and inched slightly to the right. Renzo didn't miss it, or what it might mean.

"Know that if you pull a weapon on me, I will paint your fucking office with your brain matter." Renzo nodded at the picture on the desk that had been turned to face the doorway. It showcased an older woman with blonde hair, and a young man sitting next to her on a bench. "That your wife and son?"

He didn't know.

He was just guessing.

Given the way Bill's hands dropped to the top of the desk, fully in view, Renzo assumed he had hit the nail right on the head with whoever that was in the pictures.

"What do you want?" Bill demanded.

"I told you—information."

"About *what?*"

"Not what, who. The Marcellos. More specifically, Lucian Marcello, or better yet, his daughter, Lucia. I need you to get me information. Where they are, or what they're doing. I need you to find all that shit out, and get it back to me. Preferably without you running off at the mouth about what you're doing for me. Because if you do, I keep this gun loaded, and ready. Do you get me?"

The man just *blinked.*

Like a fucking idiot.

"Do you have a death wish?" Bill asked. "You don't go around *asking* about the Marcello family, Renzo. You certainly don't go around asking about one of the three brothers, or one of their *daughters*. Not if you don't want them asking *why* you're asking."

Renzo smiled again in that cold way of his. "Well, that's the thing, isn't it, Bill? By all appearances, it won't be me asking anything about Lucian, or his daughter. It'll be you. They'll want to know why *you* are asking, and they'll come here for that information. By then, I'll already either have what I want, or be long fucking gone. So, I guess you're left with a couple of options, aren't you?"

The man behind the desk swallowed hard. "And what options are those?"

"Simple. One, you refuse and I kill you right here and now. I will move onto someone else to get the information I want. Or two, you start making some phone calls ... or maybe you call some people in who are stupid enough that they won't give a shit if you ask some questions. You make sure you're careful, so the Marcellos don't know it's you asking about them and their business. Then, you pass the information off to me, and you can go back to yelling at your cooks, and getting paid dirty money to overlook the crates of cocaine they keep stashed in the back room."

Renzo tipped his gun to the side a bit, amused at how Bill's eyes followed the weapon carefully. "See, then if you're careful, you won't have them coming back on you. You can go back to what you were doing before like this never even happened. And I expect you to do that, because if you ever even breathe my name to someone, it won't just be you I come back for, Bill."

He glanced at the picture on the desk to make his point clear before adding, "I mean, it's your choice. If you need a bit to think about it and choose, I apparently have all the time in the world. I don't mind waiting."

"You're asking for trouble, Renzo."

Not really.

This wasn't trouble.

Trouble found him months ago.

Trouble's name is Lucia.

And he loved her to fucking *death*.

• • •

Patience, as Renzo had come to learn over his lifetime, paid off for everyone who was willing to wait long enough to get what they wanted. It took Bill three entire days to come up with some kind of useable information for Renzo, but damn, when that information really came through, it couldn't have been better.

Lucian Marcello apparently did most of his business in a restaurant he owned in upper Manhattan. Of course, Renzo wasn't at all surprised that he'd never even heard of the business's name before considering he probably couldn't afford to fucking eat there, and the one time he'd made a trip into upper Manhattan was to do an exchange with a guy who was hanging out of the back of a high class bar. The alleyway smelled like shit, though.

He never forgot that.

Nonetheless, the information Bill got about Lucian's favorite spot to dine, work, and basically do everything else while he was in the city meant the man spent a hell of a lot of time there. On weekends, his family tended to join him, as well.

It was a fucking long shot.

Renzo had no reason to believe that Lucia might be at the restaurant just because he knew her father was likely to be there. But he also wouldn't ever know if he didn't make his way over, and try to find out. Besides, he wasn't really going there for Lucian. He was going there because he knew one way or the other, Lucia would find out he showed up, and asked about her.

That's all he needed.

For her to *know*.

Renzo was going to pay the pizzeria owner back by literally never stepping foot near the guy's business again. It was his guarantee. After all, hadn't the guy done enough for him? He figured so.

As he came closer to the restaurant in question, Renzo pulled his phone out of his pocket, and checked the time. A little after eleven in the afternoon, which meant, no doubt ... at least Lucian would be at the restaurant. But given it was the weekend, it was also very possible that the man's family might be there, too.

Stuffing the phone back in its spot, he pulled the cigarette from behind his ear, and the lighter out of the breast pocket of his leather jacket. Lighting it up, he took a heavy drag as he came to stand just in front of the business. On one side, he noticed wide windows that showcased regular diners. On the other side of the gold-plated doors was a wall of mirrored glass—also windows, he knew, but he just couldn't see inside.

Parked on the curb, still running, was a black Mercedes. Inside the driver's seat, Renzo found a man chatting on his cell phone, and not paying him any mind, God knew he'd seen enough black cars with inconspicuous drivers dropping shit off to him over the years to know that was a Capo's car.

Or ... a Marcello.

Perfect.

The best way to get someone's attention inside was to get the attention of whoever was watching the outside. Because that was the thing about these people ... someone was always watching their backs. They didn't get to the top alone.

Settling himself with a breath, because it was fucking now or never, he supposed, Renzo stepped up to the running vehicle, and leaned against the back. He didn't do anything but stand there and smoke his cigarette. He didn't even stare at the guy inside the car, or at the business in front of him.

Frankly, the ground seemed more interesting.

It took the guy inside the car all of two seconds to realize someone was touching the car. He got out with a scowl already in place, and looking like he was built to be a linebacker on a football field. That didn't bother Renzo a bit, though. He'd figured out that the bigger someone was, the harder they fell when they came for him.

"Hey, move your fucking ass, *cafone*," the guy barked.

Renzo passed him a dismissive look. "Lucian inside?"

That made the man hesitate in his next step. His following statement was meant as a deflection or even a denial, but his hesitation had been enough to tell Renzo he found someone he was looking for. And yes, Lucian was very likely inside.

"I don't know who the hell you're talking about, man," the guy said.

Renzo nodded, and took another drag from his smoke. "Sure. Anyway, I'm not going anywhere until I see Lucian, or his daughter, if she's here. I'd really prefer *her*, but you know, I'll take either."

It was the dart of the man's gaze to the mirrored windows that confirmed Renzo's hope that Lucia was at the business having an early lunch with her family. So, now it was just a waiting game.

"I can always move your stupid ass," the guy threatened.

"You could, but how are you going to do that when I stick a knife in your throat and let you bleed out on the ground here. You're going to tell me that the Marcellos don't have a bunch of cops on their payroll? Let me guess, you're what, *muscle*? Disposable, then. Instead of having a bunch of cops around here causing them problems, they're just going to clean up whatever mess I make, and throw you in the river to wash up on the other side."

Renzo smirked over at the man. "But go ahead, put your hands on me. I bet it'll be a good lesson for you, asshole."

NINETEEN

Lucia saw Renzo first. Kind of fucking amazing, considering she had spent most of the lunch doing her very best to ignore her father across the table despite all his efforts to engage her in conversation. In doing so, she had kept her gaze on the wall, the floor, or her untouched plate of food.

Tension really was not a good enough word for what it felt like in their home lately, but this had been her entire life for the last week. No car, no phone, and when she went home, even her laptop had been taken from her room. She suddenly went from feeling like an eighteen-year-old almost out on her own, and in control of her life, to a teenager being punished like a child.

She might have noticed Renzo first, but her father wasn't very far behind. Lucian followed Lucia's gaze to where she was staring out the mirrored windows, and let out a noise that sounded like disbelief and anger all rolled into one. Lucia might have smiled if she wasn't *still* so fucking mad at her dad.

No matter how much she tried to explain to him about Renzo, and *her*, he just didn't care to hear it. He'd made up his mind on everything, and nothing she could say was going to change it. Her mother, for the most part, rarely stepped in. But to be fair, Jordyn also didn't really take a side, either.

She was neutral ground, not stepping in between her husband and daughter's feud, but also not making it any worse than it was with her own opinions.

Lucia didn't know whether to be grateful, or not.

"What in the hell is he doing here?" Lucian asked, his voice a rough growl. "And how did he even know we were here to begin with?"

Her father's gaze swung to her, but Lucia sat quietly and unmoved in her chair.

"Well?" he demanded.

Lucia arched a brow. "You think *I* called him to let him know I was going to be here today? I didn't even know I was going to have to come here today, Daddy. You made me come because apparently, I can't just be unhappy with you at home, I have to be unhappy with you out in public, too."

Her father's gaze hardened.

Lucia was still unbothered.

Where was the lie?

"How else would he—"

"I don't even have a cell phone to use, or my computer. You've taken away my car, so it's not like I can drive to tell him, either. Oh, and we don't even have a house phone because everybody has their own cell phone, so I couldn't use that to call him. It wasn't me."

Lucian still didn't look like he believed her, but his desire to argue with her waned quickly enough. That was the thing about her father. He was stubborn as hell when he believed he was right about something, or doing the right thing. Like this whole shitshow with her and Renzo. But at the same time, he wasn't the kind of man who enjoyed discontent or discomfort in his own life and home.

A double-edged sword, really.

He caused this.

"Well, he isn't getting what he wants," her father muttered, throwing down his napkin. "I can promise you that."

"What does that mean?"

"It means get a good look at him because soon, he'll be gone."

"Lucian," Jordyn murmured.

Lucia glanced at her mother, but quickly went back to her father. "You know, I've tried for the last week to get you to understand, Daddy. I've explained over and over again that this is *my life*, and not yours. That I can see whoever I want, whenever I want, and you don't get a say about it. I have let you tell me whatever you want, take away my things, and for the most part, I didn't really fight you on it. But I'm done."

"Excuse me?"

Standing from the table, Lucia caught Renzo's form in the corner of her eye again as she grabbed the light jacket off the back of her chair, and slipped it on. It'd only been a week since she had last been with him, and yet she still felt like she had to look him over for any sign of a change. A week was too long to be away from him. Her heart *hurt*. She didn't know how to explain it any better than that, but every day that passed where she didn't get to see or speak to Renzo only made it worse.

Fuck her father.

Screw what he wanted.

Lucia was not playing nice anymore.

"I'm eighteen," Lucia said, shrugging on her jacket, picked up her purse from the floor, and meeting her father's gaze at the same time. "I can go where I please, and do what I please. I can be with *whoever* I want to be with, too."

She didn't miss the tension tightening her father's shoulders under his suit at those words. She'd said these things to him before, but not with much seriousness. More like she was repeating shit to him that he should have already known.

Lucia wasn't stupid. She knew her father thought he was protecting her, but he didn't need to. And he was entirely wrong about Renzo, but he just didn't care to understand or learn about the man she loved. Lucian was stuck in his feelings because he was terrified that what happened to her older sister, Liliana, might happen to her.

Because Renzo was the unknown.

He was not *their* kind of people.

Renzo was him, and his life didn't have to be like theirs for Lucia to love him, and want to be with him. He didn't have to be like them for her to know he was as good as he was ever going to get, and she wanted him just the way he was.

"While you are under *my* roof," her father said through gritted teeth, "you will follow my rules, Lucia."

She nodded. "Okay, so then I will leave."

In her chair, Jordyn sucked in a sharp breath, but for the most part, kept her gaze on the table. Lucia knew her mom was silently hoping her daughter and husband would work this out on their own. That soon, this nonsense would pass, and they could go back to the family they had been before Renzo rushed into Lucia's life like a tidal wave coming in from the ocean.

His wave picked her up, dragged her out to sea, and hell, she might be drowning, but at least she was going to go with him. That's all she wanted.

She didn't need them to understand or like it.

It was still going to happen.

"You're going to move out?" Lucian asked, smirking a bit. "Really?"

"I don't see why not," Lucia replied, shrugging as she pushed in her chair at the table. "Wasn't I already leaving for California, anyway? Were you going to follow me there to keep an eye on me, too, or ...?"

"Lucia, be kind," her mother said softly. "He's your father, and—"

"Then maybe he should act like it, Ma!"

God.

She hadn't meant to yell, and certainly not at her mother. Of all the people Lucia was angry with lately, her mother was most certainly *not* one of them.

"Sorry," she quickly whispered.

Jordyn glanced up, and offered her daughter a small smile. "It's okay, I know you're—"

"A spoiled girl *acting* like a spoiled girl," her father interjected gruffly. "Sit down, Lucia. You're not going anywhere, and you're certainly not going out *there*. I don't care if I have to have someone come in here to watch you, and make sure you don't move an inch. You will not be going out there to see that young man."

Really?

"Fuck you," Lucia uttered, turning for the door.

She said it. She was eighteen.

He couldn't keep her here.

"Lucia!" her father shouted.

She heard his footsteps coming behind her, but she didn't care. Spinning around on her heel to see he was only a few feet away from her, Lucia pointed at her father, and then back at herself. Right over the spot where her heart was beating out of control and in so much pain with each squeeze because maybe … Jesus, maybe if she told him how she felt inside because Renzo was too far away, and had been for this whole week, then her father might understand this wasn't something she *wanted* to do.

It was more than that.

She needed to do it.

She needed Renzo.

"Right here," she murmured, pushing the tip of her finger against her chest, "it's killing me right here, Daddy. It hurts all the time because this is not where I want to be, don't you get that? I'm sorry if you don't like that, or this scares you, but I can't keep hurting in here because I'm not with him. I want to be with him."

Lucian hesitated in his next step.

Lucia didn't move an inch.

Behind her father, Jordyn stood from the table. Her mother's gaze drifted from her daughter near the doorway, and Renzo still standing outside where he looked as though he was chatting with the enforcer whose car he was currently leaning against like he didn't have a care in the world.

"Lucian," Jordyn said softly.

"What?"

"Let her go."

Lucian's head swung around, and his gaze widened. "What did you just say?"

"I said let her go."

"How can I—"

"Because she has to make her own choices, and if those mean mistakes, then that's what it means. They are hers to make, not yours or ours. I thought we learned that, didn't we? We decided that years ago that they wouldn't be influenced or controlled by this life, and us. *We decided that, Lucian.*"

"*Bella—*"

"Lucia, you may go with the young man, if that's what you want to do," her mother whispered. "We won't stop you, and we won't step in, either. I promise."

Lucia hesitated.

She went between her father, and her mother. Both were people she loved—entirely, though sometimes, like now, her father made her wonder why. Both were pillars of strength and support, or they had been for her entire life. She didn't want to disappoint them, but this wasn't about them, either.

Jordyn tipped her head toward the door. "Go, Lucia."

"Jordyn—"

Lucia had already turned to leave when her father spoke again. She didn't stop this time around. She had nothing left to say to him. Not now. She only had one thing she really wanted to do, and that was to get as close as she possibly could to the man waiting for her outside. Each step she took that brought her nearer to him, the better her heart felt.

Lighter.

Happier.

Free.

"You will let her go because I said so," she heard her mother say. "Now, let her go."

Her parents' voices faded at her back as she headed out into the main section of the restaurant. She burst out of the entrance doors without a look back over her shoulder because for the moment, there was nothing back there that she wanted. Everything she needed was right in front of her leaning against a black Mercedes, wearing a familiar leather jacket, and grinning her way like he just *knew.*

Renzo always did look his very best when he was staring at her.

Black on black on black.

The enforcer on the sidewalk was still saying something to him, but Renzo wasn't even paying the guy any attention. He clearly had something much better to stare at, now.

Her.

Lucia came closer. "Figured you'd be around."

She hadn't. She didn't know what Renzo was doing at all this last week. She'd just been hoping ...

Wasn't that what love was at the end of the day?

Hope.

"Did you?" he asked.

One of his hands had already outstretched to reach for hers. As soon as she was close enough to him to grab it, she did just that. Renzo wasted no time in yanking her as close to him as he could possibly get her. The first kiss landed on her hairline, and the second, on her forehead.

She couldn't get him close enough.

Couldn't hug him tight enough.

God, she missed him.

"You're crazy, you know," she mumbled against his chest. "Showing up like this *here*."

She had watched bigger men with more important last names be punished for a hell of a lot less than what he did here today. She honestly believed her father when he said the one and only reason he had yet to physically act against Renzo in a way that would permanently keep him away from Lucia was only because of her, and nothing else. Because her father loved her, and maybe ... there was a part of him that knew she loved Renzo, too.

Maybe.

His chuckles rocked them both, but goddamn, she loved that sound. Loved the way it surrounded her like a melody she couldn't forget. Loved the way it filled her senses with something sinful and wicked.

Was that what they were?

Sinful?

Wicked?

She could figure that out later.

Renzo pressed a quick kiss to her lips when Lucia tipped her head back to stare up at him. "We should get out of here, yeah?"

Lucia glanced back at the restaurant. "Like *now*."

"Got it."

• • •

They walked three blocks before Lucia realized something.

No one was following them.

She kept looking back, expecting to see an enforcer trailing them on the sidewalk, but no. There wasn't anyone coming for them. She thought, maybe she might see a familiar black car circling the block once or twice, but again, there was nothing.

Her mother hadn't lied.

"What are you doing?"

Lucia glanced up at Renzo, and felt his fingers tighten around hers. "I was just ... nothing. It's nothing."

He flashed his teeth in a sexy smile. "You sure?"

"Yeah, Ren."

And wasn't that just great?

She thought so.

"This way," he said suddenly.

Without warning, Renzo pulled Lucia into an alleyway between two businesses. She had thought they were just going to walk until one of them got tired, and decided to either hail a cab, or catch a bus. Renzo apparently had different plans. At the end of the alley sat a familiar bright red, vintage Mustang.

Lucia laughed. "Borrowed it again, did you?"

He shrugged as they neared the waiting car. "I was not taking a bus all the way here, I missed the subway and didn't want to wait, and I wasn't paying for a cab when this was right around the corner. And yeah, we can go with borrow. Sure, why not?"

"Ren!" She smacked the back of his shoulder with her palm. "You didn't take it, did you?"

"Is take the new word for *steal*, or ...?"

"*Renzo!*"

He didn't give her a chance to blink before he turned quick, and caught her around the waist with his arms. The force of his kiss sent her stumbling back until her back came in contact with the hard brick. Demanding, rough, and harsh, his kiss felt like the best kind of sin as his tongue warred with hers. All she could do was fist his jacket, and drag him impossibly closer. Those hands of his hand up to wrap into the waves of her hair, and tug just enough to make her scalp sting.

Shit.

She loved that.

He only broke their kiss when her lungs were burning for air, and her lips were numb. The slight tingling left on her skin from his facial hair made her wish he had been between her thighs instead.

Renzo's thumb came up to press against the seam of her lips as his other hand curved softly around her throat. He'd never squeeze ... at least, not like *this*. Only when she asked for it, and only because she wanted it, Lucia knew.

"Don't worry about the fucking car," he murmured, his gaze drifting over her features with such intensity that she swore her heart skipped a beat. Yeah, damn. She'd missed him something terrible. "I will drop it off where the guy keeps it tucked away in a warehouse tonight, and he will never even know it was taken out. The speedometer is broken, anyway. It can't record miles driven. He takes it out *maybe* twice a year for car shows. It's a fucking *waste*."

Lucia blinked. "You're terrible."

"I fucking missed you."

Her throat went dry.

Her stomach clenched.

The best ache started between her thighs.

"How's that back seat?" she asked.

195

God knew they had better things to do.

Other things to worry about.

But fuck it. She was eighteen, and eighteen meant she didn't have to always be smart and do the right thing. Sometimes, it meant having fun, and taking risks. It meant being *risky*, and oh, so reckless. Eighteen was the time to do all of that, and there was no one else she would rather do it with than the man looking at her.

"Still big enough for the both of us," he said.

"So why are we still out here and not in *there?*"

"Good point."

His laughter echoed all around before he tugged her toward the car, and Lucia happily followed. It felt like a blink, and she found herself in the back seat of the Mustang with Renzo hovering above her. He took no time at all to strip her of her clothes, and he of his, too. They made a pile on the floor, forgotten and unwanted. God knew she didn't want *anything* between them.

Not ever.

His hands skimmed down her body, slow and burning. It made her shiver, but the way he watched her ... intense with hooded eyes that couldn't seem to drink all of her in fast enough, it was addicting.

She wondered ...

Would he always look at her like that?

Always want to?

His hands dipped lower, finding her hips as his fingertips dug in deep. She widened her thighs for him, inviting him closer. Renzo didn't move an inch, he just kept holding and fucking staring.

Driving her insane.

"Please," she whispered, "I want—"

"I want to look at you. I just ... want to always be able to look at you, Lucia."

Lucia blinked, stunned. "You always can."

She'd make sure of it.

He kissed her, then. Hungry, and desperate. His soft touches turned demanding and greedy in a flash, heating her up and telling her that he was done *looking*. He wanted to *feel*.

It never failed to amaze Lucia at how it felt to have this man between her thighs, and on top of her. The weight of him was substantial as he pushed her roughly into the back seat, but she couldn't get enough. It only felt better when his hand locked around her throat as he pushed her thighs opened wider until she felt that telltale ache in her muscles.

The word *frantic* came to mind.

The way he grabbed at her. How she pulled back, locking him in with her legs tight around his back as he slid his cock along the seam of her pussy. His hand slipped under her ass as he thrust inside. All she could do was suck in air, and lose her mind in the way it felt when he first filled her full.

"Fuck, yeah."

His words echoed all around.

Like a catacomb.

She reached up to stroke her fingers over his stubble-covered jaw, but he caught the tips between his fingers, and bit down. Pulling out of her, he slammed right back in again, making Lucia whine.

That ache was back.

Her need grew heavier.

"Harder," she breathed.

Renzo grinned around her fingers, and then sucked them into his mouth as he fucked her the way she wanted. Pinned down, a hand on her throat, and his cock pounding into her at an unrelenting pace. All she had to give herself some sense of stability was her hand against his back, but all she could do was drag her fingernails down over his skin as hot pleasure licked through her nerves.

"Are you going to give me what I want, then? Come for me like I want, Lucia?"

"*Yes.*"

Her whine felt too high.

Too airless.

Too out of control.

Yeah, even one week without him was way too long.

She'd never let it happen again.

Ever.

• • •

"Renzo, hey," a familiar face said as the two of them walked past the usual loiterers on the stairs of Renzo's apartment building. "And princess Lucia. Been a minute since you were around, huh?"

Lucia gave the guy a look, and pointed a finger at him. "I'm watching you."

"Someone better," the girl beside him joked.

Laughter followed them inside the apartment building. Renzo was quick to pull a keyring full of jingling keys out of his pocket, before he handed them over to her. He pointed to one key in particular on the ring, saying, "My apartment key, go on up. I have to grab Diego. He's downstairs with a babysitter."

She smiled. "Okay."

"Fair warning—the kid misses you a lot. He might not leave you alone for a couple of hours."

Lucia only shrugged. "So?"

Renzo's chuckles filled the hall. "You say that *now*."

He dropped a quick kiss to her mouth, and didn't miss the chance to pat her on the ass as she headed up the stairs, too. Lucia tossed him a wink over her shoulder just before she caught sight of him disappearing into the bottom level hallway. It took her no time at all to climb the stairs, and come to the right floor for Renzo's place. Throwing the door open to enter the hallway. Lucia immediately wished she would have waited and just come up with Renzo instead.

There, down the hall, was a familiar woman. Sure, Lucia didn't know Carmen Zulla on a personal level, but the things she did know about the woman were enough to say she also didn't want to know her in any kind of way.

Renzo's mother didn't notice Lucia. She was too fucking busy beating her fists against the apartment door. She looked like a mess—hair matted, and greasy. What bit of makeup she had been wearing—some lipstick, and maybe kohl around her eyes—was smudged, and ruined. The clothes she had on looked like they hadn't been washed in a week, or *more*.

Lucia wasn't the type to judge. She had a feeling this woman had some kind of trauma in her history that led her down this path of substance abuse, and addiction. No one just woke up one day and decided they wanted to be an alcoholic or a drug addict. It didn't work that way.

This was a disease.

No one chose it.

But that didn't mean Lucia could feel sympathy for this woman, now. Not after the things she knew, and shit she had seen since being around Renzo. Carmen might not have chosen her path, but she did choose to hurt her children. She chose to neglect, abuse, and disregard their wants and needs for her own selfishness.

Lucia didn't feel anything but anger about that.

When Carmen didn't get the response she wanted by banging on the door with her fists, she let out an angry sob, reared back, and *kicked* the door instead. Lucia made a sound in the back of her throat—half surprised, half confused. That was what finally caught Carmen's attention that she was no longer alone in the hallway.

It took the woman a second.

Then, two.

She blinked, staring at Lucia like she might recognize her, but was trying to place where she knew her from. Then, all at once, Carmen seemed like she figured it out as her gaze dropped to the keys in Lucia's hand, and then back up to Lucia's face.

"*You*," the woman hissed. Well, a garbled hiss might have been a more accurate description. Just how high was Carmen right then? Her pupils were pin-thin as she came closer to Lucia with careful, yet still stumbling steps. "You're the little bitch he's fucking, right?"

"I—"

"Renzo, *my* son," Carmen continued. "What, he'll give you the keys for his apartment, but he won't even let his own mother have a place to sleep, too? He's a bastard, like he's always been. Would rather keep a little rich bitch happy than take care of his own mother. Did you know that, girl? He just throws me out on the street like *trash*. But what does he do for you, huh? *What does he do for you?*"

That need to defend and protect Renzo swelled swift and harsh inside of Lucia's heart. How dare this woman insult him after everything he clearly did for her?

"He doesn't need to take care of you," Lucia spat at her, "that's not how it works. Parents take care of their *kids*, not the other way around. But I wouldn't expect someone like you to understand that. You've never taken care of him, have you? He's done your job for his whole fucking life."

In retrospect, it might not have been the smartest idea to provoke a woman who was clearly high, in a rage, and probably felt like she was backed into a corner, even if she wasn't.

Too little, too late.

Carmen struck out with a closed fist, and a screech that could burst eardrums. That first punch felt like hitting a brick wall. Lucia dropped the keys, and fought back.

The bitch wasn't getting a second hit in.

That was for certain.

TWENTY

"Lucia's really here?"

Renzo had to laugh at how excited Diego was as he asked the question. So excited, in fact, that the kid missed an entire step on his way up the stairs. He barely managed to grab hold of the back of Diego's shirt to right him to his feet so that he didn't smash his damn face off the stairs. The last thing he wanted to do today was make a trip to the closest hospital to get Diego's face stitched up.

"Yeah, buddy, she's upstairs right now. Can't wait to see you."

"Yes!"

Of course, the kid picked up his pace again. Renzo had to practically jog to keep up with his little brother. It was only when they came to the second-floor landing that he heard the noise upstairs. It wasn't uncommon for a fight to break out in the apartment building, but especially not around here. It was all too common, really. Usually, Renzo just ignored it, or if he had to pass it to get to his place, he kept his gaze forward, and didn't try to step in.

It was just easier that way.

An unspoken agreement between the tenants, really.

But that yelling coming from one floor higher was not just *any* fucking tenant. He recognized the feminine shouts echoing down the stairwell.

Jesus Christ.

No.

By the looks of Diego's horrified expression, the kid knew who was fighting one floor up, too. *Shit.* This was not what was supposed to happen today. This should have been a good fucking day.

Renzo swore the world just liked pulling jokes on him. Like it allowed him to think everything was going his way for once, only to come back around and boot him right in the ass with a bitter laugh. Something was always keeping him down.

Darting past his terrified brother in the stairwell, Renzo took the last flight of stairs three at a time to get to his hallway. He threw the door open in just enough time to watch his strung-out mother grab a fistful of Lucia's hair, and throw her against the wall. To Lucia's benefit, it looked like she had given it back to Carmen just as much as the woman had given it to her considering his mother's bloody nose, and busted mouth.

Lucia didn't really have a mark on her.

Yet.

Renzo wasn't going to let her get hurt, either.

That was the thing about Carmen, though. When her sobbing antics no longer worked, and she was beyond the point of no return, the woman quickly turned to violence to solve her problems. Like she thought it would work to just smack someone around to get what she wanted. God knew she had done that to him more than enough over the years. Renzo had never fought back when he was younger because shit, it was his *mom*. And then once, she turned on Rose ... he thought he broke his mother's arm dragging her away from his sister.

She never went after Rose again, though.

Never dared to lift a finger at Diego, either.

Carmen was also a hell of a lot more hesitant to go after Renzo, too. He took all of that as a win, and whenever his mother did go into one of her rages, he didn't mind putting her in her place when he had to in order to keep her from hurting him, his siblings, or even herself. Not that she deserved his protection from doing harm to herself.

Hadn't she been doing that for her whole life every single time she smoked something, or shot more poison into her veins?

"Fucking little bitch!" Carmen screeched.

Yeah, that was enough of that.

His mother didn't even see him coming until he was right behind her. It was too little, too late, then. Renzo bear-hugged his mother, it was the safest way to keep her arms tucked down at her sides, and not able to harm someone should she be able to reach them. Yanking her back away from Lucia, he swung hard, and released Carmen at the same time. She stumbled a good five feet down the hallway, but he was more concerned about Lucia.

Fucking nobody was going to put their hands on her.

No one would ever hurt her.

"You okay?" he asked.

Lucia straightened against the wall, and wiped the edge of her mouth with the back of her hand. "Yeah, Ren, I'm okay."

His gaze darted to the doorway of the hallway where Diego had come to peek through the crack. Fucking thing—it had never shut properly. It was supposed to always be shut for fire safety, or some shit like that, but it was jammed open. Diego's wide, tearful eyes darted from Renzo, to the spot behind him.

He barely heard Carmen's insult before his mother's hand struck him in the side of his face. The surprise slap shocked him for a second—it made his vision blurry, and his ears rang with noise. It took him entirely too long to shake the dizziness away, but when he did, he was already going for his mother again.

He got ahold of Carmen just as she struck out at Lucia. The edge of her fingernails caught Lucia along her throat, leaving behind red scores that looked painful, and *fuck* …

His rage blew out of control, then.

Maybe it was the bit of blood on Lucia's throat.

Maybe it was her cry of pain.

It could have been a lot of things, but really, all Renzo saw in those moments was the color red. Tunneling into his vision and taking over his mind. *Red everywhere.* Like it was infecting him, and coloring through his whole body. He didn't hear his brother, or Lucia. He barely even saw them in the corner of his eye as he turned on Carmen, ready to hurt her just for fucking existing.

Because how dare she touch Lucia.

How dare she.

Renzo caught his mother around her throat, and slammed her into the wall. The bang echoed in the quiet hallway. He didn't even give his mother the chance to speak before he was squeezing her throat tight in his palm, and leaning in close so that all the bitch could see was him coming for her.

"Don't you *ever* put your fucking dirty hands on her again," he uttered.

Carmen's wild eyes met his.

She was gone, he knew.

So fucking high.

Out. Of. It.

She barely heard him at all, but the little bit she did hear made her breaths pick up like she was huffing oxygen, and just couldn't get enough. Holy hell, what was she on? She wasn't usually this strong, but she did her best to fight against his hold, dragging her nails over his arms keeping her locked against the wall, and baring her teeth at him like that was something to scare him.

Really, it just made him mad.

And so fucking *sad*, too.

"Let me go," his mother croaked.

No, not yet.

Renzo had a few things to say to her. He wanted this shit to be *very* clear so that there was never a *next time* when she came back around. Even better if this was clear enough that she never showed her fucking sorry ass here again. It wasn't like they needed her. She didn't do anything for them.

Never had.

"You ever touch her again," Renzo murmured, coming close to his mother's face again, "and I will make sure you never take another breath, Carmen. Don't fucking look at her. Don't *think* about her. If you come around here again, I will make you wish for death because it will be easier than what I will do to you. Do you understand me?"

Carmen clenched her teeth, and then without warning, spat at him. Renzo didn't even blink when the saliva hit his face. Oh, he wanted to wipe it off. More than *anything* in the world, he wanted to get her spit off his face, but he didn't move. He just kept his hand around her throat, and had to force himself not to squeeze until the bitch was blue, and on the ground dead.

"Should have aborted you when I had the chance," she hissed at him.

Renzo laughed.

Was that supposed to hurt?

It didn't.

"You've been telling me that for my whole life. Give me something else, Ma."

Maybe he shouldn't have said that. Maybe he shouldn't have encouraged her, or provoked her. Clearly, his mother wasn't in a good place, all things considered.

Carmen's gaze darted to the side—to the doorway.

At *Diego.*

"You love him so much, don't you?" she said, almost tauntingly. "More than me. More than *her.* More than the world, Ren. You always have. You give him everything, and you have *nothing.* What if I took him away, huh? What would you do then?"

He didn't have a reason to fear what his mother said. How was this mess of a woman—this addict, abuser, *bitch*—ever going to take Diego from him? Legally, she really couldn't unless she got clean, sober, and took care of her life and business. That was never going to happen.

Still, even though her threat felt entirely empty, he couldn't help but react to his greatest fear being thrown in his face. It wrapped around his heart like a fist clenching tight. It felt like ice water being dumped into his veins.

Someone could take Diego away from him.

And what would he be able to do?

"You could try," Renzo forced himself to say, "but no one will take him from me, ever."

Carmen smiled—bitter, cold, and rotten. Most of her teeth were gone now, and her mouth was a disgusting mixture of black and red and *yellow.* "But I could, Ren. I've got your hands on my throat. I know what you do for a living. I know where you keep your gun. I know all the things to say to make them take him from you, and give him to someone else. *I'll do it.*"

She wasn't wrong, he realized.

How much would it take for someone looking into Renzo to realize he wasn't on the up and up? If Child Protective Services came for him, he'd be fucked. Not because Diego wasn't loved and cared for. Not because he went without—he never did, not with Renzo. But simply because Renzo's life wasn't really better than his mother's at the end of the day.

No high school education.

No job on record.

A drug dealer.

Shitty apartment.

One thing after the other …

It would pile right up.

"Yeah, you know," Carmen said, all too gleeful.

In reaction to his mother, and very little else, Renzo's grip around her throat tightened so that the bitch couldn't speak anymore. He didn't want to hear her tell him the truth. That he wasn't good enough. That no matter what, he would never be good enough for Diego in the eyes of others.

That to them, he would be *just like her*.

"Hey, hey!"

Clapping hands and the shouts brought Renzo out of his daze. He was two fucking seconds away from snapping Carmen's neck right then and there with Lucia, Diego, and fucking God to watch him do it. But the sound of his landlord shouting at him was enough to hold him back for a second.

"Let her go, Renzo!"

He did, and Carmen took that chance to dart away from her son while still holding onto her throat all the while. She stumbled down the hallway, thankfully, in the opposite direction of where Diego was now clinging to Lucia's legs against the wall. Had she gone anywhere near his little brother in those moments, he wouldn't have been able to control himself.

Renzo turned to the landlord, ready to apologize. The man didn't look like he wanted any of it, and his next words only confirmed that thought.

"I have had enough of this shit! All the disturbances, and complaints," the man spat, shaking his beefy head. "She shows up here, makes a mess, and I tried to overlook it. I *tried*, Ren. I know you're fucking young, and doing the best you can, but I just can't be having this anymore. You're to be out of here by the end of the month. Do you get me? *The end of the month!*"

Renzo felt numb.

Like he was watching himself from up above.

Dead inside.

The landlord shook his head one more time, gave a pitying look in the direction of Lucia and Diego, and then he disappeared into the stairwell once more. Renzo turned to tell his mother to fuck off somewhere—in a hole, preferably—but the bitch was already gone, too. She left through the other door at the end of the hallway.

"Ren," Lucia started to say.

He held up a hand, hoping it would be enough to quiet her for a second. He just needed to think. Plan. *Something.* "Just ... don't right now, please."

"It'll be okay. We'll figure something out for the apartment, and—"

He let out a hard, bitter laugh. "That's not going to help. That won't stop her."

"What?"

Lucia didn't get it.

Renzo didn't blame her.

"Carmen," he said harshly, turning to snatch the keys to his place that had been forgotten on the floor. He made quick work of unlocking the apartment, and slipping inside. Lucia followed him with her hand tight around Diego's who was still oh, so quiet and scared. "That bitch ... she's fucking vindictive, Lucia. If she thinks she can hurt me, she will do it."

And right then, Carmen promised to hurt him through Diego. He didn't have any reason to think his mother wouldn't follow through on her threat. That's just what she did. So fuck it, he wasn't going to give her the chance to hurt him by using Diego at all. Oh, sure, the bitch could try, but she was going to have to *find him* first.

That wouldn't be as easy as she thought it would be.

Lucia made a quiet sound behind him, but Renzo was too busy opening up the small hallway closet. He yanked out two bags—one for him, and one for Diego. Both black duffels would fit just enough shit to do them for a while, but not much more. It was also all he could carry for the moment.

"She's not going to do anything. She's *high*," Lucia whispered, coming closer. "I'm sure she says a lot of things when she's high, Ren."

Wrong.

Well, partly.

"She says a lot of things, sure, but when she's in that kind of mood, everything she says holds weight, Lucia."

"Wait, what are you doing?" she asked, following him down the hallway where he slipped into Diego's bedroom. "What are you doing with those bags?"

"Packing shit he needs. Me, too."

Lucia said nothing for a long while as Renzo filled one bag full with Diego's clothes. His little brother edged into the room, but hung out near the doorway as he watched Renzo work.

"Ren?" Diego asked softly.

Too soft, really.

He dragged in a ragged breath, and turned around to face his brother. Dropping to his knees, he put his arms out for Diego to come closer. He did, thankfully.

"They won't take me, right?" Diego asked.

Renzo shook his head. "Nope. And we're gonna go on a trip, okay? Take a drive, and see what we can find. How does that sound, buddy?"

Diego smiled, but it didn't reach his eyes. "Sounds fun. Don't forget my dino, okay?"

Yeah, his one stuffy he always needed to take with him. Still sitting on his bed where he'd tucked it in that morning before leaving with Renzo.

"I won't forget your dino," Ren promised. "So hey, do you remember what I showed you last week—the vent?"

Diego nodded. "You took the money from the freezer and your bag, and put it in the vent."

As a *just in case*, he showed Diego where he decided to hide his bit of cash. He figured he should move it because he had more than what he thought was safe to hide in the freezer, and he expected his crazy mother to show up again like she always did. Carmen wouldn't have thought twice about taking his money. Not if it meant she could get more drugs.

"Remember how to open it up?"

"Yes."

"Good, you go get it for me."

Diego turned before darting out of the room, and Renzo took a moment to regain his bearings. Standing, he grabbed the stuffed dino from his brother's bed, and shoved it into the bag, too. He grabbed the full duffle, and the empty one before heading out of the bedroom and down the hall to the bathroom.

Where he kept all his shit.

It wasn't much.

A few pants.

Shirts.

Nothing important, though.

Everything else, he kept on him.

"Renzo, you can't go—"

Lucia's quiet voice reminded him that she was still there. He could hear her hesitance, the *worry*. He didn't want her to sound like that at all, but here they were.

Spinning around to face her in the dimly lit hallway, he said, "I can't go? I absolutely can and will go. There is one thing in this life that is mine, and that is *him*. He is my life. What, you want me to sit around and wait for her to report me to CPS? For them to just come around *someday* and take him from me? You think she won't, and you are wrong. I have only gotten by this long taking care of him because I have kept moving. I have kept her away, so people didn't know what it was like for us. Not that it would matter—nobody ever looks too long at people like us, anyway, right? But when they do, they just hurt us."

PRIVILEGE

Renzo shook his head, saying, "Who is going to take him if someone comes here and removes him from my custody? His sister? Rose is *seventeen*, and still in school. We don't have any other family that would be willing to take him. An uncle in San Francisco, but he doesn't want anything to do with his sister's mess, or her shit. Meaning *us*. Where does that leave Diego, Lucia?"

She opened her mouth to speak, but he beat her to the punch.

"To the system," he spat. "That's where he will go. And I will never get him back."

"Ren—"

"*This* is my life, Lucia. It's not a nice place to live, but here we are. So please don't fucking tell me what I can and can't do to protect my brother. Okay? Just don't."

He turned around, and headed for the bathroom to grab his shit.

Lucia's voice followed behind him, never once fading as she kept in step with him. "I was going to say that you can't go without me, actually."

Renzo almost missed a step as he came to the bathroom doorway. "What?"

"You can't go without me, Ren. You're wrong—you have two things. I'm yours, too, remember? You can't go without me."

There was panic in her voice.

High, and unmistakable.

It cut him deep. Like a knife right to his heart.

He didn't turn around, but she came up behind him anyway. Those small, soft hands of hers pressing against his back was a momentary relief from the hell his life had just turned into.

"You should go home," he murmured, "back to your family. They're right, you know? I'm not good for you, Lucia. This isn't good for you. This isn't your life."

"Ren—"

He spun around, so he could stare her right in the face, and maybe then, she might hear him when he told her the hard facts about him and her. "*This isn't your life.*"

"But you are," she whispered, coming close and grabbing hold of his jacket with both hands like she was terrified that if she let go, he might disappear. "You're my life. You know what I realized today? I got up this morning, and I was looking at my calendar. It took thirty-six fucking days for my entire life to change. Do you know that? It's been thirty-six days since I met you, and nothing is ever going to be the same, Ren. You did that. And now you want to tell me that I have to do all this *alone*? I'm not me without you, and all it took was thirty-six days."

"Lucia—"

"You can't go without me. You go, I go."

"Listen to me—"

"*You go, I go, Ren.*"

He dragged in a breath.

Sharp, and painful.

It'd be worse without her, though.

He knew that.

Breathing was so much harder without her.

And fuck, he was selfish, too.

He should have made her stay.

"Together, then?" he asked.

Lucia smiled that smile—through her panic and her fear and all of it. She smiled, and her fists clenched his jacket tighter than ever. Like he needed the reminder she was right there, and not going anywhere.

"Ride or die, Ren."

Yeah.

Him and her.

Until the end …

Ride or fuckin' die.

TWENTY-ONE

"What's he doing?" Renzo asked.

Lucia didn't even have to ask who Renzo meant. He'd been asking that same question every half hour or so. Like he needed to keep checking on his little brother, even though she knew good and well Diego was still sleeping in the back seat, because the boy might up and disappear otherwise.

Glancing over her shoulder, Lucia found Diego in the same position he had been the last time Renzo asked. Facing the rear seat, his back turned to them, covered by his favorite blanket, and still hugging his stuffed dino close. He was out, and he wasn't bothered at all by what was happening.

"Still sleeping," Lucia said, righting herself in the seat.

Renzo nodded, and let out a small sigh. "Good."

"Hey."

For the first time since they got on the highway, Renzo glanced sideways at her. He'd been so focused on driving, and putting as many miles between them and the place they'd come from as he could. She didn't fault him for that, or his lack of attention. She did wish she could make it a little better for him, though.

"It's going to be okay," she whispered.

A slow smiled curved the edges of Renzo's lips. "That's debatable."

"Ren."

"But it's going to be a hell of a lot better with you, Lucia."

She smiled widely.

That was the man she wanted to see.

Reaching across their seats, she caught the edge of his jaw in her palm, and stroked the hard line with the pad of her thumb. His rough facial hair tickled her skin, and his gaze caught hers again. She wanted to believe—at first—that Renzo was just overreacting about his mother's threats. That *surely*, Carmen would not be so vindictive as to try and get Diego taken away from the one person who clearly loved him more than life itself.

And then she thought about all the other things she knew Carmen had already done to her children. What would something like this be compared to all of that?

A drop in an already full bucket, Lucia imagined.

She'd wanted to hope he was panicking.

She knew inside that he wasn't.

Lucia peered back at Diego again who was still comfortably sleeping like his whole world wasn't burning down around him. And hell, maybe it wasn't for the kid. He still had his brother, after all. That's all Diego ever seemed to want.

"Do you have an idea about where we're going?" Lucia asked.

Renzo shrugged. "Maybe."

It was something in the lilt of his tone that had her attention going back to him again. In the darkening light of the day, and with the little glow the dashboard provided for them to see, Renzo finally seemed back to his old self again. Calm, unbothered, and *hers*. All things she loved.

"What?" she asked.

"Nothing."

"It's something."

Renzo nodded ahead, and Lucia glanced out the windshield to see what he was staring at. A sign coming up, it seemed. It read the miles left before they crossed over into a new state. Away from New York, her life, and family. It was the first time since she had gotten in the car that she thought about them at all.

How long would it take them to figure out she was gone?

What would they do, then?

Still, even as those questions danced through her mind, they were quick to leave before they could linger too long and bother her. She was where she wanted to be with *who* she wanted to be with. That's all that mattered to her.

Was it selfish?

Crazy?

Not like her?

All those things and more.

It still didn't change the fact that she was exactly where she wanted to be, doing what she wanted to do, and *with* Renzo. That outweighed any reservations she might have had. That stopped her from thinking about all the rest.

"Last chance to back out," he murmured.

Lucia gave him a look from the side. "Back out from what?"

Renzo wouldn't look at her. "This, I guess. I can drop you off at the store coming up, if you want. You can call someone—your father. I'm sure he'd come pick you up, no questions asked. I'd understand, Lucia. This isn't exactly what you signed up for with me."

"I didn't sign up for anything with you."

That was the truth.

More than either of them knew.

Lucia never expected to meet this man beside her. And when they did cross paths, she never even considered that their time together would lead to her first love, or that he would change her perception of the world—that he would change her whole world—without meaning to, or even wanting to.

She meant what she said earlier.

Where he went, she went.

She was not her without him.

"I'm not going anywhere, Ren."

He gave a little nod, and then put his attention back on the road. His hand snaked over the middle to grab hold of hers and hold tight, though. There was something that felt desperate in the way his fingers tightened around hers, and held strong like he wasn't going to let go. Maybe that desperation was her, too.

She needed to feel it.

"You should stop at the store, though," Lucia said. "I need to grab something."

"Whatever you want, baby."

It didn't take long for the store that had been advertised on a billboard a few miles back was in their sights. Renzo pulled into the busy parking lot, and parked along a gas pump. Lucia stepped out of the car, but gave a look into the back at a still-sleeping Diego.

"Want me to grab some food while I'm in there? He's going to be hungry when he wakes up."

Renzo laughed as he reached for the nozzle. "He'll eat anything as long as it doesn't have lettuce on it."

"Got it."

Lucia headed for the convenience store, ignoring the looks that were passed her way as she crossed the lot. She suspected the people were more interested in the car than her. That probably wasn't a good thing—exactly how many vintage red Mustangs were there in New York, or even across America?

Not that many, she bet.

Inside the store, Lucia made quick work of grabbing a whole armful of food and junk from the shelves and fridges. Water, juice, chips, prepackaged sandwiches, wrapped cheese, and a chocolate milk for Diego. At the front, the man behind the counter didn't even really look at her while she paid for the stuff. He was too busy watching a recap of the latest game on the television next to the register. He only asked her a question when he asked her if she wanted to pay for the gas at the pump for Renzo, or if he was going to come in and pay himself. Lucia paid for her shit and the gas using a debit card that was attached to her accounts and trust fund, and it took her all of three seconds to realize her mistake but it was already too late.

It could be tracked.

The second she put it in and entered the pin, her location was known.

"Excuse me," the woman behind her said politely, trying to get her to move so that she could ring her stuff in as well.

Shit.

"Sorry," Lucia muttered, grabbing the bags from the counter.

Turning to leave, her gaze caught something in the corner of the store that she had overlooked before. Maybe it was a stupid idea that came to her mind, but she figured at this point, her card had already been dinged here … she might as well milk it for all it was worth. Stepping up to the ATM, she stuck her card inside, and punched in her pin.

Ever since her father had taken her car away, Lucian had put her on a budget with her card. Sure, she could go into the bank and pull out as much cash from her accounts that she wanted to. But since her cards were still attached to her parents' accounts in a third-party bank, her father could control just how much money she could take off her cards.

Not that a five-thousand-dollar spending limit was anything to scoff at, really.

Lucia punched in the max limit she could take, according to the machine which was two thousand, and prayed the machine had enough cash inside to accept it. Usually, ATMs only had a couple thousand dollars inside at a time. She almost fucking choked when the machine beeped, confirmation came up on the screen, and a second later, money came out the bottom in the amount she requested.

Hoping no one noticed her pull that much cash from the machine, she stuffed the large wad of bills into the plastic bags at her feet, grabbed them up, and headed the hell out of that store. Renzo was just coming around the side of the car to head for the store when Lucia met him there.

"I paid for the gas, and my stuff, and—"

"Whoa, slow down," he murmured, his hands coming up to find her face with a soft touch. "Did you grab money from the car?"

She shook her head.

Renzo stilled. "You used a card?"

"Yeah."

"*Lucia.*"

"I know, I know. But *look.*"

Renzo glanced down at the bags she was holding, and then his gaze widened when she opened them up to show the money inside. Add that two thousand onto the bit of money he had taken from the apartment, and they might be okay for a little while.

"We gotta get rid of the card," he said.

"Okay."

"What else do you have on you?"

"Other cards. My cell."

"It's all going, too."

Fine by her.

Renzo sighed, and glanced back at the car.

"What?" she asked.

"It needs to go, too. The car, I mean. There's cameras all around here. How much do you wanna bet this will be the first place someone comes to when they realize you're not in the state, they can't get ahold of you, and this was the last place you used your card."

Yeah, shit.

The car would be on camera.

So would they.

"Really love that car, though," Renzo muttered unhappily.

Lucia laughed.

Hell, they had already gone *this far.*

They did this much.

What was one more thing?

"Why don't we go find a new one you like?"

"I do know how to boost a car."

She didn't doubt it.

• • •

Diego sat on the hood of a black SUV and chugged his chocolate milk while holding his egg sandwich in the other hand. He watched Renzo with a curious eye as his brother moved around the back of the red Mustang they'd parked in a field. Lucia drove the SUV behind Renzo while he took the car. With darkness all around them, all that could be seen in the desolate field was their headlights shining through. They'd gone off the highway, and drove into a rural area for longer than Lucia cared to think about after they'd boosted the SUV from a closed car lot where they parked it in the back, and no cameras could see them.

"What's Ren doing?" Diego asked.

"Nothing. You eat your food."

"Okay."

Diego's chewing filled the air as Renzo finished his work at the back of the Mustang. Popping open the trunk, he pulled out an orange gas tank, and set it to the ground while holding onto a license plate in his other. Not only had they taken the SUV, they had also taken a license plate from another vehicle in the lot and exchanged it with the one on the car.

They would be highly unlikely to notice for a while that a license plate had been switched. And while the cops would be looking for an SUV with a license plate number that belonged to the stolen vehicle, they now had a different stolen plate to put on the SUV.

It was kind of brilliant, really.

Lucia chose not to ask Renzo how he came up with the idea.

It took Renzo a couple of minutes to get the correct license plate on the SUV before he came around the front. Diego was just finishing his sandwich and milk, holding the trash from the food out for Lucia to take.

"I gotsa pee real bad," Diego said.

She helped him down, and he headed around the other side of the SUV to do his business.

"Drive to the other side of the field once he's done," Renzo said, holding tight to the gas can, "and then I'll run across and meet you."

She eyed the can he held. "Are you going to burn the car?"

"Yep."

Well, then.

"Okay."

• • •

"Home sweet home for the night," Renzo muttered.

Lucia eyed the small motel room for anything unsavory, but found the place was comfortable, and clean, if not a little out of date. She could deal with the aging furniture and awful wallpaper as long as the bedsheets were clean.

After driving a good portion of the day, and most of the night, they needed to rest.

Renzo shifted a sleeping Diego into the bed—directly in the middle—and pulled the blanket up over the boy. Lucia set the few bags she had brought in from the vehicle to the floor, and let out a sigh. Renzo did a quick check of the room, including pulling open the sliding doors that led out to a small deck.

"Hey," he murmured over his shoulder.

Lucia was tired.

Damn tired.

She had been running on adrenaline for hours. That, and the shitty energy drink she'd picked up at the store. What she really needed to do was get in the bed, and go to sleep like Diego.

She still went to him when he said, "Come look at this, baby."

Renzo slipped out onto the deck, and Lucia followed. He was already climbing up what looked to be a fire escape ladder when she exited the sliding double doors. "What are you doing?"

214

"Breathing."

Lucia blinked. "What?"

"I feel like I haven't breathed in hours, Lucia. Come on."

Unquestioningly, she followed him up to the roof of the motel. It was only two floors high, with them being on the second. Once she pulled herself over the top edge, Lucia found Renzo had already threw his leather jacket down on the pebbled roof, and sat his ass down. He stared up at the sky for a long while, saying nothing. Lucia simply went over, crawled into his lap, and hid her face in his chest when he wrapped his arms tightly around her.

She found her happy place like that, her legs wrapped around his waist, arms tucked in close, and pretending like the rest of the world didn't exist. She needed a lot of things—a change of clothes, a shower, and a bed.

Right then, though, she found she only needed him.

"You can see the stars," he murmured against her hair. "Can't ever see the stars in the city."

She glanced up, and found he was right.

"It's beautiful."

"Mmm, no. Pretty, maybe. Interesting, sure. Not *beautiful*." His hand came up to find her chin, and then he tipped her head down so her gaze met his. "You are beautiful. The sky does not compare."

Lucia grinned. "Smooth talker."

"I don't need to talk for it to be true."

One soft kiss led to another, and that quickly turned into something else entirely. Something hotter, and faster. Hands up her dress, and bites on her throat. It didn't take Renzo long at all to get them free of her clothes, and her resting on his cock as his hands warmed her body from the cool air.

And all it took was a kiss.

"You're gonna kill me," she told him.

She had no control with him.

None at all.

Renzo chuckled huskily, and swept his thumb over her trembling lips. "I think you have that mixed up, baby. You'll be the death of me ... that was always going to be the case."

She didn't know about that.

Shifting in his lap, she silenced him by taking him a little bit deeper. All she needed was his cock inside her to be reminded she had nerves in places she never knew existed before him.

"You know, I'm going to need some clothes," she murmured, leaning in to kiss his mouth.

Renzo nodded. "Tomorrow, we'll find something. There's a fucking Walmart on every corner."

He probably thought she never shopped at a Walmart before.

She had news for him.

"Oh, leggings and yoga pants, please."

He groaned. "I bet your ass looks fantastic in yoga pants."

"Guess you're going to find out."

Renzo grinned, grabbed her ass tight, and squeezed hard enough to take her breath away. This was probably the last thing they should be doing. They definitely shouldn't have been making light about their situation.

She couldn't find it in herself to care. Or to think about what might happen now.

She was with him.

He was with her.

They were together—the way they were meant to be. Forever.

The rest were details.

She never cared for those.

"I go, you go."

It was like he could read her mind. Like he knew all the crazy shit going on in there. His words came out in a breath, barely there at all, and his thumb stroked her cheekbone as she came close enough to kiss him again.

"You go, I go," Lucia echoed, shuddering when his hips flexed upward. "That's how it's going to be."

Until the day one of them died.

ABOUT THE AUTHOR

Bethany-Kris is a Canadian author, lover of much, and mother to four young sons, one cat, and three dogs. A small town in Eastern Canada where she was born and raised is where she has always called home. With her boys under her feet, a snuggling cat, barking dogs, and a spouse calling over his shoulder, she is nearly always writing something ... when she can find the time.

Find Bethany-Kris at her:

WEBSITE: www.bethanykris.com
BLOG: www.bethanykris.blogspot.com
FACEBOOK: www.facebook.com/bethanykriswrites
TWITTER: www.twitter.com/bethanykris
INSTAGRAM: www.instagram.com/bethany.kris
PINTEREST: www.pinterest.com/bethanykris

Sign up to Bethany-Kris's New Release Newsletter here: http://eepurl.com/bf9lzD.

OTHER BOOKS

Renzo + Lucia

Privilege

Andino + Haven

Duty
Vow

John + Siena

Loyalty
Disgrace

Cross + Catherine

Always
Revere
Unruly
The Companion
Naz & Roz

Guzzi Duet

Unraveled, Book One
Entangled, Book Two

DeLuca Duet

Waste of Worth: Part One
Worth of Waste: Part Two

Standalone Titles

Effortless
Inflict
Cozen
Captivated
Dishonored

Donati Bloodlines

Thin Lies
Thin Lines
Thin Lives
Behind the Bloodlines
The Complete Trilogy

Filthy Marcellos

Antony
Lucian
Giovanni
Dante
Legacy
A Very Marcello Christmas
The Complete Collection

Seasons of Betrayal

Where the Sun Hides
Where the Snow Falls
Where the Wind Whispers
Seasons: The Complete Seasons of Betrayal Series

Gun Moll Trilogy

Gun Moll
Gangster Moll
Madame Moll

The Chicago War

Deathless & Divided
Reckless & Ruined
Scarless & Sacred
Breathless & Bloodstained
The Complete Series
Maldives & Mistletoe

The Russian Guns

The Arrangement
The Life
The Score
Demyan & Ana
Shattered
The Jersey Vignettes

Find more on Bethany-Kris's website at www.bethanykris.com.

Made in the USA
Middletown, DE
27 January 2019